AF407300

Stormführer

E. R. Everett

Chapter 1

S udetenland, 1943

A cluster of scientists moved in the shadows of wires and cables, sine waves modulating on black screens and rows of tall metal boxes. Pale white suits shielded the three men from the crimson substance in a leaden jar, held by one carrying a pair of oversized tongs. They huddled, eyes shielded behind leaden glass faceplates, focused masters of their art, as if performing some unspeakable rite deep in the earth's crust. They were in fact holding their sabbat in tunnels once hollowed out by the work of skeletal men, specters, somewhere under the low mountains of Eastern Germany. Each meter of empty space was a man's soul, torn from its emaciated form of bone and rag through the process of death by hard labor.

Each slow movement made by the hooded forms was performed with the careful understanding that, without the thick shrouds and gray glass protecting their skin, bones, heart, lungs, liver, and other vitals, all would cease functioning in minutes in a tumbling domino effect of encroaching death by particles traveling at near light speed from an indifferent pile.

This was, however, no masquerade of the superstitious, no invoking of the deaf forces of nature to be summoned blind and impotent into a world alive only to one's own imaginings. No, these were men of natural science, a dark art all its own, top men of a nation leading in the study of the deadly actinides, the pariahs of the periodic table. From this nation's stock were harvested the brilliance of Einstein and von Braun,

Oppenheimer and Heisenberg, Bosch and Röntgen. They knew their trade, its coin: arcane knowing, but more than mortal knowledge, a near-deific understanding of the inner workings of substance, of material form at the atomic level. These were of those men, men of application from theory, or what was left of them. The coven of three had once been seven.

The mass was a seed, a seed of time, a grain planted in subterranean soil, a new *Wunderwaffe,* a "super-weapon." No bomb, no rocket, no airship, no U-boat, no new spiraling germ or chemical toxin. The contingency plan of a soon to be fading Third Reich. These men were to reap a new technology, a weapon that might enable a man to move from one point in time to another. It was called *Die Glocke* — "The Bell." It was Hitler's impossible plan.

The Fuhrer had been keen on acquiring *verboten* foreknowledge through the writings and practitioners of the Occult. But he had more faith in science, and after several clandestine meetings with small cadres of men who collectively knew more about the properties of time and matter than all other men alive, the Leader had begun molding a plan of doubtful certainty for transcending space-time—the harnessing of subatomic deities as elusive as breath into the wind. He called it *Projekt Reise*.

As the Fuhrer's closest-kept secret within a labyrinth of secrets, buried in kilometers of tunnels under the *Sudetenland,* it was to be his means of waylaying errors of the recent past. Communicating with counterparts in 1938 with meaningful symbols sent across space-time, imparted to an overconfident demigod of the past, just might steer his war strategy away from mistakes already made. The War had, in fact, not been going well. But no matter. This was a contingency begun years before this day. And it would work.

The Bell was four meters high and three across. This massive upturned black caldron of matter and energy sitting atop a 70-centimeter-high honeycombed platform would utilize Xerum 525, a reddish, radioactive mercury construct. The three men poured this substance into three widely spaced meter-long lead tubes, 20 meters from the perimeter of the brooding bell-shaped capsule. This sweltering venom had killed the other four, deep within the Owl Mountains, leaving only three. Soon, there would be two.

SOUTH TEXAS, 2035

"Mr. Hayes, you have a visitor."

Not a sound. The box didn't move. The young man walked into the small room containing a single bed, empty though perfectly made, and a large box—or rather, a collection of cardboard segments pieced together with packing tape to form a large shelter—standing upright.

A delicate afternoon light poured in tiny rays through the rusty metal grating, a thick mesh with which nearly every window of the gray cinder-block facility was covered from the outside. Faint scratches could be seen scored into the protective Plexiglas serving as a single windowpane embedded just inside the grating. Light blue paint was fresh on the walls of the room.

"I'll be back in fifteen minutes to check on things," the middle-aged nurse smiled encouragingly and left, closing the door behind her in the wide doorway, followed by the metallic snap of an automatic lock. The young man, wearing jeans, a t-shirt, and a pair of flip flops, sat on the bed and waited in silence. Perhaps he was sleeping, the young man thought.

"Mr. Hayes," he half-whispered.

Nothing.

He sat and waited, faintly aware of a slow beeping from the far wall.

After some moments there was a stir. The box shifted slightly and slid almost imperceptibly against the blue wall.

The young man decided to lift the box only slightly. Bony feet protruded from beneath a thin hospital gown; the rancid toenails needed cutting. Maybe he would come back later, the young man considered. Or maybe not at all—if there was no point.

The box shifted again, its inhabitant giving an almost imperceptible groan. Worried that his former teacher might need medical attention, the young man wrapped his arms around the box, pinching at two opposing corners, and lifted it up and over its contents towards the high ceiling. It slid to fall against the side of the bed, propelling a thin wisp of dust from the bedcover and into the rays of approaching twilight. A faint odor of sour perspiration filled the room. The man's wispy, balding head lay on the desk, a set of black headphones lacking ear pads lay across a damp scalp. The wires had been cut.

The man's head, resting on folded arms, was turned toward the young man, but the eyes, fixed, bloodshot, dimmed, stared past him into the blue wall. His mouth was closed, neither in frown nor smile. His face reflected a mind surrounded by tough skin thickening over an old wound constantly re-introduced to a blunt force.

An ECG machine by the wall had revealed itself once the box was removed. Its beeping cadence began to increase in both volume and rapidity. The young man wondered at its growing intensity, trying to read the steadily increasing numbers, when a thump sounded from the desk. Then another . . . and another, each crash more violent than the one before. Shocked into immobility, the young man could only watch as the forehead lifted and dropped, lifted and dropped, a crimson pool forming between pale, encircling arms.

SOUTH TEXAS, SPRING, 2031

Farhat Farash, an India-born exchange teacher given a one-year tentative contract, stood at the front of the classroom. Today's lecture had been on the Italian Renaissance, preceded by a 20-minute introduction tying the Roman and Byzantine eras to the early 1300s in Europe. It was one of his favorite topics, and even his students seemed interested.

Mr. Farash sensed their involvement, pausing the video to further explain how the Black Plague not only wiped out one-fourth of the benighted medieval Europeans but also feudalism itself, decreasing the workforce and thus increasing wages, leading ultimately to more fertile economic conditions for the poor who survived the plague, allowing for educational opportunities before unknown for a nascent middle class. Extra money to spend, combined with the invention of the printing press, made books accessible. More people then learned to read, culture flourished, and voila . . . the Renaissance was born! Progress born from plague.

For a while they seemed to be taking it all in. Then a giggle started. Another was added.

It stung a little when Jake lifted his cheek from his desk to see what the laughter was about. He half-expected the chuckling to be about him until he squinted between rows of students' heads to the whiteboard at the front of the room. Mr. Farash seemed confused as well. He half-smiled and watched the faces of his students for a few seconds until it dawned on him to turn around and look at the whiteboard.

On the screen stood a Roman statue mounted upon a fountain in an old city square, presumably in Florence. Mr. Farash had used a small remote control to pause the video in order to make his points. At the paused image hung Poseidon's masculine parts with enlarged detail. Mr. Farash, who had the annoying habit of standing in the light of the projector as he spoke, carried the relevant parts across the center of his white chinos. He quickly unpaused the video. Water then sprayed upward from the fountain to crown the glorified spectacle as the giggling went viral, and then finally epidemic, across columns of desks.

In the next classroom, Richard Hayes, another history teacher, sat back, leaning into the black desk-chair, letting the wheels roll forward and back, propelled by his heels, as he flipped through an old paperback. It was Hermann Hesse's *Magister Ludi—The Glass Bead Game.* Hayes often fantasized about gamifying his courses, creating an all-encompassing game—like in the book—which students could play while learning all that was amazing about history, literature, philosophy, art, music, science. He would, of course, start with history, were he to create such a game. But where to begin? And, no, there wouldn't be any "starting with history" since all of these fields intertwine with one another, like the notes of an incredible symphony, when true learning and cultural enlightenment coalesce in the human mind. It had been that way with him as a college student, certainly, and nowadays he rarely even attempted to teach his history lessons without bringing in those crucial artistic, social, economic, and philosophical influences. But to do it through a powerful game, electronic or otherwise. It was a grand idea, the philosopher's stone of teaching, yet a chimera for even the most ambitious of teachers to even hope for. Hesse's description of the game was vague at best though Hayes had hoped to glean at least some small idea for its implementation in this third reading of the lengthy novel.

He heard a not-so-distant "slam." A teenager leaving the classroom next door in a dramatic huff? Possibly, but doubtful. He put the book down and counted the seconds. One . . . two . . . three . . . . Then came the tapping on the tall, narrow window of his classroom door. Oversized glasses appeared behind the thin criss-crossing wires embedded in the tall glass. Though Hayes was only a few yards away from the door, he glanced across the room nearly full of students tapping away at black keyboards, staring into screens of various sizes.

A dark head appeared through a crack in a gently opening door. Hayes joined the man in the hallway, closing the door behind him. He had been officially assigned to mentor the second-year teacher at the beginning of this school year, but it was clear in the ensuing months that Farash would rarely take his advice. "Excuse me, sir. They're at it again. They don't want to learn. I'm thinking I'm having a breakdown." Farash smiled while he spoke, but it wasn't jocular. Mr. Farash was a little afraid of his students. No, he was terrified of them. What he *really* needed, Hayes reflected, was a sense of humor of the adolescent variety, something almost second nature to all the best teachers he'd ever met. As Hayes stood, shoulder leaning against the door, politely nodding but paying little attention to words he had heard before, one of the lines from the book came to mind: *Whatever you become, teacher, scholar, or musician, have respect for the "meaning" but do not imagine that it can be taught.*

A few minutes turned into ten, then twelve. The bell would ring. Farash's kids would file out next door. The problem would be solved with a change of souls, no shots fired, no confrontations. The day would pass. Another bygone. The source of Farash's angst was this habitual focus on the anxieties of the present moment, as if there were no anon, no cold brew waiting anxiously to be sipped at the end of the school day, just the problem of Now requiring some immediate solution. Sad, really.

Summer, 2031

Richard Hayes, a middle-aged high school history teacher, had double majored in history and computer science back in college, unwilling to surrender either of his two disparate passions. Now, some thirty years later, he worked at home most summers to supplement his income, online, from his tiny cabin, buying and selling web addresses. Hayes had built what he called the "Farmer" program to target the business and non-business entities most likely to one day desire unique suffix signatures. He would spend some of what he had made that year to buy up the most likely suffixes still available, which now sold for very little—one to five dollars each, in most cases. Throughout the year some of the URL suffixes would sell for thousands, others for hundreds, most for fifty to seventy-five dollars each, the latter to virtual mom and pops desperate to secure an online presence.

Of course, most of the established corporate giants had already claimed their URL homesteads, but the far bigger pool of mid-range companies, most working across multiple continents in some online capacity, were already beginning to shed the stale ".com" for something perceived as more cutting-edge. The timing was perfect. He'd made some noteworthy sales over the last few months. If steady, these transactions would allow him to retire within the next ten or fifteen years. He'd done this sort of thing every summer for the past decade, finding some niche of the Web to exploit during his time off. He was good at it and had built up enough savings to retire years ago, but only at his present level of . . . comfort.

In an old robe of silk paisleys, grabbing on the way some coffee warmed up from the night before, Hayes walked the few steps from the kitchen to his blinking corner of wires, boxes, and terminals. Several screens littered the long foldout table serving as a desk, along with candy wrappers, crusty forks, and a half-eaten salad. Fly strips, dotted mostly with mosquitoes and fruit-flies from months past, hung every yard or so from the high A-frame ceiling beams of his cubed home, a cube but for the A-framed roof.

It was on a steamy day in late June when Richard Hayes hit upon something not quite right. Farmer was running through possible suffixes, cross referencing them with the names of companies from a database containing many thousands but excluding those that had already purchased their own unique suffix territories. Essentially, the

Farmer program pulled up company names and linked them with associated suffixes based on likely keywords. With matches formed, Hayes would buy up a few of the most relevant suffixes with the highest probability of interest and then market them directly to the company.

He watched as the company names and lists of potential abbreviations scrolled blindingly down a small, gray window on one of his screens. He lit a Habana Especial he'd smuggled in his underwear from the Matamoros border town, a mere twenty-minute drive from the cabin, some weeks back, and took a rare but satisfying lung hit. He blew the smoke through a low opening in an otherwise thickly draped window, which kept out most of the morning sun's already smoldering intensity.

After minutes of scrolling, dozens of company names were matched with potential suffixes and listed in a secondary screen. Suddenly the Farmer program froze. It stopped on the suffix ".allein" but with no associated company name. Hayes hit the "ignore" button on the screen, and the whizzing abbreviations and company names continued to scroll in their thin, gray columns.

He noticed a cadre of fruit flies beginning to accumulate around a half-eaten grapefruit sitting in a large Mexican ashtray, defying the strips, and frowned. He gave the buzzing specks a wave off and began to peel at the pulpy edges of the grapefruit. The rolling digits on the screen were hypnotic. A beep sounded, barely audible above the heavy blowing of the aircon unit jammed into the large window of the cabin's second story loft.

Hayes' modest open concept cabin had been bought from a hardware chain. Its design had been meant for accommodating occasional hunters in lonesome brush country where the deer were fed corn from timed feeders. Walking into the building's facsimile on the vast parking lot of the hardware store, Richard had fallen in love with the simplicity of its open plan, its steep staircase against one wall bearing no handrail, leading up to a tiny loft floored by one-inch plywood sheets. The loft, serving as bedroom and storage space, was where he slept on a low futon, surrounded by his boxes of dusty possessions, most of which lined the edges of the loft where the acute corners of angled roof met linoleum flooring.

Hayes had done most of the work on the cabin himself, and altogether the project had cost him a little over $25,000, land included. It was perfect for his needs, the living area floor space housing a wide bookshelf, his computer niche, a flat-screen television, and an old couch. The kitchen area stood to the left as you walked in the single door near a corner of the house, the bathroom directly under the loft and opposite the kitchen space.

Hayes heard the beep despite the hard blowing of the huge window unit. He stared hard at the screen. Again, the scrolling froze on one suffix: ".allein," at the top of the endless column of possible letter combinations. Only slightly curious about what was probably a glitch, some for-next loop ending sooner than it was meant to, he opened another window on the screen and typed the suffix into another gray box. This would allow all addresses actively using that suffix on the Web to appear in a separate column. This could take hours as every possible web address would have to be checked for an active response during the subroutine. There was not much else to do, so he decided to take a walk before the sultry South Texas 86 degrees became 97. It was 7:15 in the morning.

A two-year-old, brown eyed German shepherd named Fräulein awoke from her padded place at the foot of the futon in the loft. She heard the screen door slam and dashed blindly through the large door flap in the bottom corner of the front door, shooting out into the trail by the long resaca. She walked at his heels at first and then in front, sometimes stopping to sniff at a dead rodent or a piece of skin left by a molting rattler.

Hayes reflected on nothing in particular, strolling beneath overhanging Brazilian pepper trees planted throughout much of the twelve acres and which, like witches' fingers, surrounded his cabin but, like his thinning hair, left the pate exposed. It was his favorite thing about the place—those uncertain trees hiding the deep brown cabin from any passerby who might happen to walk near the gate. His fenced property was barbed-wired and gated, surrounded by stubby trees of neighboring farms, the dark, long resaca, and the furrows of farmland rimming it as it snaked through multiple properties usually covered with dense sugar cane or low cotton. Little trace revealed the existence of his cabin, save the dirt road leading to it and a green Subaru pickup. He took notice of the thick meshes of water plants dominating the dark water in its undulating trail through the nearby farmland. He often ate from the fresh produce of those fields, encouraged to do so by the several farmers whom he knew from the occasional visits that such land ownership politely required in this part of the world. A six pack of Corona under one arm lubricated the long moments of these awkward occasions between the farmer host and this disparate visitor.

Continuing to smoke the last of his Cuban, Richard thought nothing of the web sites and the suffixes littering his three monitors. Rather, he let his mind wander to other things—his grownup son, working construction somewhere in Montana, the woman who had taken the boy out of Texas all those years ago, the thought that he, Richard Hayes, might someday remarry, but probably not. He kicked a rock into the water. Fräulein stopped in front of him, gave him a tilted look of curiosity, then sniffed the air and continued to trot up the path. The trail stopped at a tree line behind a barbed-wire fence. There were no clouds, only the intensity of sun and heat somewhat filtered through the pepper trees rustled by a light breeze from the southeast. The chirping drone of locusts melded with the smooth brushing of the overhanging pepper pods rustling with the sound of cascading beans in a slowly upturned rain stick.

On his return to the cabin, Hayes descended to a path next to the still water and halted, watching minnows swim near the hard, clay-dry edge of the water. Several grackles squawked from the trees above, then louder as the German shepherd approached a black bird on the little trail. It was beautiful in its bluish blackness, Hayes reflected. It was also enormous, for a grackle, appearing more like a small raven or a large crow. The sad thing attempted to flap a wing that would never again touch sky or cloud. Fräulein sniffed at it and then backed away, watching attentively the bird's failed attempt at flight.

He had not heard the grackles until he noticed Fräulein looking toward him and then up into the trees at five or six black shapes, squawking as if for a fallen comrade. Fräulein, receiving no sign from her companion whether to approach the broken bird, apparently decided that the easy kill wasn't worth the noise and simply trotted on ahead past the thing. Hayes pitied the poor creature and tried to reflect in consolation on the inexorable cycles of things, life, death, rebirth, a perpetual recurrence. There was nothing to be done. He thought back to a portion of the *Beowulf* epic he'd memorized back in college and slowly recited the words as a kind of preempted eulogy: *But the raven winging darkly over the doomed will have news, tidings for the eagle of how he ate his fill, how the wolf and he made short work of the dead.*

Near the cabin, Hayes stopped to grimace at some of the green hairs of algae floating just beneath the stagnant surface of the narrow resaca. He wiped his bald forehead with the base of his t-shirt, revealing a thin patch of black stomach hair over a tiny, white gut. His eyes refocused, and he saw his own reflection in the murky water. Richard Hayes was not what others might consider handsome and never had been. He was of low-average height, thin. His nose, which needed trimming, shaded his upper lip under a bald forehead and balding scalp, a bird's nest of tangle set way back. As an adult, he had noted the resembled between himself and Larry from The Three Stooges. Well, you can't pick your face. Your nose, certainly, but not your face.

Once inside, Hayes glanced at the screens. An hour had passed, and browser screens were still opening and closing everywhere. He washed his face in the sink of the little kitchen and looked out a small window onto the watery ravine amidst the trees, still aware of a distant chirp.

The rolling of the thunderously silent browser screens finally ceased with the last remaining windows blinking out until only one small window was left open at the center of the screen followed by three long beeps. Farmer had done its job.

Richard Hayes was oblivious to any of it at 3:47 PM. He had napped hard on the old couch during the late morning and into early afternoon. Hayes was snoozing on his old couch when Fräulein barked from the rug a few times at the barely audible beeps coming from the computer. He awoke and patted her head, deciding to make some afternoon coffee before again checking the screens. Waiting for the coffee to brew, he leaned onto the table to read the screen. Centered in the scrolling area of the gray box was only one website matching what he was looking for:

http://walküre.allein

He sat down at the table, grabbing a handful of almonds, and munched through his sips of coffee. He was wide awake now. Here was a company that had already claimed its extension, so he couldn't exactly buy it cheap and then sell it back at a ridiculous profit. But such an unlikely company URL piqued his curiosity. He would have never found it had his home-brewed software not allowed for the possibility of umlauts.

He brought up an extensive Singapore-based search engine database, which he knew to be excellent in cataloging foreign sites, and did a search for "walküre allein." Nothing. Then "allein walküre." Then each alone. Nothing. He tried various spellings like changing the "W" to a "V." No result.

Hayes often wondered at how some companies had acquired their names. No well-known classical or mythological reference was spared the inglorious honor of representing some flatulent corporation, as if the said company actually bore the qualities of the deity after which it was named, or the legendary hero, or his misspelled cousin. Did any of the founders of these companies really know anything about the history of their chosen mascot? Hayes was doubtful, with names like *Janus*, a company with two-faces? Really? And *Pasiphae Labs*, a genetics research firm laughably named after the wife of the King Minos, a queen whose apparent penchant for bestiality gave birth to the Minotaur.

Walküre and especially its anglicized Valkyrie would make a great name for a cryogenics firm or health club though it was likely some foreign bank or insurance company. Perhaps he could sell them a better suffix than *allein*, which he knew to be the German word for "alone."

Richard typed the web address into a browser and pressed Enter. The screen went white and then froze. He pressed a few keys. Nothing. He pressed a few more to pull up the task manager. Still nothing happened. He frowned at the scaled-down browser which he had himself built some years back, considering the likelihood of a glitch. He pressed spasmodically at the keys. Nothing changed. He was about to unplug his computer from the wall to initiate a hard reboot when he heard something deep within the small speakers that he at first mistook for a voice from outside the cabin.

He plugged in a pair of headphones and put them on, thinking that it was probably some metallic noise caused by a short in the wiring. He turned up the volume. Still, the sound was faint, nothing more than a wispy sprite of his tired imagination. He threw off the headphones and ran up the narrow stairs to click off the rumbling beast of an aircon unit. Running back down, he thought for a moment and then unplugged every appliance he could think of.

He returned to the chair, seeing solid white screens on all three monitors, bright, almost pearlescent. Again putting on the headphones, he listened once more for the nearly silent pattern of sound. From deep within the headset, he thought he heard . . . distant singing . . . low, fading in and out.

The screens of all three monitors remained white and frozen. Frustrated, he ripped off the cushions of the headphones, exposing the bare metal, wax, and magnets, and pressed hard against both sides with his palms. Now, though it was still extremely faint, he heard a voice. It was operatic and female.

Gradually, the three screens began to glow with an even brighter white, almost blinding in the murky corner of the cabin. A small text box then appeared in the middle of the screen with a blinking cursor. There were no words to indicate that this was a login query, but he assumed that it was and simply typed in a string of digits involving his name, birthday, and street address, omitting any spaces and carefully committing the login to memory. The next box requested a password and the last a choice of genders. The boxes vanished and the music then faded into the low roar of a crowd of people speaking what sounded like gibberish. Through the mist of darkening pixels, Hayes became as if surrounded on all three screens by a crowd in what looked to be an old street market. He brought the three screens closer together and decreased the angles, almost boxing himself in. As the ambient sounds of bustle and street noise increased, he brought himself and his chair closer.

The realism was astonishing. It was panoramic. It was as if he were looking through a helmet with three wide openings. Even the space between monitors gradually went unnoticed. There was a bit of a glare coming from a window not completely covered, so Hayes reached for a black felt blanket sitting at his feet under the long table and threw it over his head, encompassing also the three screens. He reached for the cushions he had removed from his headphones and slipped them back over the metal frames. The cups surrounding his ears completed the almost total envelopment of his senses. He just sat there for a moment, enthralled by what he was seeing and hearing—the people, the old-fashioned cars, the sounds of a big city reverberating off three- and four-story buildings.

Hayes appeared to see through the eyes of a man apparently trying to tie the laces of his own boots. This movement, however, had halted suddenly. The man now fixedly held the black, oily shoestrings with both thumbs and index fingers. His hands were frozen in place. Richard tried pressing a few buttons—arrows, page down, tab—and realized that he was able to pan vertically and horizontally as well as elicit some movement from the figure on the central monitor, but that was about it. Pressing letters individually and simultaneously gave him more hyper specific choices of movement, but to orchestrate some sort of fluid mobility from the seemingly endless combinations would take days of fiddling. He crossed his (own) arms and thought. This must be a game or virtual tour of some kind. After a few moments, he dashed up to the loft and rummaged through a box of old VR equipment, finding a set of gloves and a balled trackpad, all outdated though worth a shot.

After plugging the nearly archaic devices into his PC, Richard moved his balled trackpad with a gloved right hand. The black glove had been a standard 3D mouse glove that, among other things, moved multiple black cursors with the fingertips and palm. Its surface was studded with tiny metallic nodes covering both the front and back of its faux leather skin.

Watching the man's hands at the bottom of the center screen, he positioned his gloved mouse ball with his right pinky and clicked. Nothing. Again he clicked the finger, this time with an upward drag. The man's finger moved slightly as the cursor drifted off the finger, leaving it to fall back into the same position. It was all he could do for the moment. The view of the man's polished black boots shook at times as pedestrians jostled by on the crowded sidewalk, apparently brushing against him with a faint *"Entschuldigung, bitte"* followed immediately by a louder "Excuse me, please." He knew enough German not to need the translation.

It was indeed a game of some kind, one clearly involving complicated movements. Hayes reached for the studded left-handed glove matching the one already on his right and slipped it on, hoping it might control the left side of the booted figure. He turned his left wrist and the world went sideways, and in the right-hand screen his shoulder was soon rubbing against a sidewalk curb. The shoestrings were still in his hands, but with some clicking and dragging he was able to free the man's fingers from the strings and somewhat right himself.

Hayes pushed the ball held in his right palm forward while spinning it slightly. This brought his view upward. He saw fathers, mothers, children, some glancing at him, nearly all wearing hats. An elderly woman in black stopped in front of him and shook her head with a look of sad disgust; she glared at him momentarily and then went shuffling along into the crowd, using a closed umbrella as a cane. This was like no game he had played back in the day. What fazed him most was its sheer realism. Apparently, video games had come a long way.

With some further difficulty, Richard stood the man upright. It required the lowering of the gloves, flattening them like feet against the desk and raising up the palms while leaving the fingertips upon its surface. A few clicks of the trackball buttons with his right hand

and he was stumbling along the sidewalk. From behind, he heard boots crunching the pavement towards him. He spun around in his chair to look, but all he could see was his cabin, Fräulein relaxing on the old couch. Turning his attention back to the screen, he edged the mouse-ball to the right and his character's virtual head began to turn. Dragging his left glove back, he found his character looking down at a starched black uniform. A dark cap fell forward over his face, blocking most of his view.

With a jerk, the hat fell to the ground as a gloved hand gripped the left arm of his avatar. Faintly: *"Gehen kann schwierig sein, ja Kamerad?"* Then louder: "Walking can be difficult, eh comrade?" He spun the mouse-ball left and saw the smiling young face of a soldier in uniform.

After fooling around with the keys, the mice, and the gloves, Richard found the right combinations for the movement of his legs, his head, his arms. It was slow and complicated work, but he was also being led by his upper arm, almost carried. In time, he managed to step into the back of a military truck, guided by the soldier's shackling grip. He managed to make his avatar lean toward a bench in the truck opposite his guide, who soon let go of his arm, causing the body to tip into a seated position. It was dark in the back of the green, tarp-covered truck. The sky through the entrance was overcast.

The soldier across began to talk lightheartedly, lighting a cigarette and offering one to Hayes' avatar. The man's uniform was unquestionably Third Reich. Richard quickly got the gist of what the man was saying through the sketchy voiced-over translations. Apparently, he thought that Richard's avatar had had too much to drink.

The truck began to move. Absorbed in the realism of the images and surrounding sounds, Hayes began to feel himself sliding to the left in his own chair and grabbed the desk for support. It jarred him momentarily out of what had been a brief, trance-like state temporarily interrupted when he had to grab the edge of the table, realizing again that there *was* a table in front of him.

Richard threw off the felt blanket and looked around his room and then back to the screen. The headphones had fallen to his neck. He got up to grab a bottle of water from the small refrigerator, less from thirst than a need to regain some perspective. But as soon as he left his place in front of the screens, everything on the screens went black. Grabbing the water, he quickly crawled back up into his makeshift tent. The screens remained blank. Pressing Enter, he found his onscreen desktop and double-clicked the browser icon. He quickly typed in the web address and found himself back in the truck in the same position though now on a different street. Nothing had paused in the game while he was out of it. The truck was traveling on a street between city blocks, but in front of him sat the same silhouette of the man who had helped him into the truck. Twilight was approaching.

The soldiers in the truck were talking again, two of them loudly, and there was laughter on his right side. He turned his avatar's head to the right using the mouse ball, suppressing a momentary desire to do so with his own head. The man seated next to him was wearing a uniform slightly lighter in color than the others, and on his head was a darker helmet. Seated on the bench across from Hayes and to his right was a soldier who seemed not so jovial as the other two. This soldier stared at Hayes, or rather, at his avatar. He too was dressed in the lighter colored uniform and wore the same helmet as the man seated to the immediate right of Hayes' character. *Military police?*

A tall, clear bottle of golden liquid was being passed around, but Hayes had no idea what combination of keys was needed to drink anything, so he shook his head subtly as it came his way. Richard looked to his left through the tarp's opening and past the truck's tailgate. It had begun to rain. He heard it tapping against the tarp as the noisy truck splashed through the drenching night, pausing briefly at checkpoints and crossing over bridges. The stereophonics were amazing!

His avatar must have looked ridiculous to the other characters in the game as Richard continued to test the mechanics, jerking this foot and that shoulder, standing up slightly and sitting down, tapping keys and then correcting, but if he had seemed odd, it wasn't noticed, except maybe by the soldier on his diagonal right. Richard decided to try speaking. He pulled the microphone arm of the headphones down over his mouth and spoke in a whisper into the headset microphone. "Testing, testing." The soldier beside him turned to look in his direction. The others were distracted. "Hello everyone." This time he spoke clearly. The soldiers looked at him. "'Hello,' he says! Welcome back Wicker. You look like *Hundescheisse*!" Apparently, not every word would be translated.

After some time, Hayes started to get a feel for the game. An hour had passed, then another. Keystroke combinations were needed to show emotions, like smiling or anger. A small face appeared in the bottom corner of the screen when an emotion had been registered, the face reflecting the current emotion and then fading out. On a slip of paper, Hayes jotted down the seemingly endless combinations existing between the keys, the gloves, and the mouse, noting actions and reactions, difficult but strangely intuitive. The soldier across asked a question that he didn't quite catch through the noise of the truck. The best thing to do was simply to narrow his eyes in the direction of the opening with a face of what he hoped was exhaustion and nausea. The soldier laughed and started passing another bottle.

Events didn't involve the immediate or constant drama of a video game. Rather, they played out gradually. One second was one second. Hayes found the biggest thrill in the reactions his avatar's movements would elicit from the other characters. He had his character focus his eyes on the man in the seat diagonal from him. With the mouse-ball pushed forward, he leaned towards the seated figure. He raised and closed his right gloved fist. He saw the same fist on the screen, repeating the same actions. He rotated his fist. The fist on the screen responded. The soldier scowled in his direction. He lunged the fist forward, moving the mouse-ball only a few inches. His whole body went with it as it launched toward the chin of the man. The soldier saw it coming and jerked his head back, missing the punch but clinking his helmeted head against one of the steel braces supporting the truck's tent enclosure. Faintly, *"Vas war das?"* and loudly in almost the same instant, "What was that?" The man stared at him, confused. The others watched in silence. He chose to try it again, this time with the other arm. Coming from the left side of his body, it reached the soldier but with greater difficulty. The soldier was alert and easily deflected the blow with the open palm of his right hand. The man then stood up and grabbed Hayes' avatar by the head with both hands, pressing down, forcing his head to the floor of the truck bed. He hammered down hard on the back of his neck with one hand. Hayes' character fell flat.

A second later the screens went blurry and then faded to black. He tried various keys, but nothing changed. He exited his browser back to the desktop and reopened it, putting in the address over and over. Nothing. Staring at blank screens in the dark of a now sweltering room, Richard began to feel sick and a need for sleep overtook him. He closed the browser and dragged himself up to the loft. His head throbbed as he switched the massive aircon unit back on.

After a few hours of sleep, Richard Hayes awoke in a daze and placed the headphones back on his head. He tried numerous times to return to the game, but the screens remained a two-dimensional landscape of pearlescent white.

Hayes lay on the old couch. He forced himself to wait a full thirty minutes between attempts to reopen the browser window now fixed on the walküre.allein location. Staring from the couch at the distant beam holding up the a-frame of his roof, he considered the complexity, the realism, drawing him to the game. Occasionally, especially when many images had gone by—like when he had looked out from the back of the truck bed into the midst of the city—the screen would lag a bit with tiny freezes, as if the processor in his computer weren't enough to handle the tremendous detail. But in reality the lag had been almost imperceptible, taking away nothing from the experience.

At first, he checked the website every thirty minutes, then every hour. It was twelve hours before he could make something reappear on the screens. One apparently played the role of a German soldier, stationed probably in Munich, by the looks of the buildings and architecture he could somewhat recognize. There was no login, no company name, no title screen. Once your browser opened the game, there was a brief fade-in, and you were simply there.

When Richard was finally able to return to the game, he had left the truck, had perhaps been carried out. He found himself in what appeared to be an infirmary. There were large, high windows behind his bed, spotless. Everything was spotless. A few nurses were moving silently in what he soon realized was a long room of beds. He stood his character up. His uniform was wrinkled.

The action wasn't constant as would be expected in a first-person shooter. But it wasn't the appeal of bloodshed and heroic aggression drawing Hayes to the game as he played for hours at a time, for days eventually, with little sleep. It was the complexity, the reality of the situation in which his character was involved, the seemingly endless world, the exhaustive research that must have gone into his character's creation and the creation of the world within which he interacted. Tremendous detail had been put into every little piece of it. Normally in a first-person shooter, a trash can, for instance, might be a copy of all the other trash cans in the game, but in this game each trash can, for he found himself looking around for such details, was unique. He could detect no repeated patterns in the textures.

For weeks, Hayes pulled himself away from the game just long enough to sleep his four hours a night, to make coffee, to feed Fräulein, or to heat up a frozen dinner. By early August, Hayes had come to a few realizations about the game. First, the game might be some sort of language-learning program. The longer one stayed into the game, the more German and less English was used by the other characters as repeated words became no longer instantly translated. Secondly, the characters in the game reacted to the words of the player in a convincing way. Over the weeks, Hayes began responding to his fellow Germans in their language, haltingly at first, often receiving some curious looks. He would use German words as he learned them and replace the others with English, usually in the same sentence. The word order wasn't perfect, but he did what he could. At times he could detect a second or two of lag during which a translation program must have been hard at work attempting to transform his broken words into something intelligible. Other characters' reactions then reflected responses more or less appropriate to what he had said or intended to say. Such complexity! Everything happened in real time. When his character slept, he had to wait—usually about four to eight hours—before playing the character again. In these instances, the screen would go gray, and he knew that meant sleep. In these instances, he had no control. He simply had to leave the screen where it was and wait for the avatar's eyes to open again. The avatar would then awaken and perform movements on his own for a brief moment until finally under Richard's full control.

The character was SS. He worked in a prison camp, in Dachau, the Bavarian camp near Munich, one of the first camps to spring up during the Third Reich. It wasn't a mass extermination camp. In fact, based on dates he would see on calendars and in newspapers in the game, it was 1939, years before the mass deportations and the "final solution."

One afternoon, Richard received a package. He took the box to his corner and cut the shipping tape with a pocketknife. From the box, Richard pulled out the black helmet he'd ordered online, dripping with shipping peanuts, the connecting wires trailing to the floor. Richard detached the audio hook-ups from his computer and tossed the old headset into the box, stashing it behind his computer table. When all the wires were hooked up, it would display a wide screen about six inches from the wearer's eyes, wrapping around his face from ear to ear.

Experimenting with the shiny black helmet, once his avatar was semi-conscious, he found that he no longer had to use the mouse ball to tilt his head, for with the helmet on, he could tilt his own head and the avatar would do the same. When he turned his head to the left, the image in front of his eyes shifted at nearly the exact same moment, the virtual reality almost matching reality itself. Incredibly, the visual experience almost seemed three-dimensional, and the audio was flawless. This was truly a thing of beauty.

Chapter 2

Sudetenland, 1943

Projekt Reise had once sat ominously at the corner of a mountain cave a kilometer underground. It had been moved to a small above-ground facility in the Bavarian foothills. Originally a metal sheeting factory constructed in the early 1930s yet only briefly used, the space would be clear of any obstructions and human beings upon the Bell's reemergence in 1939, or thereabouts. The machine certainly couldn't have been tested underground, for those caves hadn't existed then. The Bell would have rematerialized in solid rock.

Metallic arms were folded into the grooves of its circular form, its small head centered at the top of its rotund mass, squatishly implanted in the sloping shoulders. It slept though vented a faint hum on its meter-high platform of steel and black cables snaking their way into the frosty form, a chemical like ice caking on the surface of its ponderous shell.

The three forms, moving with slow hesitancy like aging sloths. The dark denizen on the platform heeded not its sparse cadre of devotees. And for their part, just standing near the deity unprotected by the white leaden suits would carry the penalty of an excruciating and liquefying death.

One votary measured the radiation with a clicking box raised and lowered before the silent form, while one snaked venom-filled cables into projections at the base of some metric tons of steel and lead. A third watched, a veritable Atropos, ready to pull a switch at a box protruding from a corner of the platform, should the need arise to terminate the aggressive un-life of the leaden idol. They, three left from seven, were impressed even now by an unswerving faith in their own god—calculation. Control was theirs, and fate had no hand in the construction of this indecent caricature of a common church bell. Two thick rings of lead and steel were contoured into the base of the Bell, barely visible as separate from it, yet so balanced were these counter-rotating cylinders that the smallest wisp of breeze would tilt either into a slightly new position on its unapparent axis.

The man at the lever, the tallest of the three, was given a nod, once each by the remaining two. Then all stepped back as a reddish glow could be seen faintly illuminating the nearly invisible cracks between the rings of steel at its base. The tall man walked behind the machine and knelt to crawl through a tunnel beneath the platform upon which the Bell sat. The other two checked instruments standing outside the perimeter on metal crates, cabled together and to the edges of the Bell. Unseen, the third and most learned of the three entered the blackness of the *sanctum sanctorum*. The Chosen then, feelingly, shut the hatch in the floor of the hollow structure and stood up, completely enclosed by seemingly infinite layers of artificial night.

Outside, the brightening rim of the bell's base throbbed and the humming increased as if it sensed the intruder's presence. The two rings of thick metal spun in opposite directions, slowly at first, then building up speed. The upper portion of the Bell remained stationary until a great momentum had been achieved. The man inside looked up into the empty skull of infinite darkness and put his gloved hands against his ears, bending over as the throbbing hum quickly became a jaw-ripping screech. He looked at where his feet would have been, and as he strained to peer into the darkness, he fell into oblivion.

SOUTH TEXAS, 2035

Two nurses rushed into the room. The young man, still standing, quickly moved out of the way to let them through. One stood by the door while the other, the one he had seen earlier, looked to the man and to the blood pooling over the desk. She gasped and turned. "Did he . . . did you . . . the box must not be removed!" She reached for a stack of small towels from the closet and mopped up the blood, wiping the man's forehead. She held up the forehead with a free hand, calling to the other nurse still standing by the door, "The box, Nancy. Quickly, please."

The other nurse hurried over and grabbed the box. The first nurse quickly replaced the bloody towel with a clean one, resting the forehead on the folded padding. Both nurses then lifted the box, gently placing it over the man at the desk.

Gradually, the beeping subsided into a slow, faint rhythm. "I'm sorry," the young man said, sitting heavily at the edge of the bed. "I really had no idea."

SUMMER, 2031

The summer of Richard Hayes' discovery was approaching its bittersweet end. Because of the game and the time it seemed to require of him, Richard knew he wouldn't be able to muster the focus needed to prepare for a completely new year. He decided to teach on autopilot as his thoughts, he knew, would be filled daily with the game's most recent scenarios. He used lesson plans from the year before. A tiny fraction of his own time would be sacrificed. The rest could be devoted to developing his character, his Nazi avatar.

As the fall semester progressed, however, Richard Hayes began to see the teaching potential behind his new obsession. He himself learned much about the period, the details involved in running a labor camp, the relationships between persons of equal and unequal rank. What possible educational objectives *wouldn't* be met if students played it during class time, perhaps as an extra incentive, so long as he supplemented it with further context and background? It touched on sociological experiences, psychological, even anthropological ones. He could team up with Perry, the English teacher across the hall, and assign all kinds of projects allowing students to connect their experiences in the game with the more complicated elements of their own lives.

Still, he doubted that all students would want to play the same avatar. Could they vary from student to student? Doubtful, since there was no login of any kind, no sequence of entries telling the program who had logged in. They would all play the same avatar—*Sturmführer*

Heinrich Wicker, SS, guard at Dachau. But their differing reactions might cause widely differentiated game results between students, results that could be compared, students' decision-making skills honed through an analysis of their differing reactions to identical stimuli.

In November, Mr. Hayes decided to give extra credit to a student in desperate need. It would be an experiment, an after-school endeavor lasting two weeks. He would have the student open the specially created browser, his own invention, taking the user directly to the site address without revealing its URL. This, he figured, would keep things controlled and centralized, at least until he had a better understanding of how this miraculous teaching tool actually performed. Then, he would simply monitor the student's progress and reactions as he played the Game, scoring points to be added to quizzes. He had no idea how points might be awarded, something he'd deal with later.

Richard had a classroom full of computers of various makes and computing speeds, collected, with administrative approval, from the classrooms of teachers who had left the district over the years. He sat Marcus at the newest and fastest model, watching over the kid's shoulder, letting him use a somewhat worn pair of studded gloves and two mouse balls.

Once Marcus had logged in (by merely typing his name) and the screen transitioned into a city environment, his avatar stood in the middle of a street intersection. The bright sun revealed all the details of the surroundings, the people, the cars, the street, the square buildings. Marcus was startled and made quick movements with the gloves and ball. The character immediately collapsed. Cars of the late-1930s moved slowly around him. Some beeped their horns, drivers staring as they drove by. One car stopped at a shoulder. A man in a gray coat got out to direct the traffic around him. Richard intervened, taking over the headset and directing the gloves and the ball by gently raising the boy's wrists, "just for now." He expertly brought the character to a standing position, "Excuse me," he said. A few taps at the keyboard and the character smiled. "It must be the heat." The man in the gray coat smiled back and waved as he walked back to his car. The usually soft-spoken Marcus was impressed, amazed even, looking back and forth between Hayes and his avatar on the screen. His mouth was wide open.

Hayes transferred the devices back to Marcus and deftly taught him the basics, raising his arms and positioning the trackballs for him until the young man was able to maintain some control over the character. In twenty minutes, Marcus' avatar, in a gray uniform, was directing traffic passably well. It wasn't Heinrich Wicker.

Knowing what he now knew, Hayes gradually sought ways to incorporate the game into his social studies units. With only twelve computers exhibiting the power to run the game without annoying lag, he would have to rotate students through the stations while prepping the others with background needed to make the best decisions in the game, based on their avatars' unique situations.

Planning anything, however, was difficult since there was always the Game. The distraction ate up his spare hours like minutes and fed on his days.

Of course, there were many justifications for including the game into his curriculum. Not the least of which was the linguistic slant it gave to his history lessons. Perry, his team-teacher from across the hall, would love that. Certainly, by May Perry would be covering 20th century literature, which would work well within the context of the game. Over the last months, Hayes had relearned the essentials of the German language very quickly. There was no reason why students couldn't also be immersed into a second language this way. Perhaps in the years to follow, the game could be introduced early in the school year, about the time when Perry had the juniors studying *Beowulf*, for instance. The German language encountered in the game would provide an excellent Anglo-Saxon linguistic tie-in to the work while Hayes would give them history lessons regarding relevant Saxon and British migrations. There were plenty of English words—originally Old German or Saxon—survivors of the later French-Norman invasion of England in 1066. The most frequently used words, in fact, like fish, hand, arm, nose, hair, water, cow, grass, stool, boat, and gold, had near-identical German cognates. As far as learning nouns was concerned, German was the easiest language for an English speaker to master. Literature (they would have to read newspapers, pamphlets and possibly reports in the game, after all), geography, cultural awareness, even science for some students, all would be worked into Game-based history lessons.

Spring, 2032

By early May, Mr. Hayes had introduced the game to all his students. Student buy-in was slow, however. Lag made the game almost impossible to play on some of his units. He would need faster computers, and more of them, to feasibly run this game as a significant teaching tool, tied to a much wider range of bandwidth for 30 students to play it simultaneously in a single classroom. It was a huge challenge to consider for next year, but not an impossibility. In mid-May, Hayes applied for a last-minute State grant that might mean getting more powerful computers and faster Internet flowing into his classroom. Fortunately, he had come across an advertisement seeking applications for a grant open to every school in the South Texas region. His part would be to convince the readers of the application that his plan for the new computers was more worthy than those of any other applicant, which wouldn't be too difficult since many teachers and administrators were essentially intimidated by the new teaching technologies emerging in education, and the few who weren't were likely years behind understanding its possibilities. He doubted that any were aware of the obscure but powerful tool he had discovered that summer.

Hayes spent a week in May planning the idea that, he knew, would sell his application to the grant readers, like hawking lottery scratch-offs to adults equipped with third grade math. The plan involved including some off-the-shelf software he'd never use, at least not for long. Any reasonable justification he could make for the purchase of computers combining increased student confidence and improved State test scores would surely be placed at the top of the list.

Fortunately, there was a new software suite on the market which was supposed to "tap into a student's cognitive gateway" to somehow reveal the real-world value of the education s/he was receiving, intrinsically motivating him or her to achieve better scores on the StatSat IV, the State test for low-performing juniors attempting to graduate. The software was the Aris MindMage Suite, and it *required* updated equipment and wide bandwidth. To get VR gloves and trackball mice, he added to his projected lesson plan a set of free online virtual reality tours of historical sites and museums. Hayes' administrators signed off on the application with barely a thought and proffered his submission. By July the grant for improved bandwidth, a lab license for using the MindMage software, headsets, mice, VR gloves, special desks, and 30 high-speed computers were all his to use as he saw fit.

Fall, 2032

The computers bought with the grant money were installed in Richard's rather large classroom over the last few weeks of the summer. His room was almost double the size of a normal classroom since it was originally intended for use as a computer lab. The computers themselves were embedded in special one-piece student desks. One merely had to sit down and press the top of the angled L-shaped box to watch the wide screen pneumatically raise itself up from horizontal. A keyboard would then glide out of what looked like a low mail slot and position itself under awaiting fingers. Interactive gloves, headsets, and mouse-balls were stored in large cavities on either side. The Internet flowed in by means of a satellite dish which pushed connectivity into the room through cables like a firehose, all mounted just outside and above the classroom's small window.

There were 30 computer stations positioned in five columns of six with nearly a yard of empty space between and in front of each desk. The walkway between the columns was covered in cables of various thicknesses and colors, eventually to be zip-tied together in bundles and placed out of the way along the edges of the units.

Hayes' next move was to put a box around each station—to help with the realism. Each student would be enclosed on three sides and above in his or her personal, virtual space by refrigerator boxes, little cubicles they could slide forward or back around themselves at their discretion. Interactive helmets, like the one he used at home, would have been ideal to achieve this private realm for each player, but the grant money had been maxed out by the units themselves and by the ridiculously overpriced MindMage software installed on the units. Instead, he had come up with the idea of allowing students the option of using the boxes to encapsulate themselves while involved in the Game. He had no idea whether or not this would even work or how many students would be interested in learning in a cardboard cave, but he thought the idea deserved some merit. Within a few weeks, he had most of the needed boxes, willingly donated from various appliance retailers.

Mr. Farash had dropped in during Preparation Week, the workweek before students returned, when mandatory in-services could be gotten out of the way, the time when teachers put up their class rules and decorated their doors and walls and bulletin boards. When he walked into Mr. Hayes' classroom, the middle-aged instructor was at the opposite end of the room near his desk, cleaning out the contents of several filing cabinets, tossing out stacks of manila folders bulging with copies of assignments. Large refrigerator boxes, monoliths of somewhat unequal heights, stood in front of desks, in rows like a memorial he had once seen in Berlin. Hayes noticed him, nodded, and kept working. "How goes it my Indian friend and fellow educator? Ready for a new year?"

"It goes well, thanks for asking, Richard. Just cleaning out a few things. I see you've been busy."

"I got the computer grant."

"Exceptional! Where are the computers?"

"In the desks. The keyboards and monitors slide out."

"So why the boxes?"

Hayes explained, as he would to others, that full implementation of the Aris MindMage software required total concentration on the part of the student. The more focused the student, the higher the StatSat scores would be, or so the spiel went. Still standing at the classroom door on the side of the room opposite Hayes, Farash was intrigued with the setup, so intrigued that he did not catch the part about students actually working inside the boxes. Rather, he simply thought the boxes were the containers in which the computers and desks arrived. He thought their sizes a bit large to justify their probable contents, but this wasn't the first time he was confronted with the over-packaging of American products, always boxed to make the contents look like more than what they actually were.

It was a month into the school year before Farash made his first visit to Hayes' classroom for a round of occupational therapy. It was mid-morning, and some students had been sleeping through one of his lectures. He'd had enough. He looked through Hayes' narrow window and saw . . . nothing. There was no light on in the room. Perhaps Hayes had taken his students to the Learning Resource Center.

Farash tapped on the window and waited.

No response.

He tried the handle.

Locked.

Farash went back to his room, pretending all was routine. At the bell, Farash rushed into the hall to see if Hayes would appear at his door. Hayes was at his open door and students were filing out. The fluorescent bulbs in the ceiling above the classroom were fully lit. He and his students had been there the whole time.

"Mr. Hayes, if I could speak with you for a moment."

"Sure."

"These students have no respect for authority. Why do they sleep so much? Do they not sleep at home? Are they not given curfews?"

"Hmm." Hayes stood at his door, non-committal. He watched the next group of students shuffling past, some smiling in recognition, most ignoring him completely.

Farash now smiled broadly and sadly, showing bone-white teeth and dark gums above his bleached button-up shirt. "It is funny, do you not think so, sir? I have barely had them a month and they sleep in my class like zombies." Hayes shook his head in condolement but said nothing. He was distracted by an idea and barely heard the man. Farash sighed and walked back into his room, shutting the door with some force; it was now his conference period. Hayes felt a twinge of guilt, but whatever advice he chose to give Farash, the man would never implement any changes in his teaching style. In the time he had known Farash, giving both encouragement and detailed critiques seemed equally pointless.

Later that day, Farash returned. The room was dark again. This time, the door was unlocked. There was, however, the barely audible sound of typing coming from some of the boxes, like distant rain tapping on a flat pane of glass. Though fully daytime, only small specks of light pierced through a window painted over from the inside with black paint.

Hayes was sitting at his desk near the window on the far side of the room. He was reading a hardcover book with an attached reading light and looked up briefly before returning to the page. Farash shouted to Hayes from the door, "Where are your students?" "In those boxes, mostly," Hayes said, looking up and then glancing back at the novel. Indeed, a few of the high-achieving students up front chose not to work in their boxes, thinking the idea absurd, and instead left them pushed forward, but these were hidden from Farash by all the other boxes in the room almost completely covering each student. Most had taken to the idea of using them fairly quickly once they were introduced to the Game.

Farash's eyes were starting to acclimate to the dark room. Some tiny hints of light radiated from the base of some of the boxes. Cables snaked along the floor at the sides of the boxes, leading ultimately to about a dozen newly placed sockets along the walls. It was like being in a dark warehouse after hours. Farash came up and sat on the desk next to Mr. Hayes, looking at him with the most apparent question mark that he could muster. Hayes looked up, smiled, and said nothing. Farash sat quietly and looked out upon the cardboard monoliths, listening to the drone of the aircon and the light tapping.

After some moments, a cry could be heard. It was as if a student in one of the closer boxes was laughing or crying or perhaps both at the same time. The sound stopped and typing continued. Hayes left his desk and motioned for Farash to join him beside the box from whence the curious emotion had been emitted. He pushed the box forward, exposing a female wearing a headset, completely immersed in what was happening on the screen, apparently no cause for alarm. As Farash tried to figure out what the student was looking at, the student's head turned and directed at Farash a sightless stare, making the teacher jump back involuntarily. Her gaze returned to the screen as if she hadn't seen the man. The student's fingers were busily moving in the studded gloves, suspended in air at the sides of the monitor. One held a wireless mouse-ball in midair. Occasionally, the girl would lift one hand or the other, waving fingers as if putting the screen into a trance, and then, dropping the ball, resumed typing. Hayes was quietly sliding the box back over the student when he and Farash heard another student from a box in the back row: "Oh shit . . . damn rifle cut out on me . . . uh, forgot ammunition."

This is indeed a unique teaching method you have implemented Mr. Hayes," Farash said enthusiastically as Hayes led him to the door. Hayes knew the man would seek a further opinion from the campus principal regarding this "new teaching method" prior to forming one of his own. Hayes shut the door behind Mr. Farash, flipping a pen through his fingers. He knew the man's mind and expected a visit from the Principal after Farash had seen the students "playing games" in Hayes' classroom. With the many contradictory teaching theories floating around, he could spin his ideas into any form he desired if boxed into a difficulty. He could argue traditional drill-and-kill and get just as many proponents on his side as a project-based or quasi-synaptic method. He knew this idea had serious potential and was unlike anything anyone else was doing.

Currently, Richard was using the MindMage software the grant required during about 10% to 15% of the instruction time, for appearances. When a student had completed a subunit, s/he would then open up Hayes' simplified browser which took the student directly to an historical, fact-based virtual world of the 1930s and '40s. Each avatar was different, each character somehow tailored to a student's own personality, at least as far as Hayes could gather from the questions he would occasionally ask them. Algorithms apparently gathered data from the movement of the gloves and mice, the spacing of keystrokes, the audio input, timed reactions, and so forth. These things could predict much about one's mental state, especially over time. He had no idea how the game placed students in their personality-appropriate scenarios so quickly at the onset, some only a few minutes after first opening the browser. Richard silently gave homage to the Valkyrie builders responsible, whoever they actually were.

Hayes incorporated the Aris MindMage into his curriculum because he had to. It was part of the grant, and he'd have to submit reports, eventually. This meant students finishing a certain number of subunits each semester, according to his proposal. Mr. Hayes therefore required each student's completion of a brief subunit of the MindMage every period before joining the Game.

But it wasn't long before the class time devoted to the Aris MindMage soon dropped to ten percent, then five, though Hayes hadn't decreased the workload. Students were scurrying through the Aris MindMage to get to the Game before losing valuable class time. Their scores on the MindMage, however, hadn't dropped, only the time it took them to finish lessons, which meant overall performance was improving. Some students were even coming before and after school to get subunits completed beforehand so that all their class time could be devoted to what actually mattered to them, the Game.

A few weeks had passed before Farash would approach Hayes' classroom door again. This time, Farash knocked rather solidly on the oak-veneered door, left arm akimbo with a fist resting on his white chinos. It wasn't long before Hayes opened it and Farash squeezed in gratefully, as if now shielded from what had followed him through the hall. Hayes' classroom was fully lit up this time.

"Can I observe?" He smiled, pitifully.

"Sure. What for?" Hayes knew what for. Farash needed to hide. Passing the boxes, Hayes invited Farash to sit next to him on his desk, as usual. The aircon blew hard into the room, masking much of the sounds coming from the columns of monolithic boxes. Occasionally, one box would stir, bumped from within by a gloved hand or elbow perhaps raised too high.

On screen, Daniel Mesa's avatar opened its eyes to a blurry room, a hard bunk, a little metal whistle in his hand, and a young doctor seated beside him on a rusty stool. He looked about him, noticing a peeling wall and a door missing an upper panel. "*Habst du der Husten heute?* . . . Do you have the coughs today?" the man was asking. A nurse looked indifferently at the boy who lay swaddled in dank sheets. "*Mein Kind. Hustest du heute?*" My child, are you coughing today? The doctor seemed friendly. Daniel felt comforted by the young doctor's presence, and the woman's. He didn't think his avatar had a cough.

The man in the white coat took the boy's wrist while looking down at his own wristwatch. He soon dropped the boy's hand and walked towards the door. The nurse asked, "*Doktor Gross, haben sie die Medizin für der Junge?*" Do you have the medicine for the boy? The man in the white coat stopped, turned to look at the boy, and walked out the door with a clipboard in hand. The nurse followed, shaking her head. Then there was a partial silence. Distant groans began penetrating the walls, but Daniel had no idea who or what made those sounds, or where they came from. A stench from the stale mattress and sheets seemed to intrude upon his own senses, somehow even reaching faintly into the cardboard box. He looked down at his avatar's arms. His hands were turned in, bent and shriveled, wrists yellowed. His legs looked blue with cold and, somehow, ridiculously small. He couldn't move them.

The nurse returned with the "*medizin.*" He watched her jab the needle into his leg and press down to plunge the clear liquid into his unresponsive, deformed body. "What is it?" he asked her. She pretended not to hear him, removed the syringe, and quickly left the room. Perhaps his avatar hadn't spoken.

Fall, 2032

Coach Mason, Principal, stood by the flagpole listening to Farash's frenetic report one sunny Thursday afternoon. "Aren't you, sir, curious what Hayes is doing with all those big boxes? Do you know his students work *inside* of them? I couldn't believe it when I saw it with my own eyes!" The large American flag attached to the metallic pole gave palpable pops and forts as the students piled out of the school and, by increments, into the dingy black and yellow buses. Farash was attempting to convey his concerns dutifully. He was also a little jealous of Richard's computers.

Coach Mason looked straight ahead at the buses coming and going. "Hayes. Well, he's a good teacher. It's likely he's doing something new, probably an Internet thing. If Hayes is one thing, Mr. Farash, he's solid in the classroom. Maybe one of the best teachers we've seen at this school in years. Did you look to see what his students were working on? He wrote the grant all by himself."

"It looked like they were playing video games."

"Video games, you say?" Mason frowned. "Well so much of the new stuff is made to appeal to kids. I wouldn't worry about it."

Farash reflected, then frowned. It just seemed suspicious. The exclamations of students, hidden away in their confining cubes, and the guilty grin on Hayes' face when he looked out across the cardboard boxes told the tale, at least partially. He liked Hayes—though Hayes wasn't always the best mentor, rarely helpful when help was truly needed. Mr. Farash had a duty to his career, to the students, to doing the right thing. That's why he had approached Principal Mason.

The afternoon was waning and students were becoming scarce in the parking lots and around the doorways. Mason smiled and thanked Farash for "keeping an eye on things." Farash smiled and half-bowed, turning to walk to his little sub-compact.

Mounds of charred cloth and scorched human and leathery animal remains lay thick in the fore while the tanks continued their unrelenting climb, interminable in their approach, towards the foothills of Warsaw. Before the fall, Lionel had just about given up, seeing most of his comrades beaten into the dirt by the rapid fire of the small tanks and the pistols aimed by men riding solo in the sidecars of buzzing three-person motorcycles.

Lionel watched from his horse, standing just inside the tree line as his fellow countrymen attacked a group of German tanks from horseback with primitive lances and muskets. He had run out of ammo and so had to find a bit of shelter to reload. The explosions seemed amplified by a choking black smoke rendered from a nearby pit. Between ear-ringing bursts, grinding mechanical tracks plodded forward, setting off their own projectile explosions emitted from the dark pipes protruding from mobile engines protected by a thick layer of *dunkelgrün* steel. But those were still some distance away, too distant for Lionel to consider much as his horse contorted itself oddly and landed upon his thickly clothed body while his antiquated musket flew off in another direction. He struggled to get free of the horse, which already lay unconscious across his chest and shoulders.

He pulled himself out between mud and horse, just enough to watch the advance of the smoking metal beasts. The screen was fading as the avatar closed its eyes, Lionel expecting to die at any second, when everything went dark.

Chirping could be heard through an open window, a warm breeze hitting Lionel's face, the discernable smells of both his cluttered room and the earthy scent of dry farmland. He was back home, it was early morning, and he had played most of the night. Lionel's laptop sat on his chest as he lay in bed. He smiled and threw off the gloves. He had done it! Hayes' special browser, which he had copied from his school computer using a surreptitious flash drive, was now his to use. He'd spread to a few others of the junior class, attached to an anonymous email, of course. It would take a few days to package it as an executable installation file, allowing anyone to download and install it on their own machines with a few clicks. Granted, their machines would have to be high-end, like his, and most juniors at the campus didn't possess much along those lines. But a few did.

On presentation days, Mr. Perry, the tall, thin English teacher across the hall, would combine his classes with those of Hayes. On these days, usually once or twice a six weeks, they would pack Perry's classroom, some students sitting on desks and standing along the walls.

Hayes enjoyed working with Perry on these collaborative endeavors though they didn't get a chance to collaborate much, both teaching seven-period marathons each day with 30-minute lunches and a period off to decompress. The two teachers in the small school district basically had the same students enrolled in their classes, so this sort of teaming worked out pretty well. Hayes had told Perry everything he needed to know about the game for the joint project to be successful, which, in reality, wasn't very much.

A hefty boy in baggy pants and close-cropped hair pulled his speaker notes from a front pocket and unfolded them, his left forearm tattooed from his wrist to his elbow in a way that made the arm look cybernetic, with cables and metal gears seeming to snake through the flesh. He looked at his audience, looked down at his feet and gave an embarrassed grin through reddened eyes. "Don't laugh because I already know it sucks." He paused. Then he began giving his report. "I was a horse trainer in Poland. I am now thin with long arms, so I'm having a tough time with the cold. My character doesn't heal well. He has a cut on . . ."

Perry cleared his throat from the side of the room. "Remember the rules, Pete. Refer to yourself as the character, in first person, not to your character in the third person." Pete nodded and continued.

"The camp is surrounded with barbed wire and towers. On one side runs a track with regular trains blowing and screeching to a halt before a long platform of men with the lightning bolts on their collars. It comes and goes twice a day.

"I sleep in the second tier of bunks with two other guys." A few giggles came from the middle rows. "It's not always the same guys though." More giggles. "I mean, some die right next to you while you're sleeping, and then you wake up and they're staring at you with their dead eyes and you can't wake them up so you just push them off the bunk so you can go back to sleep." Silence.

"Of course, most of us have a choice of bigger and better things in the camp, particularly if we carry the dead—and the soon-to-be dead. I haven't done that. Or if we can convince the people that they're only getting a shower. I haven't done that either, but you hear things from other players during the game."

"'*Inmates*,' Hayes pointed out. Don't refer to it as a game. Talk about your experiences as if they are real."

"Inmates. . . . OK. Now devices. First, imagery. My ribs show through my loose skin and my bunk, filthy with lice, is only five feet long so my feet hang off the end. I work at the digging spot with nothing but the pathetic striped clothes. The pants are loose and they just come to my calf. They took my shoes away at the train platform and gave me some brown moldy ones that don't even look like shoes any more, more like pieces of stringy beef jerky. My feet are always worse off than the rest of me. There's dried mud between my toes. Like others, I tried wrapping them in whatever I could get, newspapers and dirty strips of cloth mostly. The Germans have separate trash bins, but I realized that the more generous of them—and one is actually kinda generous—leave some of their trash at the top where some prisoners can get at it. I would have starved once except for that guy.

"Simile. A few prisoners are like the dogs that some of the guards walk around with, wanting to bring you down to build themselves up. They just want to please the guards. They have it pretty good, and it makes me want to volunteer for their jobs, the ones that take away your humanity."

"Very good, Pete," Mr. Perry encouraged.

"Personification." He continued. "My sad feet. Once they are gone, the rest will quickly follow.

"There is a guard. Herr Spiegel. The guards just call him 'Spieg.' He sometimes inspects the area where we work and even dropped a part of his sandwich near a prisoner once, the prisoner in the worst shape who was about to die. He tried to avoid stone-cutting or carrying the blocks since he could barely lift his own head. Because if you can't work, you're taken behind the ovens and shot in the back of the neck and then you fall into one of the pits I helped dig. I've seen it many times. They don't even kill you and drag you. They walk you to your grave and shoot you there. Less work that way.

"Spiegel has fewer medals and patches than most of the other guards I've seen.

"Metaphor. He doesn't bark orders like the others. Just patrols, mainly the workers' areas. Once, he accidentally dropped his wallet beside a rock I was chopping at with a broken spade. It fell open and there was a picture of his family. There was a blonde woman in the picture holding two babies. I picked up the wallet and handed it to him. He put it in his front pocket, nodded to me, and walked on." At this point Pete lifted his fleshy chin off his chest and looked at his audience for the first time.

"A nod? What am I? Just a Polish Jew. A nothing in their eyes." He was going off-script. "And here is a member of the great Master Race, no, one of its inner circle, nodding to me as if I were more than a pigeon crapping on his favorite car. Spiegel became my favorite Nazi from that point on. He shows me not all Germans regard us as non-human. But if they let on, they'd be in here with us or sent to the front, so they play along, kicking, yelling. The rest just beat us for fun. You can tell the difference. I'm not sure, but I think he smiled when I handed him the wallet."

The boy returned to his seat in the front-row beside a red-headed girl with braces. The speech was over and no one clapped. No one moved or said anything. Then the clapping began in the middle rows and spread to other students. Finally, the whole room was all howls, whistling, and clapping. Pete turned to the girl with the braces, looking past her, grinning. "Yeah, I told you it sucked."

A sizable jock wearing a gray t-shirt started to stand up in the back row, staring fixedly at Pete, thought better of it, and then sat down again, working his hands together while staring at the fake wood grain on his laminate desk. He began to stand up again and sat back down, shaking his head. "Oh my God. Oh . . . my . . . "God," repeated Blockführer Spiegel's human counterpart.

Chapter 3

All that came to mind was the likelihood, the probability, that he was in hell. *Endless. Dark. Die Nacht* spoken of by the Mormon diggers.

There was indeed darkness. Silence. Nothing.

He spoke in whispers as if sipping at the words. Endless. Darkness. Night. The faint words seemed to surround him, traveling directly from mouth to ear. Echoing mouth to ear yet filling the space around him. He tried forming the words of a prayer long ago forgotten and then gave up.

He heard the crinkling of the paper into an enormous ball and stopped moving. He stirred and imagined a beast of infinite size scooping him up and compressing him like a discarded paper bag.

He lay in a fetal position. As he lay still, the sound of paper was replaced by a throbbing. He felt pain throughout his joints and muscles. His head throbbed and the pounding seemed to echo off the walls of a metal chamber.

He reached up to touch his eyes, to check if they were open or closed. He could feel nothing, as if his fingertips had been removed. His hand stopped short against a flat, smooth surface. They were gloved fingers. His head had been covered as well.

For a moment he couldn't decide whether he had been spun into a cocoon or simply left inside a petrified egg to suffocate. The heat was getting unbearable and he imagined himself curled up on a frying pan. As memory began to flash in and out of his thoughts, he stood up, panicked, and rushed forward, immediately knocking his helmet and suit against a curved surface. He fell flat on his back and groped towards the center.

His head touched something. A curved handle. A wheel protruding from the floor. He was hyperventilating, gasping at the thinning air. On all fours and pulled at it, attempting to turn it first in one direction and then the other. Nothing moved as his gloved hands slid around its edges.

After three attempts, he stood up and ran back to the wall. The direction didn't matter. He pounded with both fists and screamed with what little air he could muster. In his delirium, he thought of the blackness of space and what space travel might be like. Blue dots exploding before his eyes, he made a final attempt at the wheel near the center. It gave. He was free.

SOUTH TEXAS, NOVEMBER, 2035

For a few minutes, the young man had been lying on the now-wrinkled bedspread, staring at the high ceiling of the quiet hospital room. He wouldn't stay long.

There was a "tap tap" at the wide door of the hospital room. Rain was likewise tapping against the Plexiglas window on this side of the metal grating.

The usual nurse walked in, tall, blonde, young, certainly enough to grab the young man's attention as his eyes moved, gradually, to her face. "Well, two visitors on the same day? This can't be a coincidence."

"I'm sorry?" He was confused as the nurse stepped over to the box, ignoring his words. "Someone else to see you, Mister Hayes. She says she's your aunt."

A small, bent octogenarian female shuffled in behind an aluminum walker, the hump in her tiny upper back almost as high as the wisps of curly white hair growing in clumps over a pink, spotty scalp. She looked at the floor as she shuffled in, then stopped and turned to face the young man as he sat up, about to stand. "Don't bother," she murmured in a heavily foreign accent. "I do not think I am here to see you, young man."

He sat against the bed frame in the far corner and watched. The nurse quietly shut the door behind her as she left the room. The old woman spoke up so as to be heard through the box. "Hello, Richard Hayes. My name is Selma." Her German accent was heavy.

"Selma," came a muffled voice, rough and hollow from apparent disuse. Selma sat on the edge of the bed and leaned her spotty, wrinkled forearms across the top of her metallic walker. After a few moments she turned to look at the young man. "Who are you?" she asked, her bulbous eyes looked tiredly at his neck rather than at his face.

"I was a student of Mr. Hayes. I just came by to say hi."

"Very vell," she said indifferently. "You von't believe anything you hear me say to this man. Though it doesn't matter one way or the other—no one vould believe you. Perhaps you can write a book someday. But for that you might have to take lots of notes," the old woman paused, then nodded, and her gaze fell back to the box. "Does he sleep in this bed?"

"I don't think so," he replied. "When I first sat on it, it was covered with dust."

"He is a sad man."

A GERMAN NURSE TOOK a syringe and smashed the point into a wooden beam along the wall. She was angry. The avatar's counterpart almost collapsed into a crying fit, seated in the dark in her big cardboard box. *The Doktor* returned. He was a bespectacled German, tall, stooping, and bald, carrying a wet towel into which he smeared the foul contents of his hands, tossing the towel into a metal canister on the floor in a corner.

"*Anke, das ist deiner kiste,*" *that is your box,* he stated, pointing to a small box on a metal shelf of cardboard boxes and glass beakers. She turned to the shelf and reached for the box. She opened it. Inside were more syringes along with some small vials containing a white powder, one of a clear liquid. She shut the box and squeezed her eyes shut.

"*Ein Problem?*" suggested the tall doctor, putting a fatherly hand on her shoulder. "No. No problem . . . *Nein. Kein Problem,*" she responded, not knowing from where the actual words derived but knowing them to be a reflection of what she did say, or wanted to say, or thought. She wasn't sure.

Emerging from the *Provisorische Krankenhaus*, Karen stopped before one of three large, makeshift tents inhabiting a wide yard surrounded on three sides by a small network of administrative buildings. The tents resided nowhere near the regular prison barracks but rather near the fence at the side of the camp. It was starting to rain. Karen clutched the box tightly under her arm. To turn around and walk the other way would be to commit herself to a similar camp, if not the same one, as an inmate. A good German did what she was told. Ask no questions, except to clarify, and then do your job. Otherwise, you are perhaps a collaborator, an enemy of the State, the worst scum soon residing at the bottom of the prison roster.

She stood before the door of the largest tent. The avatar, Anke, shook, seemed about to collapse . . . from exhaustion? Fear? . . . when a soldier opened the door and motioned her in. She followed, seeing several cots, two containing women. The one in the far cot was unconscious. The woman in the closest cot was staring at her, wide-eyed, talking desperately in another language. Sounded Baltic. Possibly Lithuanian. Karen didn't know how she knew, but she knew.

She was to administer euthanasia to this dark and attractive woman, beautiful though extremely thin. On any other woman, the features wrought by the emaciation would have seemed cadaverous. Her belly showed her to be about five months pregnant. The woman knew why Anke, Karen's avatar, was there. She stared at the German nurse, backing up on her cot to its furthest corner, ready to strike with her feet. Clutching the side of the tent nearest her head, she began to scream, as if this pointless cry were meant to save her life, hers and that of her unborn child.

Karen, an advanced sophomore taking Hayes' class with juniors, knew her role in the game very well. A part of her hated it but thought it must have a purpose that she would eventually know. She knew she didn't belong here, in this place, this time, this situation. She was someone else, from somewhere else. For a split second it was actually difficult to remember who she was—the realism of the game was frightening at times. You could get so lost in the game; your own identity starts to retreat somewhere or blend into that of the avatar. The current scenario dominated one's thoughts and a faint glimmer of something else nagging at you as you made your decision, often the decision to either survive or to do the right thing—and be roasted for it.

She opened the box and took out the vial of clear liquid. The soldier who had led her into the tent stood just inside the door and looked on. The screaming of the woman had brought him back. Anke pressed the syringe into the vial and filled the syringe until it was about half full. "Nežudyk mano kūdikio!" the woman screamed. Karen had no idea what she was saying, but she did know that though this woman probably suffered a fear greater than she had ever known, and though this small mound of child just beneath her skin was indeed human like herself, it had been growing in an overworked, malnourished mother for months in the camp and would probably die anyway, would certainly die when the mother died of malnutrition, which appeared all but inevitable.

Anke sprayed the syringe of fluid into the air to eliminate the bubble of air within. A pointless life-saving gesture, but still there was protocol to follow. She took the syringe and bent toward the unexposed thigh of the thin Lithuanian woman who quietly pleaded for mercy. Anke held a finger to her lips, shaking her head slowly. With a quick swing of the arm, she embedded the needle deeply into the leg, the liquid filling the muscle of a hard thigh in dark pants.

The soldier fell, gasping, grabbing his leg and yelling "*Helf mir! Helf mir!*" while Anke struggled to cover his mouth with a hand towel. Gradually, he lay unconscious just inside the tent, staring sightlessly into the dark canvas roof. The young woman stared at the nurse in horror, shaking her head. It would mean all of their deaths. So pointless.

After Karen emerged from the tent, she materialized from the cardboard cave and the Game, throwing her backpack over her right shoulder, almost tripping over the cables. The bell rang for second period while another much louder siren pealed in a distant camp, 83 years in the past.

When the bell rang and the lights came on, students slowly and reluctantly began to emerge from their cardboard caves, taking up their backpacks from along the back wall and saying little while filing out of the room; some exchanged a few excited whispers while others walked out in morbid silence.

Dana Murphy didn't want to return to this avatar. It was part of the class, so she got in, hoping it was already dead. It watched as smoke seethed through the chinks of a hastily built chimney. She saw fire behind a semi-rusty grate with "*Achten*" chalked across it and was briefly and strangely soothed by memories of her grandmother's cabin in the cold, windy woods of Maine. She could somehow smell the wood fire behind the black metal door. She couldn't move anything but her left hand and arm. The right arm seemed broken and useless. She brought up the dirty left hand and held it before her eyes. It was real enough, but not quite, in some respects. The spaces between the bony fingers were dark along with the fingers themselves, all stained with dirt. She gently touched her belly, swollen with malnutrition and pregnancy.

The metal door of the furnace, rounded at the top, was pulled open by the spindly fingers of a hand protruding from a dirty, striped uniform. The *Sonderkommandos* tried to work quickly but often stumbled from lack of sleep. Their stumbling was frequently rewarded with sharp yells from the SS soldiers watching from a distance, but not from kicks or rifle butts. They were too important, even kept separate from other inmates, housed in rooms rimming the crematorium, severely warned not to speak of what they saw or did.

The flat iron gurney upon which she lay was fixed to move in only two directions, its wheels seated atop rails. Dana could almost feel the hands resting on her own shoulders, gently pressing. She heard a faint whisper in her left ear: "Go with God, pretty woman. Tell him what is happening here and be at peace." Her body was rolled toward the small, open door, feet first. Soon her avatar's feet were catching fire, sizzling, blistering, as they slid over the red-hot coals and the bits of charred bone, superheated in the orange and yellow shimmer.

Dana reached for her tightening throat. She could move her arms freely now, and as she did so a new awareness penetrated her mind, cooling her skin, and the angle of her body gradually inclined until her upper body was vertically positioned. Dana found herself once again seated in the dark box, at a student's desk, before a now black monitor closing to its hidden, horizontal position. Her feet still tingled as if just taken from the flame. She removed the headset covering her entire head and became aware of a square of light around her sandaled feet. Shaken, she heard the end-of-class bell and pushed the box forward, grabbing her backpack, then dragging her feet down the hall, almost tripping down a flight of stairs, then to the left, past a row of blue lockers, and into the classroom where she would sit through a period of Calculus Fundamentals, nauseated and very weak.

She knew that she would be assigned another avatar, one in a comparable situation, if Mr. Hayes was correct about how things worked. Its death was terrifying, and she didn't want another avatar. Right now, she just wanted to sleep.

Dana's Calculus Fundamentals teacher, Mrs. Villarreal, sat beside the overhead projector and called on students at random to grade the homework of their peers, a daily procedure. Having switched papers with Julia, the quiet girl with long black hair sitting next to her, she dug out a red grading pencil from her small purse and signed her name next to the words "graded by" on the back of the single sheet of paper torn from a spiral notebook and handed to her. Julia's homework was only half-finished, so she kept her regular pencil out in case she could squeeze a few right answers in without Mrs. Villarreal noticing. Dana's and Julia's handwriting weren't so different.

Dana couldn't focus on mathematics. Her mind kept drifting back to the game, what she may have done wrong resulting in her avatar's death. Maybe she didn't do anything wrong. The inmate's death may have simply been unavoidable—she was fragile, skinny, weak, and pregnant—had been all of these when Dana first began using her in September. The cards were stacked against her from the start. Dying early wouldn't cause even a single point deduction in Mr. Hayes' class, but still it kinda sucked that some students could be guards, some politicians, some military police, some soldiers, and she had to be a pathetic little Lithuanian Jew stuck in Dachau, skinny and, as in real life, pregnant.

The German nurse had saved her life, the one with the syringe who'd killed the guard. They were going to take the baby then, she thought, or maybe kill her and the baby with one injection. But kill a guard? It was stupid, really. What would the nurse accomplish by wasting her own life? And what was Dana supposed to do about it? Certainly, the nurse knew that she, the inmate, was going to die either way.

She wondered whether the girl who saved her was an avatar or just a computer character. Maybe everyone in the game *was* a person behind an avatar. It was even possible, she thought, that hers was the *only* avatar in her game. *Were* all the other characters simply computer generations? Was everyone in Mr. Hayes' classes simply playing their own independent games? He never came out and said this *wasn't* the case. He rarely talked about the inner workings of the game, only about how we should report on our own experiences, what we were learning, how it applied to history and our own lives.

Dana was called on to work on one of the problems projected on the screen. She worked it without having to look either at the book or at her own paper sitting on Julia's desk beside her. Julia had left the problem unfinished. Dana's answers, however, were perfect. Another student was then randomly called upon to work on the next problem.

When the grading session was over, Dana handed Julia's paper back to her. It had no marks on it, and, noticing this, Julia grinned. Though Dana hadn't filled in blank answers with correct ones, she at least hadn't marked any wrong. It would be Dana's ass, not Julia's, if Mrs. Villarreal happened to look at some of Julia's answers and notice the grading errors, but Dana didn't care.

Apart from a few rare exceptions, no one really encountered the other players in-game, as far as they knew, though discussion of the game between students was common. The European war involved millions. There were literally thousands of camps both inside and outside of Germany, and there were only 183 juniors. Not all found themselves in camps, but many somehow ended up in one or at the front, one way or another. Some students had been in several camps by the end of the first semester, and it was all in real time, so an eight-hour drive in a truck took an actual eight hours; a week on an overcrowded train took just as painfully long.

Closing the browser didn't mean everything would continue as it was when you opened it again. Things would happen in your absence, during the other 23 hours of the wakeful day, and, depending on your role, you'd have to catch up, without letting on to other characters in the game that you hadn't actually been there, for unnatural behavior was often punished by ensuing circumstances. After dying, one could expect to appear as someone in a remarkably similar situation, surviving in a camp perhaps a thousand miles away, though stuck in much the same circumstances as before. Whether you were a politician, a clerk, a bus driver, or a grave digger the rules were the same no matter how you died . . . or how you chose to live. Still, for every player, no matter how mundane his or her avatar's life might seem, scenarios always came up that involved life and death situations—and choices had to be made, always tied in some way to the War.

Working late one night in his classroom, Richard Hayes decided to take a break and sat at one of the desks in the back corner. He had bought an additional VR helmet to see how it worked on these machines. Perhaps someday he could chuck the boxes and give students the helmets to use instead, maybe pay for it with candy sales and donations. He certainly hated asking for money, and fundraisers were always a pain in the ass. Still, there might be some way to get them. He pressed and the pneumatic screen and keyboard offered themselves in a slow but steady draw. The unit powered on. Soon the gloves were on, and the video, audio, and mike wires of the helmet connected to the side of the unit. He pressed it on his head and watched as the wide screen in his helmet hummed into a picture.

Soon there was movement. He found himself in a small, dark room littered with stacks of old clothes, linens, piles of old rags. Richard pulled Wicker's Zippo lighter from his left pocket and snapped it into use. There was a girl lying in the mess wearing a white smock over the gray stripes of a prison uniform; she turned slightly and ran thin fingers through roughly cropped hair. Startled, she brought the hand back down, looking straight into Richard's eyes. Another nurse was picking through the rags nearby. The woman seemed no younger than 30, but considering the conditions of the camp, she might have been no older than 18. As he held the lighter closer to her face, she rolled over, shielding her face from the light—or perhaps from the stench of the burning naphtha that fueled the lighter.

"Savina?"

"Hnn?"

"Savina. That's your name, right?" His words were followed by a quick translation in German.

The girl turned and looked up at him, at first perplexed, and then scooted crablike backward with her back to the wall.

This was the second time Richard Hayes had seen the woman. The first time had been very brief, some nights before, and he had overheard her talking with a kitchen worker for the prison hospital, so her name had stuck in his mind. "Are you hungry?" he whispered and almost simultaneously heard his own voice in German: *"Haben sie hunger?"* Her eyes widened. She seemed even more confused. Richard felt around in his coat pockets and found a candy bar and a small tin of crackers. He handed these to her. "My name is Richard Hayes. I'm not who you think I am . . . ." It was a ridiculous thing to say.

She wouldn't take what he had handed to her, so he placed them on the floor. She said something in a mumbling voice, and "What do you want?" came whispered into the helmet just a moment later. And then, "What more can you take from me?"

Richard was startled. "More?" . . . *Mehr?* spoke his character. But he'd never even spoken to her before. He looked around the room. At that moment, she sprung towards the door and was out of the large, dark room in an instant. He went looking for her and found himself in a makeshift kitchen. Prisoners were shuffling about with large sacks of potatoes, cabbages, and onions. She was nowhere amongst them. He spent some time wandering around this part of the camp looking for the girl.

Then, at nearly 10:00 PM, Richard heard something else, something outside the game. It was his classroom door being tried, easy to hear in the echoing silence. He heard keys tried in the door, one after another.

Richard's heart beat quickly. Probably a custodian or security guard. He quickly removed his helmet and slowly pulled the refrigerator box over him and his desk as a form moved across the door's narrow window. After trying a few more keys, the figure paused and then departed. No security guard or custodian, the man was wearing a tie.

Students often came in to play the game before school, some as early as 6:15. Others trickled in at 7:00. Some would ask to come in on Saturdays and others just showed up when he happened to be there on days off, apparently after driving by and seeing his car in the parking lot, playing well into the afternoon as he graded papers, mended gloves, and straightened up the room. From the obsession that some students acquired for the game, Richard assumed the visitor of the previous night to have been one of those who somehow obtained, or tried to obtain, a copy of the room key—not a tricky thing to do, he mused, as nearly all teachers had master keys. But students rarely wore ties. He thought he might just ignore the fact, maybe even invite the person in next time for a history lecture. That would get rid of 'em. But he had the suspicion that this wasn't the first time that someone had attempted, and possibly succeeded, in entering his room uninvited as evinced by junk food wrappers left the next morning after the trash cans had already been emptied.

He knew well the game's addictive nature, and he also understood the odds against anyone procuring the means of playing it outside his classroom, making the idea of someone coming in after hours when no one was around even more likely.

The Dictator, recently named *Time Magazine*'s "Man of the Year," walked into the Bürgerbräukeller beer hall as cheers flooded the nighttime streets. The vocal din came from the sidewalks and windows of surrounding homes and shops selling clothes and kitchen implements, wine and red flags. It was November 8, 1939, the anniversary of the 1923 "Putsch," a small clash between National Socialist demonstrators and Weimar Republic soldiers and police, a movement begun in this beer hall that poured out into the streets like dregs from a cracked barrel. It had been a failed attempt at wresting control for the man who later won Germany without firing a shot. The leader had always claimed this as a victorious day for Germany and had given a speech here every year since his rise to power.

A few thousand people sat waiting in the beer hall or stood outside watching for an opportunity to listen from windows and doorways. He was flanked by his *Leibgarde* or "LifeGuard," the *Leibstandarte*. Its head, a robust man with a pronounced scar just above his left cheek, walked backwards, behind the dictator as he approached the entryway, with his back to the man, eyes scanning the crowd. Two other men well known to the people of Deutschland walked closely at each side.

A third man, good-looking though thin, with dark hair, nervously paced on a far sidewalk just behind the crowds. His hands were in the pockets of his overcoat, one of them fingering a folded note. He was a Swiss astrologer named Karl Ernst Krafft.

The retinue entered the beer hall and made its way up to the dais where a podium awaited the speaker. The edges of the room were filled; in each corner a tall, jacketed man stood looking over the crowd. The dictator was frowning; it was the dark before the dawn of one of his most hysterical speeches, and he had to bring himself into character. It was also the twilight of one of his most daring decisions. Plans had metastasized quickly, and a war-ready Berlin awaited a mere word from the dictator. Here, in the capital of Bavaria, the leader rose to the podium at the punctual German hour of 20.00, expecting to take the next train back to Berlin so as to be there by early morning.

With a gaze of cold indifference, the room was silenced. He seemed to have little patience for introductions. The speaker began immediately with a belittling of the British economy. Germany and the values of National Socialism required the end of this capitalist behemoth, even if it took five long years of war. He then turned on the French, took a few shots at the now subjugated Poles, and said almost nothing about his current political comrade, Joseph Stalin, except to express a distant regret that communism and all communists wouldn't be so easily deterred from their infectious designs by a mere war.

"No. They fight Germany from within, through her alliances, attacking her literature and her art. The sources of communism and Jewishness are aligned in the servile attempt to unite weak men against the powers devised by Nature to perpetuate the strong. Power is the key to the survival of every species that has ever walked, crawled or flown across this world. And those attempting to move against it, failing to adapt to its immovable laws, became extinct.

The enemies of Germany act against this very nature, for they enact laws to fill the bellies of the undeserving by taking from the naturally strong and fertile and giving to the weak and underdeveloped.

"We are the strong. And they want to take everything from us. The human race is a dying race if this is to continue. If the strong of humanity die, humanity itself dies. We, Germany, must be even more united than the enemies of National Socialism, but not like the communists, in their huddled, backward, herded mass, attempting to defeat the laws and principles of natural selection by giving 'to each according to his need.'

"We together are far stronger, for we support what nature has dictated. The strong adapt. The strong survive. We are that strength, and our sacred duty to this land and to our race, our breed, our species, is to allow nature's law to flourish, and in fact to refine it to an even greater degree where the strong *must* destroy the weak so that humanity, and by humanity I mean the *best* of humanity, the *highest* of humanity, can grow and progress."

The speech continued for about an hour with pronounced repetition, stirring up the emotions and feeding the nationalistic glory-lust of its cheering listeners until the head of the dictator's protective retinue, the robust man with the scar above his left cheek, handed the leader a piece of paper recently unfolded. The leader paused; such an action of passing such a note at such a moment would only be done if absolutely necessary. He knew the man well enough to know to read the note quickly. He knew his audience well enough to show no emotion, no matter what was written there.

The scowling speaker glanced up at his security head and saw nothing on the man's face except a side nod towards the cellar entrance. The dictator then looked toward the entrance to the beer cellar where a tall, dark-haired man was held between two SS officers. The man was holding a yellow handkerchief to his face. The note read

My Leader, there is a bomb ticking
in the pillar behind you.
It will detonate at 21.20.
You must leave NOW!
Know me by the yellow cloth I hold to my face.
If this is a lie, have me executed.

The dictator glanced at the man who nodded from behind the yellow cloth and then calmly at his watch. 20.58. He would cut his two-hour speech to one hour and summarize what was left over the next five minutes. When finished, he walked calmly toward the entrance of the beer cellar where he waved to the officers to take the man outside. His protective retinue followed, nonplussed by the leader's inclination to make an abrupt change in plans.

The man between the SS officers smiled and nodded at the leader as he passed; the dictator never gave the man a further look. After whispering something into the ear of the *Leibstandarte* chief, the dictator hopped into the back seat of one of a string of black cars and headed to Munich's train station, *Der Hauptbahnhoff*. Later, an explosion ripped through the beer hall, pulling down an entire balcony section, killing mostly restaurant staff. Riding in the back seat of the curvy 1935 black Mercedes Benz convertible, the dictator turned his head at the distant thud and saw smoke rising from the blast many streets behind.

Blood oozed from both nostrils. The man's beaten face had vertical and diagonal wounds destined to become faint scars. His arms were pulled behind him into a sling of rope and from these his body was suspended from a metal hook. He screamed and played the part well, yet he never changed his story. Why should he? Farash didn't feel a thing.

"How did you know of the assassination attempt on our Leader?" The German SS men asked the question again, and again. He had been handed over to them the minute this special detachment had arrived in Berlin. The man suspended from the hook would pause, spit a quantity of blood, and tell them something else about the Leader that few people (or none) in the present time would actually know, hoping it would give him some sort of credibility. Farash had studied the Second World War almost as deeply as he had the culture of the Sumerians. The little-known facts he could produce, however, were only making things worse. "You know he only has one testicle, which is why he won't submit to physical examinations." Two men behind him simultaneously beat at his elbows with truncheons, clearly taking the comment as an insult. The interrogator sighed, shaking his head. Unfortunately, he had orders to keep the man alive.

Karl Ernst Krafft was taken from the hook and led into a cell in an underground bunker beneath Berlin's Gestapo headquarters. The walls of the bunker dripped with frigid moisture. The bloody avatar could barely move at his commands and shook uncontrollably. Farash would simply have to wait for the character to heal. He decided to let it sleep as he slept himself. Besides the beatings, it had been tiring business to withstand 18 hours of the same boring sort of questioning—a weakness in the programming, no doubt, thought Farash. It really had been tedious.

It seemed impossible to convince the men in the interrogation cells to believe the story of a Swiss astrologer who purportedly only had the Leader's best interests in mind. The "stars" had warned him of an attempt on the Fuhrer's life to be carried out on the day and at the time written in the note. But the more statements he made which turned out to be accurate regarding the historical bombing, the more of a suspect he became in the plot to kill the dictator.

The bomb-maker was found attempting to cross into Switzerland. Farash, through Krafft, had not only given the man's name and where he would cross but also the fact that detonators and bomb drawings would be found in his luggage. Krafft was either the greatest of guessers, a man possessing significant extrasensory powers, or, and most likely, a radical intimately involved in a plot on the Fuhrer's life. The bomb-maker, Johann Georg Elser, a cabinet-maker by trade and staunch protestant union man, was caught just as Farash had predicted, carrying drawings, fuses, and all.

What saved Farash's character, keeping the social studies teacher in the game, was the fact that Elser, under severe torture at the Sachsenhausen concentration camp, admitted to nearly everything they already knew—and some things they didn't—except for ever having known or even having heard of Karl Ernst Krafft. Elser was shipped to Dachau but kept in "good condition." The National Socialists would need him to "confess" for propaganda purposes to conspiring with British agents in attempting to assassinate the Leader.

The Reich Minister of Propaganda, Joseph Goebbels, soon heard the story of Krafft and his marvelous "prediction" and sent for him at the *Propaganda Ministerium* in Berlin, across from the Reich Chancellery.

Today, Richard had begun the game standing at the center of what was referred to as the "parade grounds." There had been rows of prisoners in every direction. It was early morning and diesel engines were grinding away in the distance on the other side of the two rows of barbed-wire gates.

He had a whip in his hand. He was clearly flustered and in mid-strike, slapping the but-end of the rider's whip against the back of an aging female prisoner who, apparently, was still strong enough to work yet had for some reason refused to do so. This scenario wasn't like anything he had yet experienced. Whenever he assumed the identity of his avatar, Richard was usually sitting in a mess hall or walking the perimeter of the camp, or sleeping in a cushioned cot in the officers' barracks. Unlike many of the officers who lived in town, most with wives and children to go home to every night, Heinrich Wicker lived at the camp.

Hayes let the whip fall from his avatar's hand. The woman was silent, with her hands over her ears, crouched and rocking forward and backward on her knees, awaiting the next blow. Richard looked up. The nearest prisoners, forlorn in their striped rags, watched peripherally while others seemed not to pay any heed. He looked around for other officers. There were six, placed variously about the perimeter of the furrows of sad humanity in this great yard. Thousands of prisoners were lined up for "roll call." They might have been there for hours.

He lifted the old woman by her left arm, and she straightened, staring in front of her, tears and dirt blotting her face. Richard Hayes finally realized something about himself, his other self. He thought back to the room filled with old clothes and rags and the woman named Savina whom he had approached there. Her reaction then, this situation now, confirmed it. The character he played must have been one sadistic son of a bitch. How could he not have known after all these months?

He picked up the whip again. He must act the part to be successful in the game. It was only a game, after all, and he would advance as far as he could—certainly farther than any of his students would. That was his challenge to them. Maybe at some point he would become a Gestapo chief in some big city like Krakow or even Munich or even perhaps one day take over as head of the SS. Feeling sure of his role now, he played the part. The woman was ridiculed, stripped, humiliated and frightened. He beat her unconscious with his fists and had two male prisoners drag her body far back to her original place in line, leaving a thin trail of blood over the hard ground.

Then they stopped dragging, reporting that she was "dead, *Herr Offizier*." There was no point in moving a corpse back to its place in line. It might as well rot where it lay, as a warning to others unwilling to do their part. A wind flitted through his avatar's ears and hair. He looked around. His uniformed comrades gave a few casual nods from the far corners of the large assembly—there would be no more work refusals after this little show. There was more silence, save the frigid wind rustling through the camp.

Richard pulled at the helmet and then began reaching frantically for the helmet's straps. He couldn't get to them in time and was sick in his helmet. He choked on the vomit; it had gotten into his lungs, making every acidic attempt to breathe a sharp and painful endeavor. He fell from his chair, still grabbing at the straps. The helmet had saved his head from a hard thud against the floor as he fell, nevertheless, into unconsciousness.

Richard Hayes awoke in a state of pitch-black burning filth. His nose and eyes were raw. He could barely breathe; all was dark in the plastic helmet, his chin and neck coated with drying chunks of vomit. He reached back for his pocketknife, opened it, cut the straps, and flung the helmet off his head and across the room, hitting the floor with a crack and finally rolling across the kitchen's linoleum. Fräulein had been lying next to him. Her whimpering had awoken him.

Staggering, he stood up. He thought of his classroom, the computers, the cables, the painted window, the speckled sound-absorbing schoolhouse ceiling tile, the aircon blowing against the cardboard boxes. It all looked different in his mind. He thought of the students, some probably having experienced what he had experienced—maybe far worse. Which were guards? Which were prisoners? He pitied them. As of this morning, this wasn't just an online game. That its ugliest side had never actually occurred to him made him furious with himself.

He stayed home the following week. He had months of sick days saved up and used up a small fraction of them while recovering from the mental and physical exhaustion of that Saturday morning. He didn't touch the game in that time but rather took long walks with Fräulein across the scrubby fields and even worked a little in his small, weedy garden of spicy peppers and cilantro. He also started to plan classroom routines divorced from the game, like in years past. Daily, he faxed new lesson plans to the school secretary. Most of the students wouldn't be happy, though the more he thought about it, some might be relieved. The refrigerator boxes would need to be flattened and moved out of the room.

When Hayes returned to school in early December, a few students showed some concern for his absence. A rumor had begun to circulate regarding his "chemotherapy treatments." Cards and small gifts filled his desk and mail cubby: "To the greatest teacher ever! Get well soon!" A shiver ran up his back as he read these, looking out at the classroom and wondering about the individual experiences lived within those dark cubes.

Over the next weeks, Richard Hayes still used his computers, and students worked collaboratively through applications via the normal browser. He had discontinued the use of the game, avoiding any reference to it when he could, almost as if it hadn't ever been played. When students started to complain after the first few days of his return, realizing that this wasn't just a temporary stay in their educational routine, Hayes would simply mutter something nebulous about the browser not working with the new software upgrades. Several of the brighter students offered to help him get the problem fixed. "Thanks guys. We're doing what can be done."

Hayes pretended not to notice when students insisted on the game, repeated daily for a while, during every period by some of the more vocal juniors. Gradually, however, routines began to reshape themselves. Learning continued in his history class though enthusiasm waned well below what it had been. Over several weeks, junior attendance dropped. A few students had just stopped showing up.

Chapter 4

The German scientist crawled through the hatch in the floor of the humming Bell, passing through a honeycombed metal platform. His gloved hands touched concrete, dimly lit with a reddish glow, less than a meter below the platform, and he twisted to pull himself through. He peered past the wide legs of the low structure, through a thin layer of smoke emanating from the Bell, finding himself and the Bell completely surrounded by a glass enclosure, its walls standing a meter from the platform on all four sides. Crawling with his forearms, he managed to slide himself to the edge of the platform to get a better look at his surroundings, his head emerging just past it; he looked up. Beyond the enclosing glass structure was a vast structure, its ceiling some twelve to fifteen meters overhead.

In the dim light, he noticed a pencil lying just under the platform and a few sheets of paper scattered here and there. He saw crates stacked along walls, tables and chairs spaced evenly outside the glass. He heard two sets of quick footsteps clomping down metal stairs; there was then the distant slamming of a door and another slower set of footsteps descended. He scooted back beneath the platform like a bug. Soon there were three men in lab coats standing in front of the glass door wearing rubber-soled trainers. He worked to stifle a cough from the light smoke filling the glass chamber. *Not now, Kurt Debus,* he thought to himself (in German) as the three men spoke to one another just outside the leaden glass. The glass was quite thick, but Herr Debus could just discern what they were saying. They were speaking in English with American accents, most of which he understood.

"I tell you, the rims got brighter," said one. "Hell, you could see it from the control room. Must be a power flux."

"Seems to be a bit of smoke in there. We'll probably have to shut it down to check against the calibrations," spoke another.

"I don't see any smoke, and sometimes the rim pulses a bit—you know that. Anyway, we're not shutting it down," spoke a third voice carrying clear authority. "Rads are normal." He tapped at something attached to the glass. "See . . . not even above a thousand."

Spring, 2033

Naturally, it started with armbands.

The word was written in white on a black background: "*Erwachen*!" Wake up. Some, for some inexplicable reason, displayed it in Chinese. ◇◇. Some of the junior girls wrote it in pink, some with pretty hearts and matching bracelets. A few football players included their jersey numbers on the armband along with "Seniors 2034." Toward the end of the spring semester, nearly half of the juniors had armbands. Others, however, sported a small green button, almost invisible, on their backpacks, some on their shirts, reading "*Schlaf!*" Sleep! It was likely, thought Hayes, that the buttons began as a rebuttal to the armbands, so he asked around. It was all tied into the Game. It was as if the game continued, though it hadn't been part of Mr. Hayes' lesson plans for months. Were they still playing it somehow? Had someone discovered its obscure URL, or were they just playing it out in their heads?

Hayes well understood the Game's addictive nature; it wasn't like studying indifferent equations or disembodied facts in a history class or memorizing forgettable terms like iambic pentameter and endoplasmic reticulum. The Game had appeal because, unlike nearly all other educational paradigms, it had slant. You couldn't avoid choosing your side. Being and choosing *was* the game. It wasn't about drafting an indifferent essay on the narrative structure used by a bright little Jewish girl writing in a journal while hiding with her family behind a bookcase in Holland. You were either the little girl on a train or in a camp or in a ghetto trying to stay alive past the next culling, or you were the one dragging out a family from hiding, climbing the ranks with every capture. You could find a family and drag them all to an awaiting truck or lock them into a windowless, packed boxcar and hose them down through the high bars on a cold winter's night, with frigid water meant to bring frostbite to maybe eliminate some of the weaker ones. That sort of thing could mean promotion. You could also be a camp commander and issue reprieves to a group of political prisoners at will, risking a stab in the back by an inferior or the possibility of becoming fodder for Polish bayonets on the front lines the very next week. That had been the Game, and, apparently, it wasn't over.

By April, when it was clear that Mr. Hayes wasn't bringing back the Game, the cliques began to form. In the lunch lines, for instance, some noticeably allowed those wearing the *Erwachen* band into the front while the juniors wearing the green buttons lingered behind; many even stood behind burly undergraduates wearing armbands, underclassmen who had no idea what the Game was about. The seniors were generally noncommittal. They were on their way out in a few months.

Administrators and some teachers had condemned the armbands from the first day, some even giving wearers in-school suspension. A particularly vocal parent, however, an equal rights lawyer who had a particular interest in school law, defended the students' rights to freedom of speech, citing eerie similarities to a recent incident in California where a court unanimously upheld students' rights to wear armbands as an expression of political voice.

After a few weeks the legality issue went to the School Board. The Directors, already busy with the State's new testing models and the hiring of several school principals in the district, gave in, trying to avoid an ugly and expensive legal battle in which there was already a precedent. Ultimately, the students only went a few days without the freedom to speak from their respective cliques in the form of buttons and armbands and stickers on the shoulder straps of backpacks.

It was in this climate of Game withdrawal that something really disturbing began to happen, as far as Richard Hayes and some of the other teachers were concerned.

STEVEN IS A GAY JEW. HE MUST DIE.

This first appeared on Mr. Perry's whiteboard one Tuesday morning in red lipstick. Steven Berg, an awkward sophomore, known for keeping to himself and wearing shirts displaying favorite death-metal bands, hadn't been seen in his classes for several days. Then, according to the more reliable teachers' lounge gossip, Steven was placed on homebound services for the rest of the year, having suffered a car accident the previous week. Administrators kept tight-lipped on the matter as it was still under legal investigation.

The principal, Coach Mason, called Richard Hayes into his office in early March. It was a mild afternoon, and Richard had been chatting with a female colleague during bus duty. He was summoned through the intercom.

Mason stiffened as Hayes walked in and sat himself down in a chair opposite the principal's desk. "What do you know about the armbands and the green buttons?" Mason wasn't wasting any time.

"Juniors playing politics or something. Fairly harmless, as far as I know," Hayes responded. He of course had his doubts. But it had all started after he *ended* the game, so he still thought others might not see the connection before it fizzled out.

"Do you know about Steven Berg?"

"I know he's homebound. Was it a traffic accident?"

James Mason paused, staring at Hayes. "He was beaten by one of the armband-wearing thugs. When he recovers, he'll be attending another district."

"Beaten?"

"It was what they're calling a 'hate crime.'" Mason, a principal for many years at the school, spit into his trashcan and adjusted the wad in his lower lip with his tongue as he spoke, revealing small, discolored dentures. "They were wearing clown masks."

Mason hadn't been so direct with him before. No talk about the rising prices of food or the high taxes the local people were paying to keep the State's nearly bankrupt system afloat. Nothing about the travails of his wife, a French teacher at another district, where teacher-student ratios were nearly 40 to 1.

A huge fish tank stood in a corner, the large goldfish and some snails brought in to keep Mason's blood pressure in check, which was odd since nothing seemed to faze the man. He'd seen it all. Until now, maybe.

"Do they know who did it?" Hayes was by now sitting up in the faux-leather black seat.

"Nope. Do you know anything about it?"

"Nothing," replied Hayes.

"Well, I have to ask. I'm asking all the teachers and staff what they know. No one seems to know anything. He was found in a ditch in front of his house on Monday morning, October 21st. He was gagged and bound with duct tape. I won't go into too much more detail, I can't really, but he had been . . . impaled."

"What?"

"A pole or something was . . ."

"I . . . I know what impaled means." Hayes frowned. He felt a chill of fear run down his back and arms. His heart was beating fast. Both men were silent for some time.

Hayes began, "No suspects? No evidence? What about fingerprints?"

"Whoever he or they were wore gloves, we think. He had been in a nightclub parking lot in McAllen. His car was found there with the keys in it. Since the thugs were wearing masks, he couldn't ID any of them. He said they disguised their voices."

Hayes thought for a moment and looked down at his own hands. He remained silent.

"You still playing that game in your classroom? What is it . . . that Nazi game?"

Hayes shook his head. "No. Not anymore." Mason already knew the answer to the question. "Just trying to cover all the State objectives, you know. Can't hit them all with just one method."

Mason was old fashioned and thought textbooks were still the best way to teach. Still, he knew a good teacher when he met one, and it didn't take many classroom observations to convince him that the school had scored a rare one in this Richard Hayes. He spit again into the can and readjusted his wad.

"They're gonna want to look at that game of yours. It's just too weird all these arm bands and cliques, gangs really, more than the usual nonsense, and then the Berg kid. He didn't have many friends, but his parents don't know of him ever having been threatened before either."

"How do they know it was a bunch of students who did it? The armbands?"

Mason mused. "Yep, somebody saw kids with armbands around his car that night. That's all we have . . . that and talk about your game. Somebody had written, 'Steven is a gay Jew and must die' on Perry's whiteboard. You heard about that, right?"

Hayes thought quickly. As much as he hated the idea of a student he'd seen walking the halls getting hurt, self-preservation began to fight against the desire to learn anything more that might tie it to him. "I heard about it. Still, it doesn't seem to have much to do with waking up or sleeping . . . or any of the stuff they put on the armbands and buttons." No, he didn't want to know any more for still another reason. Sure, the less he knew, the less he'd be dragged in. But to know for certain that there was a direct connection to him was a terrifying idea. Still, he knew.

"You know the armbands didn't start until weeks after I moved on to another method. They weren't playing the game when the first armbands appeared."

"That's what I gather," Mason responded, smiling, standing up to put on his coat. The meeting was over. "If you hear anything, let me know. This is a butt-ugly business. Retirement sure is sounding sweet these days . . . what with all the teacher cuts and what not." Not so subtle.

Hayes motioned to leave when Mason sat back down with a growl, dropping his coat on his desk as he did so. "Wait. Just one more second." Mason sat with the fingers of his meaty hands locked together. He looked at his hands for several moments with eyes narrowed but sharp.

"I want you to bring back the game."

"What?"

"Like you said, there's no clear connection between the game and this kid's situation. In fact, maybe he was attacked because the kids *stopped* playing it."

Hayes closed his eyes. He wasn't liking where this was headed.

"The fall semester's senior attendance was the highest it had ever been in the history of this school—even compared with the 1950s. Hell, their absentee rate last year was lower than the other three classes combined. Teachers were starting to collaborate around what you were doing . . . trying new things of their own."

"I'm not thinking that's such a good idea."

Mason continued without seeming to hear Hayes' comment. "You know, I was in a conversation with one student—the Martinez kid, the one always in and out of Alternative. Well, he didn't get written up all first semester, and all he talks about is your game. No, that's not right. All he talks about is what he's *learned* in your game, history stuff. He actually said he was afraid of getting into trouble because if he was taken off campus, he wouldn't be able to play your game."

"It isn't *my* game. There are other ways to . . ."

"You know, I sat in on a geography class a couple of years ago—won't mention the teacher by name of course—and not one kid in the class could point out where Poland was on the map. In October, I believe it was, I listened in on some kids talking back by the back stairwell. You know what they were talking about?"

"Not a clue."

"They were working up what they called a "counteroffensive" in case the Germans decided to invade Russia. Must have been playing the game as high-level politicians or something."

"Barbarossa . . ." Hayes began.

"Yes, I figured that out pretty fast. I did teach world history for twenty-seven years." Mason smiled, giving his head an ironic tilt. "Well, they were detailing out between three of them how they could get such and such numbers of horses and supplies to the troops in Ukraine to bolster the border's defense against Germany. The game is teaching these kids about planning. There's math in it, there's military science, there's history."

"Yes, sir. There's also morality. They're forced to make choices about whether or not to sacrifice themselves, their careers, their lives, for others, for what they know to be the right thing. But it can be bloody, and at their age . . . ."

"Exactly! Moral dilemmas . . . right and wrong. We need to be teaching that kinda thing nowadays! God knows too many parents don't!"

"The problem . . . at least this is what I suspect . . . is that they were mostly making the wrong choices. Promotion . . . sometimes survival . . . in the game often requires them to make choices which hurt . . . ."

"They're learning dammit!" Mason's face was turning bloodshot.

Hayes was quiet. "They were learning," he repeated. It was hopeless trying to convince Mason to keep the Game out of the school. Sure, the school got more funds when attendance was up, which didn't completely explain why, even in the face of a lawsuit down the road, a guy like Mason wanted to keep the game going. Hayes himself knew the incredible educational value of the Game, and Mason thought it might act as an outlet for the students, a relief valve for their teen angst, but Hayes saw a danger Mason simply wasn't seeing. Bringing it back wouldn't make the armbands disappear. Probably make it worse.

Mason, as rare as he was—old school, but an intuitive instructional leader among managers and well-paid state exam clerks—didn't see the Game as a safety issue. Which meant he didn't really link the Game to the Berg boy's assault. To him it was just an online game that made kids think—and increased attendance.

Richard left the man's office after tentatively agreeing to restart the Game. Hayes' balding crown was sweating, and the edges of his curly tufts of hair had become damp. He wiped his pate and looked at the perspiration on his hand. It wouldn't be long before everyone in the small town realized that the Berg boy had never been in any car accident. It was even likely that Hayes was one of the last to find out. It was a tight situation, and there would be hell to pay if anything like this ever happened again.

Hayes went back up to his classroom. Late afternoon approached and the room was dark. He made his way to the front of the room near the window where his desk sat. Hayes lay back in his rolling chair, well hidden behind his desk and oversized flatscreen, and stared at the ceiling, his arms hanging limp at his sides. Even though there was no direct link between the Game and the boy's severe injuries, Hayes felt responsible. Guilt rose up in him, and he felt like he himself had been at the scene of the crime, some part of himself watching and doing nothing. He decided that he would force himself to sleep in his classroom tonight. There was no Game for him now, no desire in him to play, revulsion rather, but he owed the Berg kid this tiny piece of sacrifice, this time to think things over. He might even talk to some of the juniors in the morning, get some details from those wearing the armbands who might connect with him based on some lingering idea of loyalty. It was Thursday, and knowing he might not sleep at all tonight, he could make up for it with a long slumber in his little cabin over the weekend.

Richard lay sprawled in his big chair, scratching a little box into the spray-painted window until some black flakes of paint got under his nails. He looked through the little transparent box he had made. A bright streetlamp positioned over the students' parking lot sent a shaft of light through the aperture into his eye. He stared at it until he had to blink, and, feeling a chill, grabbed a small, folded blanket from his bookshelf. The cover over him felt soft and warm, protective somehow. The aircon was blowing lightly against the blanket and the night outside the window was silent.

It was 10:15 PM when the door handle began to rattle at the far corner of the room. Hayes looked up from his chair, instantly alarmed. He thought about the thick steak knife he kept in his desk; then his mind leaped to a long, whittled stick he'd confiscated from a student four years before, which he'd neglected to turn in to the principal's secretary. He reached for the stick, which stood behind a corner of the bookshelf behind his desk.

He couldn't remember if he had locked the door or not. It opened slowly. A figure glided to the first console nearest the classroom door. The cardboard boxes had all been removed.

The screen blinked on, brightening one side of the room with a ghostly light. Hayes could now see the figure, clearly male, slim. The man shook his head as if to throw off an unwanted idea and mounted the thick headset upon his dark head. After putting on the studded gloves and sitting down into the unit, he began tapping his fingers across the keys rapidly, expertly.

Richard sat in near darkness at his desk. He eased up in his chair as the tapping of the keys filled the room. The figure had covered himself with one of the dark afghans folded on a nearby desk, which some of the students had brought to keep themselves warm when the aircon blowing directly on them became unbearable. The intruder was like a giant web-covered insect, waving his arms and murmuring low into his headset. He kept his eyes no more than 12 inches from the monitor and quickly became wholly absorbed in what was happening on the screen. He was, of course, playing the Game.

Richard's chair creaked a bit as he sat up. The man at the far end of the room was absorbed, oblivious to all else. Hayes could have jumped up and down just behind the man and gotten no reaction.

He wanted the man gone, but he was also curious. Since the Game was still officially forbidden, he also felt a duty to see what was happening on the screen. Apparently, his mandate against the game had had no effect whatsoever on this particular student. Sure, he'd never actually said the game was officially *verboten,* just "broken," but he also no longer made the room available for the game before or after school hours, never allowed time for it outside other planned activities during any given class period. It was a *de facto* rule this kid had decided to break.

Richard Hayes stared at the figure for some time. The figure leaned forward, unlike a teenager or a young man. He seemed older, bent over in his afghan shroud, but alert. Richard crept up to the figure from behind, intent on perhaps scaring the daylights out of him if his, Richard's, presence were detected, as it eventually would be.

The figure was covered bodily by the black afghan, its knots loosely woven. Fingers busied themselves in the gloves, with one hand occasionally lifting or slapping at the mouse ball or tapping a word or two across the keys. Hayes crept along the wall, out of the immediate view of the figure. Gradually, he stood behind the man and looked into the holes of the woven fabric. On the screen stood a figure dressed in a white suit with horizontal shoulders perpendicular to a thin, vertical neck. The character on the screen nodded frequently and spoke quickly.

The figure under the afghan was barking his whispered orders to the man in the light suit as the man nodded quickly but with dignity. Eventually, they walked down a long hallway together, the figure under the afghan still barking orders in a low murmur. Some of what he was saying was in German and thus heard more quickly by the character on the screen than his English phrases, as they passed through the lightning-quick translation matrix.

Hayes, from several feet behind, saw the men enter a room in which a large red banner was draped down a wall, covering an area of chimney above an enormous fireplace. About six feet in front of it stood a large table laden with papers, files, and the vegetable makings of salads in individual glass bowls. A fire was raging through the grate below the banner, giving off light in the otherwise dimly lit but well-furnished room. "Clearly playing a character of huge importance," Hayes mumbled to himself.

Hayes decided to retreat, letting the man finish this sequence of the game. However, he watched from behind his desk. The player never moved his head enough in Richard's direction to reveal details about his face, but he could tell from the accent who it was. As much as he was *amused* by Farash—the only description for his attitude regarding the foreign teacher—the man was sneaky. He wondered how long Farhat had been playing the game in which he had previously, at least on the surface, shown so little interest.

At some point during the early morning, Hayes fell asleep in the chair behind his desk. He knew he had nothing to fear from the visitor and had completely forgotten about the penance he had assigned himself for the night. When he awoke near dawn, the figure had already slipped out of the room.

Summer, 2033

Hayes had struggled with the decision from the end of the spring semester into the early summer. However, he finally decided to reinstate the game as part of his curriculum for the following year. Perhaps Mason was right about the students needing an outlet. It had been a long, rough semester keeping them engaged—the most difficult semester he could remember. *Maybe it wasn't the game causing problems at all but rather the ending of it*, Hayes lied to himself. Some of the more Darwinian aspects of the Game might continue to manifest in the relationships between the students themselves, but perhaps they were heightened now by the kids' inability to work out their frustrations through the choices they made from the endless options the game provided; hence the armbands. At least one could not refute the educational benefits of the teaching tool. Still, they needed some sort of warning, some guidance.

Richard himself would also return to it. In the many months he had played as a camp guard, he'd been promoted, moving in the Party from mere Block Operations Foreman to Cell Leader in only a year and a half. As far as his military rank, his effectiveness in the camp had propelled him from *Obersturmführer* (First Lieutenant) to *Sturmbannführer* (Major) just below the camp commander, the *Standartenführer*. This had been the only character he had ever used in the game, in fact the only one he *could* use with his login unless it died somehow while he played it—or during his absence from the game—an inexplicable situation he had seen with a few students' avatars. His killing of the old woman on the parade grounds had faded somewhat in his memory, and he had always wanted to see if he could, at some point, end up running the camp. Besides, wasn't he responsible for making sure the Game stayed within the reasonable boundaries of what was appropriate for students? How better to do that than to participate? More lies.

He would start to play again the following evening at 10:00 PM. Time flowed in the game exactly as it did in the real world. An hour equaled an hour. Since a character needed regular periods of sleep, Richard could come into the game with a refreshed avatar at about the time the character was supposed to wake up. The seven-hour time difference between Texas and Germany would bring him into the game at 5:00 AM in Dachau, which is when the performance of his avatar's duties normally began.

When Richard Hayes first went back to the Game in his tiny cabin, he had a difficult time understanding where he was. When his avatar opened its eyes, a dizziness made the screen in his helmet waver, or perhaps this was merely the result of his regaining his sense of visual perspective.

When he entered, it was early morning, as he had expected. But lights burned from raw bulbs above his head. These were screwed into the ends of thin, long cables suspended from thick supporting beams beneath an A-frame barracks-type roof. The beds of the sick ward were positioned as one would expect, parallel, with the pillowed ends nearest the walls. There was a walkway between the two rows of beds lining the walls of the long, narrow building. The walls beneath the high roof were made of cinder block, thickly painted a light tan.

Hayes lifted the cursor control with gloved hands and *Sturmführer* Heinrich Wicker, Hayes' character, began to sit up. It was difficult keeping the character from falling off the bed. He looked to a metal nightstand to the right of his own bed and found several medicine bottles beside a half-glass of what he assumed to be water. At his feet lay a porcelain bedpan.

A number of the iron beds contained sleeping inhabitants, but the majority were empty and tightly made up with dark woolen blankets and white sheets.

A kitchen matron, a prisoner, was pushing a cart through the walkway in the center of the room among the beds, ladling soup into bowls from a large, stainless-steel tureen and placing the bowls on the night stands by the occupied beds. Her black hair was covered by a yellow rag. Hayes recognized her immediately but said nothing. He lay back in his bed, playing his part. When she finally came to his bed, he touched her arm.

"Savina."

She placed the bowl and looked at him steadily.

"Savina, why am I here?"

She just stood, glaring at him. Eventually, she brought her face close to his ear and whispered rapidly in response: "If I could kill you, I would, Herr Sturmführer. I would put rat poison in this potato soup of yours. And do you know why? Because I don't care anymore, you bastard. Kill me if you want. Go on." The young woman was clearly shaken by her own words. Her eyes, though dark and beautiful, went bloodshot and her tightening mouth trembled, but she seemed to be waiting for a response. Surprised, he said nothing, and she returned to her tureen and continued passing out bowls of soup.

He had been away for a while, true. Months in fact. Things could change greatly during one's absence. "Life," as in reality, didn't pause between human interactions.

She had addressed him merely as "Sturmführer," a second lieutenant. This was odd. He looked around for a jacket, a cap, anything revealing his current rank. He looked under the sheet. He was dressed in a hospital gown. Nothing else he saw around him gave any more meaning to his situation. Additionally, the screen in his helmet blurred now and then. His character was apparently very tired or terribly ill. Richard too was getting sleepy and until now hadn't realized just how little sleep he had gotten in the last few days. As the screen went dark with the passing out of the avatar, Richard too fell asleep at his table in the small cabin.

"You almost died, Wicker."

It had taken a day and a half for Richard to again return in the form of his avatar. The man simply wouldn't wake up. Now he was back in the game. The image was still a bit shaky, but Hayes recognized the man standing over him as *Schutzhaftlagerführer* Alexander Piorkowski, the economic functionary of the camp. From all appearances, he had become the new camp Commandant. He wondered about Hans Loritz, the previous commandant, a man with an especially cruel streak where the prisoners were concerned.

As much as cruelty could go rewarded, it could also be taken too far. Hayes had seen guards relieved of duty for repeatedly committing acts of cruelty. As far as he knew, his character had done so only one time—an excusable offense in the eyes of his superiors though an event on which he himself did not easily reflect.

This man, about 36, looked almost exactly like his predecessor—thinning blond hair, pot-bellied middle, acne scars. He took a seat at the side of Wicker's bed and after taking off his gloves felt the forehead of his officer. "Still has a fever though his skin isn't quite as yellow as it was."

"Herr Wicker! Hello? Can you hear me?" He snapped his fingers a few times in front of Wicker's eyes. "I'm sure you've heard about your demotion." The new camp commander wasted no time getting to the point. "It was the most disgraceful thing I've ever seen committed by an officer of the SS."

"What did I do?" Richard was able to cough out a few words. The officer that had accompanied the Commandant chuckled inaudibly.

"What you did do, you drunken bastard, involved several female Polish inmates, a mop closet, and a case of Russian vodka. So, other than 'What did I do' . . . what do you have to say for yourself, Sturmführer Wicker?" Commandant Piorkowski was frowning, his small gray eyes staring directly into Richard's own eyes from below a high forehead, his thin blondish hair slicked way back.

"I . . . I what?" Richard stammered into the helmet and then thought for a few seconds, wondering what *else* Heinrich Wicker might have actually done in his absence. At first, Richard thought to mask his confusion with the appearance of self-loathing, maybe even tears; he knew the keystrokes for bringing them up. But then the Commandant spoke again, this time in a whisper near his left ear. "I would have thrown you in with the scum in the fourth block as a state criminal had it not been for the fact that we're so damned short-handed. We need everyone. And we need them sober, not stinking drunk and breaking the Fuhrer's racial purity laws."

The Commandant looked genuinely disgusted, scowling at his inferior officer. "I've put in to have you transferred to the front, just as soon as a decent replacement can be found. Tomorrow, you'll be back in the courtyard, and since now every officer in the camp knows you to be a *betrunken Arschloch* you may as well keep to yourself until you leave. It would be the respectable thing to do though the concept of self-respect seems to elude you completely." The Commandant rose from the bed and directed a German nurse that "under all circumstances, Heinrich will be fit for duty by tomorrow morning. For tonight, let him sleep—Herr Doktor tells me that Wicker's liver has swollen to the size of his head. I would not have thought it possible." He abruptly left the room. Wicker's consciousness waned.

Hours later, the screen embedded in the helmet, six inches from Richard's eyes, brought a faint light but no distinct images. As Wicker gradually re-entered consciousness, a vague figure stood over him. A female voice then whispered into his left ear. "I will cut your throat as you sleep." Darkness returned to the helmet screen once again and lasted for hours.

Richard, Wicker, awoke once again to find himself staring at the dark wooden beams. Light originating from poles outside the building fell through the high windows in a slant across the hospital beds. Otherwise, everything was dark. The room was empty save a few soldiers sleeping in nearby beds. Richard himself felt an itch just below his sternum—he hadn't bathed in days. Scratching with his left hand, he then directed Wicker with his right to rise and put on the uniform now draped over the back of a chair. This took some time. He then walked about the room, testing the health of his stumbling avatar. Not good. Soon, he was walking out of the hospital room and amongst the camp's prison barracks, an agonizing headache seemed to penetrate the distance between avatar and player.

It was very dark even under the stars, with spotlights from corner and side towers probing the distant woods and hills, then along the perimeter of the camp, and finally across barracks windows. Wicker stumbled along the inside of the barbwire's perimeter, along the barracks-side of a ditch that lay two yards away from the electrified fence. He nodded to a fellow guard he met walking the other way. A spotlight flooded his location for a few seconds and then turned again to the rooftops of the barracks. He walked the perimeter, trying to consider his current role in the game. He was Heinrich Wicker, newly demoted to mere Sturmführer, second lieutenant in the camp SS squad. He had been a major. It would have been tremendously humiliating if it were real. He had dropped three ranks; his collar lapel now displayed three diamonds instead of four; several of his medals were gone. The large iron cross no longer hung from the center of his collar. Hayes thought about the many months he had worked to gain his title of *Sturmbannführer*, all for nothing. *Sinlos*... Pointless.

Another SS officer walked past, nodding to him, as if he didn't notice the new lack of metal on his jacket and the simplified patchwork on his arm. Sturmführer. He felt like tossing it all, like grabbing a gun and killing every soldier in the camp. *I'll start with this guy*, he thought. He knew he wouldn't get far—three perhaps, maybe four. He had never done anything so remotely volatile with his avatar. It would ruin his place in the game, but he was starting to not care. It was already gone. The spell of its enchantment was continuing to wear off, this game, this other-life so much more real than his own—the life he'd led as Richard Hayes, the stale life lived long before its discovery.

Richard felt in Wicker's pockets for some food, forgetting that feeding the character would do little to assuage his own pangs. He brought out a bar wrapped in soft tissue. He munched it and could almost taste the dry, fruity, nutty texture in his own mouth. After eating it, he felt strangely satisfied though fatigued. Still walking the fence perimeter, he crumpled the tissue and tossed the wrapper just outside the first layer of barbed wire.

A dreary, cold stillness pervaded the spaces between the long cabins with a windless silence. Faint breathing could almost be heard through the empty spaces between A-frame roofs and walls. He found Savina's wooden barracks, near the hospital and not far from the long row of narrow cells where some of the political prisoners were taken and held, often indefinitely. He knocked lightly. Nothing stirred. He knocked again and then unbolted the door from the outside. As he entered, he whispered among the stark wooden bunks, three high. "Frau Bender . . . Savina."

"She is at the other end, Herr Offizier," replied a female voice.

"Danke."

The bright artificial lamps just penetrated the horizontal chinks between roof and wall. He found her nevertheless, under a thin, gray blanket. Her head was turned toward the wall, but he knew her dark, cropped hair and profile well enough to recognize her. On her other side lay two other women, both sleeping heavily.

"Savina. I need to speak with you." he whispered.

There was a pause. She didn't move.

"Savina, you don't know me. I . . ."

"And why should I care to know you?" was the whispered reply. She knew who it was without turning to look.

"Because I can get you out of here."

Another pause. "And become what, your slave, your prostitute?" Her head was still turned to the wall.

"Your friend."

"Friend. Get out. I want to sleep." She turned to look at him. "Why are you here? To rape me again as you did in the commissary closet?"

"What?" Richard was taken aback. He repeated her words under his breath back to her.

In the corner of his little cabin, Richard Hayes removed the interactive helmet. It was all too real. Much too real now. He had to look at something, anything familiar. Richard looked at the helmet. It was not enough to leave after beating a woman to death at the parade grounds. He had to come back. She made him come back. Not the old woman. Savina. He had fallen for a computer-generated fiction. It was the real reason he'd returned, the lie he had to face.

He had grown feelings for someone who amounted to nothing more than a sequence of electrons passing through circuits and motherboards. Or perhaps he was simply acting *as if* he had feelings for someone who was real, playing a role, and doing an excellent job of playing make-believe in a world permanently separate from his own pathetic life. "Maybe she is an avatar played by someone else," he thought, which would explain the attraction he had to her, a genuine affection for another human being—a rare quality for him. He actually cared about what happened to her, not something he could say about most people, even in *this* world.

When he was in the Game, she was right there, alive. When his avatar touched her, *he* touched her. Back in the hospital barracks, when she had scorned him, he could swear that he knew her scent and could now sense her thoughts from the expressions on her face. Thoughts?

He put the shiny black helmet back on. His eyes readjusted to the dark vision and his ears to the tiny chirping sounds of the German night, emitted from the living trees and fields surrounding the camp.

Chapter 5

As the men on the other side of the glass argued, Debus lay as still as possible. A streak of cold dread ran up his spine. His head ached terribly. *Americans? Impossible!* he thought to himself. There hadn't been any Americans working in the sheet metal factory in 1939 or at any time before, as far as he knew. Perhaps he had gone back too far, to when a bigger structure possibly existed at the location. This place was certainly much bigger than the factory he had just left.

When the men had left back up the metal stairs, the German scientist tried to take further stock of the situation. *Did I move ahead in time? After the war?* He concluded this to be the case. The Allies had won—not a big surprise considering the state of things in 1943. They'd taken the Bell and had been experimenting with it. They'd kept it in Bavaria, considering the massive effort of transporting the thing, and rebuilt a larger facility around it. No, that wasn't right. This construction had a bluish tint and was missing the swastika making up part of the original molding. This Bell, though nearly identical, wasn't the same Bell.

Now, what to do. He could somehow get past the contingent here, whatever that entailed. No one was currently on the floor level of the massive wide-open structure, as far as he could tell. He hadn't seen any guards or military presence of any kind. But what if he was stuck here? The glass door looked well secured. Probably locked. Unless he could get past it, he'd have to make his presence known if he were to avoid eventual dehydration and starvation. He felt the strong urge to urinate.

Debus considered just giving himself up. It would be a betrayal of the Fatherland—or would it? If the war is over, what would it matter? Others had left to work for the Americans before the war. Perhaps he, one of the key scientists on Projekt Reise, could offer his help in perfecting the device. Science, after all, should have no political boundaries. Besides, secretly, he had never been much of a Nazi.

SOUTH TEXAS, NOVEMBER 2035

"You're his aunt? Aren't you too old . . . ?"

"I am not really his aunt, but yes I am too old. Too old for this earth. I was born in Switzerland."

"I bet you have tons of stories." He was really into history.

"I was little when the second war ended. I only have one story, my boy. One life, one story. That's all you can ask for." The young man was silenced by the tone of what sounded like a terse reprimand but seemed amused by her irritability.

"What does this man mean to you?" she asked after a while.

"Excuse me?"

"Are you his son? Nephew?"

"No, nothing like that," the young man replied. "He was my history teacher."

"You seem to like history."

"It's all I think about. When I was in his class, he assigned a game for us to play. It changed my life."

"For the better, I hope," she gave him a wry smile.

"I owe a lot to this man."

SAVINA WAS LOOKING at him now from an upper bunk, her eyes squinting, eyebrows low. It must have been strange for her to see the character Heinrich staring forward, stock still, saying nothing for those few moments while Richard's helmet had been off. Luckily, the browser had stayed active the whole time and the real Wicker hadn't come back.

Richard hated this other self, this Heinrich, this alter-ego. He was certain now that this . . . this computer-generated demon had control when Richard himself didn't. It had its own personality. This avatar, when Richard wasn't him, was a self-destructive beast and had cost him his rank. No, he had cost him *much* more. How could she be made to believe that two men lived, alternately, in one body? That he, Richard, bore no responsibility for what had happened to her? To her? What the *hell* was going on!

He shook his head. "Take a walk with me."

"To the showers?" she remarked with clear derision.

"To a place between the barracks, where the searchlights don't reach. I won't hurt you."

"I can't. I'll freeze to death." It was a very frosty night.

"You're freezing now. Bring your blanket."

Richard, as Heinrich, led Savina out of the barracks and several rows of buildings away to a dark area. There was a spindly tree somewhat shading them from the bright moon above. Most of its leaves had been stripped off, probably eaten. Her thin, gray blanket wrapped around her and his dark coat made them both all but invisible.

"Now, I want you to listen carefully. I'm not the pig Heinrich Wicker. I'm somebody else. I'm an American. My name is Richard Hayes."

"Why are you playing this game?"

"What game?" He was confused. She looked at him questioningly.

She continued, "You seem to have some special interest in me. And it's physical. I get it. But then sometimes, you want more, something else? What is it you want?" Her eyes began to tear up, but she was firm. "I know what *I* want. I want you to leave me alone." Her hands and a piece of her blanket covered her face. "Why are you doing this?"

"You don't understand. I'm not who you think..."

She quickly reached for the SS dagger hanging from his belt. He held her wrist as she clasped the handle of the dagger, still in its sheath. "You think I'm pretty? Is that it? Would it be better for me to cut off my face? Would you leave me alone then?" He dropped his hand from her wrist. She slowly eased the dagger out of its sheath. She then brought the point quickly to his throat. He looked at it. The words across its gleaming blue surface read "*Meine Ehre Heist Treue.*" My honor is loyalty.

He loosened his coat and exposed his neck. She lowered the knife, positioning it near his chest, her other hand covering the hilt, ready to push the blade past the layers of uniform.

"Kill me. I deserve it. Or at least kill the man you think I am. The man I am when I'm not me . . . you'll be better off. But you can't get caught." He stumbled on the words, not really knowing how to phrase what he needed to say in a way that might make sense. She brought the knife back up to his throat. In the helmet, Richard could almost feel it pressed against his own Adam's apple. She stared into his eyes from the darkness. Neither moved. Her eyebrows narrowed. Her cropped hair covered some of her face and part of her ears; even though her hair had been brutally shorn, she was nonetheless stunningly beautiful. She seemed to see something in his eyes. He hoped she saw Richard Hayes.

After several moments, the young woman dropped the dagger and ran off in the dark blanket, screaming. Richard saw the flickering of watchtower searchlights bouncing across the camp in the direction of her shrieks. There were yells coming from the nearest tower as she reached the ditch. She jumped in and quickly climbed up the other side towards the fence. She had almost traversed the six feet between ditch and electrified fence but was stopped by a mesh of barbed wire covering the ground between like metal weeds woven into each other. It caught her feet, her blanket left behind like the skin of some molting gray snake.

Richard began to run towards her when he heard a single gunshot. It was the tight, steel-pounding, low and explosive sound of a Luger. He stopped, still hidden in the shadow of the thin tree. Then there were only the intermittent voices of soldiers running towards her body as it lay across the top of the wire mesh, just inches in front of the electrified fence, mangled and unconscious. Richard watched from the corner of a barrack as they approached the inert body of the girl tangled in the thin mesh of wire. He watched, for some moments unable to move his avatar from the shock he himself experienced.

Guards had rushed in and began to pick the body from the wire. Hayes was surprised by this gesture as other attempted escapees had simply been left overnight, even for days, after such an event, as a warning to the other prisoners. He watched as her motionless body was carried away on the shoulders of a guard like a side of butchered meat.

He let the helmet fall to the floor, staring at the black screens of the three monitors he rarely used anymore. He was exhausted and faintly sobbing.

Late Summer, 2033

Hayes left the game like one waking from the vivid conjurings of the type of dream so intense that one finds oneself spending half the day trying to bring it back. Yet it wasn't something he wanted to relive.

He had been playing for 27 hours straight and hadn't slept properly in days. It was night. Summer was over for the teachers, but students had another week off. He had time enough to sleep and still be ready for the first workday of the school year. Otherwise, he would end up passing out during a faculty meeting.

He considered the need to replace the refrigerator boxes, but quickly decided against it. He would make sure the units were all functional on Day One, but that was about it. Mason had made it clear. Reinstate the method. Sure. But he would ease up on the intensity. No boxes.

Before long, it was late Monday afternoon. Training sessions were over for the day and Richard awoke with a start from a short nap at his classroom desk. He had dreamed of the woman caught in the wire. He lay beside her in the stifling space of a third bunk in a barrack on the women's side of the prison. The barracks was empty of its usual, thin, hair-shorn inhabitants. There was much more space in the bunk than he remembered. The roof had been removed completely and the night sky faintly lit the rows of empty bunks around them. They stared at each other and touched hands. They were both wearing hospital gowns. The camp guards were gone, and they were alone in an empty barrack, in an empty camp. He felt a wet stickiness and lifted her hand still enclosed by his. He saw black, soggy roots wrapping around the flesh of her arm, growing from jagged scratches she'd made across her wrist. She smiled at him, and he realized that he had never seen her smile before. He remembered thinking it was all over, and the thought brought peace. She was happy to be there with him in these last unifying moments.

When Richard awoke the browser, he found his avatar once again in a hospital unit, this time in a small, isolated room. He was seated across from a camp Doctor. The doctor was tall, graying from blonde, and his small pince-nez-type eyeglasses sat at the tip of his nose. Above these, the Doctor's eyes stared at Heinrich with narrowed lids. "I want to make sure you are beginning your recovery with some chance of success. Now, you are quite sure you don't remember the events of the 30 hours mentioned in your report, Herr Wicker?"

Richard was at a loss and needed a few moments to assess what the doctor was looking for. He had entered the avatar amid a conversation already begun. "Can I have a cigarette, please?"

The doctor handed him a flat beige box with the German eagle imprinted in red ink above the brand: "Regie 4." The tiny cigarettes were Austrian. Richard took one and lit it from a box of matches that the middle-aged doctor had taken from his lab coat. As he lit the cigarette and his avatar inhaled, Richard noticed green folders on a desk just outside the room. Black and white photos of what appeared to be cancerous lesions and tumors spilled from their contents. Some had formed on the arms or backs of patients while some had clearly been taken out of bodies during autopsies. The doctor noticed Richard's glance.

"A fixation of my colleague's, Doctor Rascher," the man remarked. "He's new here, and they say he has some interesting ideas with regard to curing cancer. I wish I had the time to read more of his work."

"Perhaps he may have some ideas about my condition?" Richard threw him a wary glance but only saw a sort of falsified compassion in the doctor's eyes. "You may have guessed correctly, Herr Wicker."

"What do you mean?"

"Your blackouts usually last for several hours; some are days long, correct? I would attribute it to your heavy drinking, but it also happens when you've been sober for extended periods. A brain cancer might explain it. I would call it amnesia, but there have been reports that your behavior changes during the periods you've described. Perhaps it is a tumor-induced schizophrenia."

"So I have a . . ." Richard searched his mind for the German word for tumor though the program would translate it for him if necessary. "A *Geschwulst?*"

"We won't know until we get x-rays, but even then it might not show up. Your behavior is certainly erratic, and you seem to be suffering from a crippling depression as well, probably an emotional reaction to your blackouts."

Richard thought hard. Heinrich, his alter ego, of course knew there was something wrong. But it didn't make sense to program this concern over a blackout into a game's avatar, particularly when no one was playing it. It was as if the game makers wanted to draw the user in with these added concerns, make him or her play more. You were to play the game and do nothing else with your life—if you wanted things to flow smoothly. And here he was. His ex-wife would have called it "sick." It was indeed a compulsion, he knew, one offering a reality so life-like that one only regretted having to come back to this one. It wasn't just a diversion—it had become a necessity.

An insane thought began to occupy the space of his thoughts, one he had many times considered briefly and dismissed. Perhaps being Heinrich full-time wasn't so much of a stretch. He could time his own sleeping habits to those of his host, placing the demon in an indefinite coma. He'd have to retire early from teaching to make it happen, to live as Wicker full time. There was just enough of the rational side left in Richard Hayes to know that there was something very wrong with this scenario, but that part was dissolving fast.

"Herr Wicker?" The doctor waved a hand in front of Heinrich's face. "Are you having one of your blackouts now?"

"*Nein*," replied Richard, bringing his mind back into the doctor's gray examining room. He had walked into the room to examine the pictures almost without even realizing it.

The doctor wiped his glasses on his lab coat. "I'm sorry to have to tell you this, Herr Wicker, but I'm afraid you are no longer fit for duty. I'm sure this comes as no surprise."

"No. Not really. It's not just an illness though, is it doctor?"

"How do you mean?"

"It's a death sentence. They won't send me back to Berlin to shuffle papers if I can't keep my mind together, will they? They'll probably send me to the front as artillery fodder."

"Oh, I'm sure it's not as bad as that. Besides, we are winning. You know, there are many things a man in your condition can do, like work in munitions. For instance, epileptics . . . "

". . . are terminated," Richard finished the doctor's sentence, "like the mentally ill, as you know. *Lebensunwertes Leben.*" Life unworthy of life.

The doctor was momentarily silent. "Not . . . always."

They talked for a while about some of the possibilities open to a man in Richard's, or rather Heinrich's, condition. Richard wondered if he was simply playing the part well or if the doctor knew Heinrich personally. He couldn't remember speaking at any length with the doctor before, but the doctor seemed to be talking with him on a more personal level than one would expect. Richard didn't seem to pick up even the slightest clue that he himself had been saying anything out of character for Heinrich Wicker, anything to tip off the doctor that he was not who he claimed to be. Or perhaps the doctor was making allowances for his mentally ill patient. When at the point of complete helplessness, a man's personality can change for the better, making him more agreeable. The biology of self-preservation might force him to want to please those in whose hands his life had been placed—once self-reliance becomes impossible. This could explain, for the doctor, the lack of arrogance in Wicker's demeanor, as Richard spoke from the countenance of a brute. Still, Richard wanted to try to stay in character as best as he could. He also wanted some news about where Savina's body had been taken.

"Too bad about that nurse orderly. I heard she did a respectable job in the ward, for a Polish Jew, of course. Did you know her?" Hayes asked.

"Who?"

"The dark-haired girl who tried to escape through the fence."

"Oh, you're referring to Savina. Yes, she has lost a lot of blood, but she should recover. The bullet wound in her leg became infected, you know."

Richard was shaken. He asked as nonchalantly as he could, "She's alive?"

"Oh, yes."

"Why'd she do it? Wasn't she treated okay, compared to some of the others, I mean."

"Why do any of them do it? Sometimes I wonder why we don't."

"Don't? Don't do what?" He wasn't sounding like a doctor.

The doctor was hesitant. Then he whispered, "Kill ourselves in this *gottverdammten* death factory."

Richard had not considered it a suicide attempt. She was trying to get away in a panic, from him, from the camp. Then again, the fence was electrified. Wasn't it obvious? She had run at it, slowed by a few yards of ditch and a wide mesh of barbed wire lying across her path. She had had no chance of escape. This was indeed becoming a death camp, and she was a prisoner wanting release. She was being abused, perhaps regularly, by this bastard Heinrich Wicker. It certainly happened at least once—she had accused *him* of it, and it was clear that the man would have other opportunities to attack her physically, despite losing his consciousness during the increasingly lengthy periods when Richard took control of the character's . . . no, the *man's* . . . body and mind. But suicide? She was too strong; her will was far too resilient—he knew that just from their brief instances of contact. Perhaps she just wanted to end up here, in the camp's infirmary.

She hated him as Heinrich; she didn't know him as Richard Hayes. He would make her know. He hadn't had the chance to really explain it to her. Of course, she would think it nonsense if he tried again.

Savina was alive. He would have to stay at the camp as long as he could and await her recovery. He couldn't be discharged from his assignment now, not until he'd had a final chance to talk with her. Sure, she wouldn't believe it. But maybe as surreal as this place was, as incoherent as any of this chaotic veneer of order—or more appropriately, a framework of order for the sake of invoking chaos—actually was, just about anything could be believed, and the truth would certainly fall under the category of "just about anything."

The doctor motioned Richard to his office, carrying the green files with him. He wanted to show Wicker pictures of normal brains and those with tumors resulting in acute amnesia. Richard sat on the doctor's desk as if it were *his* office, trying to recreate something of an arrogant demeanor in an attempt to get back into character. He lit another of the doctor's cigarettes and offered one to the doctor who declined. Hayes flipped through pictures.

He questioned the Nazi doctor, trying to stay as hypothetical as possible. "So, you've thought about it . . . killing yourself." The doctor didn't look up from his reading. He wanted to show Wicker a page from a journal that would help make more sense of the photographed images. "I think about it all the time," Richard threw in. The doctor seemed guarded and picked up a random file, appearing to look through it.

A thought came to Richard during this hesitant flow of conversation. He really cared about Savina. Even if she wasn't real, in the sense of flesh and blood, she was more real than any woman whom Richard Hayes had met. He loved her in his own bizarre, obsessed way, which didn't make any more sense than the camp itself or this game, or anything. He hadn't fully realized it until her apparent death. He was sure she had died, but there had been a faint whisper in his mind suggesting otherwise, an inkling of a thought of which Richard himself hadn't been fully aware, keeping him from surrendering to a feeling akin to sitting in a courtroom and hearing the words of his own death sentence.

Now that she was alive again, as if willed to life by his own self-sustaining need, his role in the Game had to change. He hated the options before him, but there was really only one choice to make, now that his feelings for her were clear. If he got near her again, alone, what then? The Internet connection could suddenly fail, as it had done on occasion, and there she would be, alone with the demon. He had to get Wicker as far from her as possible. If he had to never see her again to spare her from the hands of a monster, then so be it. But the prospect of his life without her in it was an empty container.

Finally, the tall, thin, middle-aged doctor dragged the stool close to where Richard was sitting on the doctor's desk. "You care for this girl," he said, frowning, shaking his head. "It wouldn't be the first time. I saw it at Buchenwald. So, you want me to fix her so that you can again hurt this girl you care for, correct? Or should I say, in the parlance of the Party, that she is non-human, like the rest, and ask you why you care so much for this . . . animal?"

Hayes had no idea that his off-hand remarks had revealed so much. He certainly didn't think of her as non-human, though as a computer character she was exactly that. But Wicker did. A thought occurred to him once again . . . could she really be an avatar? Is someone controlling her?

"She has use," he replied.

"Indeed. Perhaps more than her duties in the infirmary suggest? Perhaps she can do more than clean bedpans and ladle soup to your . . . Kapos . . . when they come in with strange infections from the brothel at the corner barrack."

"I'm not liking your tone, doctor." Hayes pretended anger. "Rewarding Kapos with such privileges keeps them from thinking too much of what it is they're made to do here. They are betrayers of their kind, but to keep them useful we can't let them dwell on it. We must supply diversions. And we can't run this camp with just the SS. There aren't nearly enough of us."

"I don't judge, Herr Wicker. I only see my role here as . . . ironic." Hayes completely understood the doctor's meaning. Here was a man expected to heal those soon to be gassed anyway or worked to death. Here was one of the men whose job it was to make the quick decisions upon each detainee's arrival, each of whose general health decided hard labor or gas. Those in the first category would likely die in a few months anyway. The life expectancy for the average prisoner was only a few months.

Was the doctor one of the "Good Nazis"? Did he really care about his patients? Hayes ventured a statement which he knew could cost him his role in the Game. He couldn't help it. "They are like us as much as we say they aren't. Killing them or just letting them die—both are murder. Not just Savina. All of them have value. They're all human, Doctor. I think we both know that."

The doctor looked casually into Wicker's eyes. It was clear he didn't trust Wicker to say what Wicker really thought. He was a manipulator. The doctor didn't even seem shocked, though he might have if he had thought Wicker was being candid. "Then *you* are a murderer."

"As are you, Doctor."

The doctor nodded almost imperceptibly.

They sat silently in the room for several minutes, each possibly wanting to trust the other with his truest sentiments regarding the war, the Jews, the Leader. Hayes broke the silence first. "Clearly neither of us likes what we are doing here."

"Clearly."

"How do we make it stop?"

The doctor only shook his head, looking at the floor. The wispy gray hair only partially covered his otherwise spotted pinkish-white scalp.

"I'm getting out of this," Richard whispered. "I want to be able to trust you when the time comes."

The doctor looked at his hands. "I know what kind of man you are. You would say or do anything suited to your needs."

Hayes felt a slight sting from the comment but understood. "I'm not that man."

The doctor looked at him and smiled. "Even if you weren't, I couldn't help you more than you could help yourself by simply walking out the front gate. Driving would be more practical though."

"What if we took over the camp? We could let everyone go and get ourselves out of here, to Switzerland, maybe. Let them scatter in all directions while we simply vanished! We'd make them think we were tracking down prisoners, giving us plenty of time to get hundreds of kilometers away."

"If you tried, I would take sides against you," the doctor replied, firmly.

"So you *enjoy* being a murderer?"

"I enjoy the idea of my wife and children being alive. Besides, the inmates would all be hunted down. It would be pointless. My wife and children would be next."

Hayes had finally crossed the line. His position in the game, his avatar's career, his implicit "score," was no longer important. Hayes exclaimed as he jumped up from his chair and ran into the examination room, "Living isn't the same thing as just existing, Doctor!" He had seen a large syringe filled with a clear liquid, residing in an ominously open box. Instinctively, he knew its purpose. He reached across the metal table and grabbed the syringe. He stabbed his own chest with it one time, deeply, leaving the needle nestled well between two left ribs. By now the doctor had entered the room and lunged at him, trying to keep him from mashing the piston into the liquid. Wicker's own blood began to swirl into the now pink liquid of the syringe as the doctor wrestled feebly with it. The syringe stuck out horizontally from Richard's chest, empty, lodged there and suspended by the thick needle.

"You stupid man!" The doctor was breathless and leaned against the table.

In moments, the tiled floor met the side of Heinrich's face. Richard's head jerked inside the helmet as it filled with darkness and cold silence, save the rhythm of his own quick breathing. That was the end of Heinrich Wicker.

FARASH SNUCK INTO HAYES' classroom one late afternoon during Trainings Week. He sat at the desk furthest from the door.

A pale, emaciated, but fully formed death mask stared blindly from the wall and past the Reichsminister's bony left shoulder. Just below it, a huge globe sat in a wooden frame of semicircles, like ribs meeting around the amber heart of a dead giant.

The face that met Farash was equally thin, the eyes set back in the skull of its owner, dark in their recesses but bright with ideas. The man's brown, double-breasted suit jacket enclosed a long torso below a wondrously thin neck. His nose was sharp, angular above a thin and lipless mouth.

Here was one of the most powerful men in Germany standing before Farhat Farash's avatar, Karl Ernst Krafft. Smiling, this short and skinny man who couldn't have weighed more than two sacks of Indian grain was convincing a nation that the Jew, making up only two percent of the population, was Germany's biggest threat. Farash didn't linger much on this sort of rhetoric. He was out to not just survive the Game but to become the Fuhrer himself, if it were possible. It had to be possible. To accomplish this, he would first prove to the Fuhrer through this thin man how winnable the war was for Germany—at this period in history. Farash had the hindsight of history and could frame his exceptional foreknowledge as a supernatural oddity. He wasn't a man from the future but rather a mystic in whom Hitler would come to trust completely. Ultimately to become Fuhrer *must* be the point of the Game, the *ultimate win*—to gain the trust of the most evil man in history, to prove his merit in a political battle that would so gain the trust of the man who would name him his second. THAT was his method of winning. It was the only method of winning in Farhat's estimation. To win the Game he would have to become Hitler's Deputy Führer, his second in command, his political heir. Only *then* would he kill Adolf Hitler.

To do this, he had to show up Goebbels, to put the Reichsminister of Propaganda, and others, in low esteem with the Führer, to have Goebbels disgraced by mere comparison to a brilliant strategist who would draw upon a "supernatural" knowledge of forthcoming events. Getting close to Goebbels in this way, and so quickly, couldn't have been a coincidence—it *must* be an element of the Game. This would have been all but impossible in reality, but Farash had one power over the propagandist empowering him with an infinitely greater advantage. He had history. He knew, as any high school world history teacher would, of the blunders that took the German Fuhrer prematurely from the world stage, a victim of his own arrogant and mistaken assumptions.

The Reichsminister of Public Enlightenment and Propaganda stood up from his studded maroon leather chair. He didn't even pretend to be busy when Farash, in the avatar of Krafft the Swiss astrologer, was led in by an SS guard. The thin man in the double-breasted suit met Krafft in front of his desk. In some ways they were remarkably similar—both about the same height with dark hair combed straight back, oiled. Only Krafft was slightly taller and better looking than the man with the cavernous eyes.

"Mister Krafft, I am Joseph Goebbels." They shook hands. The thin man was very friendly, seating himself casually at the front edge of his own desk. "Please." He pointed to a chair in front of the desk where Krafft was to sit. The man then sat back down behind his desk. Farash directed his character to sit, smiling, making consistent but slightly deferential eye contact with the speaker. It was just a game, but he was unaccountably nervous.

"I hear you saved our Fuhrer's life." It sounded more like a question than a statement. "He saved his own life, Herr Reichsminister, by heeding the veracity of my note," Krafft replied.

"Yes . . . Yes. So what 'powers' do you have? I understand you are an astrologer." The thin man's elbows were on his desk, his long fingers folded together under a narrow chin.

"I can predict things. Things that matter."

"Predict something," responded the Reichsminister, obviously amused, "something easily verifiable, like what I will say next."

Farash almost responded, "As I said, I predict things that *matter*," a clear insult. No, he must mount the horse before spurring it, he thought. Instead, he said, "Events are chain reactions, and there are two theories with regard to future events. Either the future is set in stone, and we cannot change it no matter what we do, or the future changes with each action taken that is divergent from its current path."

"Which means?"

"If I predict something and it doesn't happen, it doesn't mean that it wasn't going to happen *at* the moment I predicted it. In other words, I might predict what you are about to say, but in the seconds before you say it, intervening variables may change the result. Thus, I may have actually been right though thought to have been proven incorrect."

"Ah. So you are of the second school of thought, that the future is malleable. Very convenient for a soothsayer, isn't it?" Goebbels leaned back in his chair, smiling, comfortably repositioning himself but without taking his eyes off Krafft.

"I'm not sure I know what you mean."

"Well, if you predict a lightning strike on that pole just outside in sixty seconds and it doesn't, well now, it's okay because perhaps an uncertain event occurring between the prediction and the event kept it from happening, like a crow or something might have flown into the cloud, causing the lightning to redirect itself. Perhaps the wind shifts ever so slightly because of the crow's flight, stirring up the static molecules in the dark cloud which would have produced the lightning, but it doesn't. That sort of thing."

"I suppose so, though it isn't likely a crow could alter the path of a lightning strike."

"Indeed. But if it did, then what would have put this crow outside your scope of prognostication?"

"I'm sorry?"

"In other words, why did not the crow figure into the original prediction of lightning striking the pole? What made it a thing outside of your original prediction? Certainly, it should have been figured into the equation from the beginning so that no prediction concerning the lightning and the pole could have been made, assuming the prediction were accurate and the soothsayer not a pretending fool." He smiled to soften the brunt of his statement.

Farash was silent. If the Reichsminister and Farash had been playing a game of chess, Farash would have already lost his queen.

"So is it true," the Propaganda Minister continued, "that some predictions are truer than others in your expert astrological opinion? That some predictions take into account more variables leading to the occurrence, making them more accurate?" Goebbels was giving him a pass, probably the last he would receive.

"Exactly. One prediction can be assumed superior to another if it takes into account the greatest percentage of accurate factors."

"Perhaps, then . . ." the man behind the desk went on, seemingly impressed with his own deductive capabilities, "the prediction made closest in time to the event would prove most accurate, having the least number of variables interfering with the chain of events leading to the predicted event."

"Yes. That's also true." Farash knew better than to give in too easily, but he didn't seem to have a choice.

"Yes." The speaker paused, one finger touched his nose and then pointed to the ceiling. "Yes. Of course, there is the other possibility. The first school of thought that you had mentioned. The one suggesting that the future is static, predetermined by the first cause, that all factors should already have been taken into account by a legitimate soothsayer as they are unchangeable, and that those who say otherwise to hedge their predictions as resting on possibly uncertain or merely intervening variables . . . are . . . mere frauds?"

Krafft was again silent. Why had the Reichsminister called him here if he simply wanted to accuse him of being a common charlatan? If he were to be tried as a conspirator, it wouldn't be necessary for him to be brought here first. He would simply be executed—after signing a confession of course, admitting to knowledge of a plot against the Fuhrer through his own treacherous connections. *He is playing with me*, he thought. *He wants to take the superior role. He believes that I may be able to predict future events or else I wouldn't be here. But in any case, he doesn't want to acknowledge that such a power would give anyone so much control. Or maybe he had already made up his mind: Krafft had been part of the conspiracy and—torture having been unsuccessful—simply wanted to whittle him down to a nub of information-providing graphite through rhetorical fencing*, of which Joseph Goebbels was a virtuoso.

After a long pause, Krafft spoke. "I understand that the Fuhrer believes my powers to be genuine. Otherwise, I would already be dead." Farash was taking a risk.

"Hmm." Goebbels stared into the eyes of his frail adversary. "*Are you a fraud, Mr. Krafft?*"

"I am not a fraud. And if I might be allowed, I can further prove it."

"Please continue." The man leaned back in his chair.

Farash paused, thought, but decided to continue. He remembered a number of trivial facts from Goebbels' diary, which had been published piecemeal and in 2033 still didn't exist as a complete historical document. "Respectfully, Herr Reichsminister, you didn't start out as an anti-Semite."

"What is that?"

"You had a Jewish professor whom you greatly admired at Heidelberg. You must have learned much from him."

Goebbels reflected, unfazed. "That is true. Of course, no farmer begins his vocation with a true understanding of the locust's role in destroying his fields. Once he sees and experiences the problems caused by the pestilence, however, his view of it changes. These bits of a man's history can be found out with little effort. Go on."

Krafft closed his eyes as if concentrating deeply. He placed the fingers of both hands to his avatar's forehead. "You vehemently defended the Jews to your lover, Anka . . . or Anda, who wrote to you that Jews were 'as greedy as pigeons after a crust of bread.'"

"Some of my letters are missing. I believe them to be in the hands of my enemies. Perhaps you know their whereabouts?"

Silence. Farash was trying to dig more out of his stubborn memory.

"Go on."

Krafft continued. "You were in love with her, but with a clubbed foot, you hesitated to make love to her, thinking she would reject you. In fact, you never made love to her. Respectfully Reichsminister, and I only say this to prove that I am who and what I say I am, you only first made love to a woman just after your 33rd birthday."

The Reichsminister stared intently at his guest. Farash had taken a big chance. A part of him wondered how such candor would be viewed by such a spinner of self-created truths presented as undeniable facts. He could simply deny all of this— both to Krafft and to himself.

After a time, Goebbels nodded. "Have you read from the works of Nostradamus?"

"Not really."

"You will." He took out a book from his desk entitled *The Quatrains of Michel de Nostredame*. It had been translated into German, its original publication dated 1555. Goebbels turned to a dog-eared page and handed it to him across the desk. "You may find a more far-reaching enlightenment in there."

Farash flipped through the book of poems, all grouped in lines of four. He read one of the quatrains aloud.

An emperor will be born near Italy,

Who shall cost his empire dearly;

It will be said by those who gather around him,

That he will prove to be less a prince than a butcher.

"One of the Medici?" Farash inquired.

"Mussolini." Goebbels corrected.

"Are you sure?"

"Does it matter? What matters is how convincing you can be of your own interpretation."

"I'm not sure I follow."

Goebbels grinned. "It's not about what it says or even about what it really means. It's about what you can convince people to think it means. Turn to quatrain five dash twenty-nine."

Krafft turned to the stanza mentioned and read aloud:

Liberty will not return,
They shall be occupied by a dark, fierce, sinful villain;
As the laws of the people will be overruled
By Hister, and Italy, a fascist republic.

"Hister?"

"Hitler or perhaps Ister—the Latin name for the Danube River, not far from the Führer's place of birth. Nostradamus played with names, some believe, to hide the truths of his prophecies from those who would have him burned for witchcraft. He was obsessed with a ruler named 'Hister.' Perhaps his oracular chickens just pecked at a few of the wrong letters and really meant 'Hitler.' Now read quatrain two dash twenty-four." Farash, as Krafft, obeyed.

Wild men insane with anger will cross the rivers,
The largest part of the battle will be against Hister;
In steel armor they will make their great attack,
As Germany's child heeds no one.

Krafft (Farash) looked up from the thick, heavy book and at the enormous globe. Through the lens of history, the "wild men insane with anger" could easily be the Russians from the East or the advancing Americans and British from the West—or both. He thought on Hitler's stubborn refusal to accept defeat until the very end, spending his last days in a Berlin bunker, even while the Red Army approached from only a few kilometers away. Krafft looked hard at the propaganda minister.

"So. You want me to find out what happens to Germany by reading this? Doesn't look good, but the words seem pretty elusive. Could be taken to mean anything."

The Reichsminister looked disappointed. "I want you to find Germany's victory in this book and publish it. I will distribute what you publish to the masses. It will help the war effort."

"And if it says Germany will fall. . ."

"It won't because you won't let it."

"Do you believe what this book may actually be saying? That there may be some truth in here?"

Goebbels again looked disappointed and shook his head. "It doesn't matter what it says, only what you can *make* it say. Do I personally believe Nostradamus to have been an accurate predictor of future world events? Not really. His words are too nebulous and his images too blurry to be of any real use in that regard. Neither matters. What matters is what you can make others, who are gullible enough to take a side, believe what you want them to believe. Mr. Krafft, I have the tendency to think of you as an absolute pretender, a dangerous prevaricator, an enemy of Germany and possibly a man with detailed knowledge regarding the highest levels of resistance against National Socialism in this country and maybe even abroad. But you have, for now, somehow convinced our Fuhrer of your veracity, and have thus barely saved your own life—after 'saving' his. I can use such a man. At the same time, your reactions to certain points of our discussion paint you as naive, a guileless and simple-minded person with powers, if he had them, which he couldn't begin to use to the Reich's advantage. Thus, I choose not to take a side with you, Mr. Krafft, one way or the other. I only wish for you to work for me here in the Ministry of Propaganda. You will interpret Nostradamus, convincingly, as one who, four hundred years ago, predicted the rise and thousand-year perpetuity of the Third Reich. As you read through this book, what you might think this occult prophet may have actually meant in any particular stanza, line, or word is completely immaterial."

Soon Krafft was led to a small office where he was confirmed in his new role as secretary to the Reichsminister of Public Enlightenment and Propaganda. Alone, and under regular surveillance, he would work to find in the stanzas of Nostradamus a glowing future for Germany and its Third Reich. His new cell in the old Leopold Palace had tall windows, a wide desk, and a clean, waxed floor.

Chapter 6

A day had passed before the German scientist Kurt Debus nearly mustered the courage to confront his Allied captors. They weren't captors, really—they didn't even know he was there. Still, he had seen soldiers and other personnel walking through the facility, delaying his decision to make his presence known. That delay would not be long, for he was beginning to have difficulty breathing in the nearly airtight glass structure.

However, as the scientist edged closer to giving himself up, two men in radiation gear made their way towards the glass enclosure. Each was fully suited with self-contained breathing apparatus. Debus, lying prone in his own sweaty rad suit beneath the humming Bell, panicked. He positioned himself against the furthest leg of the platform, watching and listening intently. One of the suited figures, still outside the glass, made his way around to the side of the Bell where thick cables and hoses joined the Bell to a massive control panel, the cables and hoses passing through the glass within dense grommets. The other slid an access card into a slot and opened the glass door, entering the enclosure, the door automatically closing shut behind him. He began vertically passing a hand-held Geiger counter over the massive form, its clicking loud and frantic. The German scientist took in a long and silent breath of fresh air.

Debus saw the hand holding the device as it made its way down the Bell and past the platform. It was all he could do to resist retreating back up through the hatch and into the massive form, knowing that any sound he made would be amplified both by the hollow Bell and the glass walls. After a few moments, the man at the console knocked on the glass and gave the other man a thumbs up signal. The man inside the glass nodded and began making his way towards the glass door.

The German scientist shuffled slightly, again noticing the pencil that had inadvertently rolled under the platform. He grabbed it and stealthily inched his way forward. He had one shot at this. The man inside the enclosure pressed a few buttons on a black panel and the door clicked open. As he stepped through, a pencil slid across the concrete floor between the door and frame. The suited figure met up with the man from the console, together ascending a distant set of stairs, oblivious that the door had remained slightly ajar.

⸻

FALL, 2033

As if life could continue as before.

Before . . . before what? What was there before? There was nothing before the Game, nothing in his life that Richard would consider worthy of garnering his attention, aside from family members who rarely cared to contact him—though he had made his own attempts, in a way.

Wicker was dead, and starting a new avatar was unthinkable—it simply took too much out of him. After speaking with the doctor, Hayes had realized that escape from the camp was impossible, as was the childish idea of emancipating the prisoners. He had killed off Wicker's sorry ass with a phenol injection to spare Savina. He hoped the digital gods would find an especially grisly place in hell for their new tenant. Still, he could have tried. It was just a game, so why didn't he rebel, taking out as many Nazis as he could in a blaze of satisfying retribution while *still* accomplishing Wicker's death? He cursed his own impulsivity.

Fräulein licked his knee and then jumped up to plop next to him on the couch; he surfed the cable channels on his big flat screen, wondering how many channels he was actually paying for. He remembered that he was on a minimum plan—a term applicable now to pretty much all of his life's required exertions and expenditures, except with regard to the Game.

He patted the dog on the head and switched channels. She gave a low whine. Apparently, she wanted something. He flipped to the local news, always amusing on those rare occasions that he watched it. There would be rain, lots of it, coming in from the Gulf of Mexico. It was still only a tropical storm, but it was sitting in warm water, building strength, had been for a day or so.

Richard's water boiler in the kitchen clicked off, and he got up to make some tea. Grabbing a canister from a kitchen shelf, he pulled out a packet of generic green tea and opened it, placing a bag in the yellowing German *Bierkrug* used for pretty much all hot and cold drinks. Another part of him remembered that he didn't especially like tea, especially green tea. Tea gave him nausea and bad dreams, particularly if he drank it right before bed. It was 3:17 A.M., and he'd be sleeping soon. But didn't he always drink green tea before bed? Something wasn't adding up.

Letting the tea steep in the boiled water, Richard Hayes fed his dog with a mixture of kibbles and dry cat food. Adding cat food was the only way he could get Fräulein to eat right away. Otherwise, the dog food would sit there until extreme hunger brought her to it. He scooped a good portion of the mixture from a lidded 20 lb. trash can into her metal bowl. She trotted immediately to it, sniffed it, and looked up at him, staring as if he had done something wrong. Her left eye was blue. Richard was startled at this and then was surprised that he had been startled. When did the eye change color? Hasn't one of her eyes always been blue? No, he would, of course, have remembered. He leaned against the counter, watching her. She eventually walked back to the couch and jumped on it, staring in his direction, as if this might get him to change his mind about the food.

He sipped the tea and winced as a succession of five electronic beeps followed, recalling the frozen dinner he'd placed in the microwave though he couldn't remember what kind. Swedish meatballs, he finally recollected.

Hasn't one eye always been blue?

The futon brought a welcome sleep, and he awoke the next morning at 10:05 with the realization that today was Saturday. It was October, and Richard heard and felt the reverberations of an autumn wind sweeping against the side of his A-frame house. The compression of it made the floor shake slightly as Fräulein looked up from the foot of the futon to sniff the air. She whined briefly and lay her head on the cover, raising one eyebrow and then the other as she looked past Richard and out a small, round window just below the arch of the high roof.

Now, what is there worth doing? Nothing came to mind this windy Saturday morning except thoughts of the Game. He thought of Savina, safe . . . if the word could apply, convalescing in a concentration camp on the other side of a make-believe world over three-fourths of a century ago.

Mr. Farash hadn't had a decent conversation with his wife in weeks. He practically lived at the high school after school hours, and an occasional late night phone call to his classroom would always result in an answer from the man, though brief. Amala even came to see him a few times, always calling first. He was always alone and always absorbed in thought, often sitting at a desk in the classroom next door. He was doing "research," the kind requiring a tremendous amount of computing power, something his classroom somehow didn't possess, and a connection they couldn't afford in their modest apartment just above a store in town selling flowers, mums, high school spirit shirts, and various birthday party supplies.

On weekday mornings, he woke up, showered, got dressed, ate whatever Amala had made for him, took the subcompact to work, taught for the day, and then when the workday was over, he would sneak into Hayes' classroom and return to the Game. There was a time when he had to look out for his colleague, as Hayes himself would sometimes spend a night in his classroom. Lately, though, Richard Hayes had been staying away from his classroom outside of school hours. He no longer came on weekends. In fact, he'd even started to use his sick days regularly, once or twice a week. Mr. Farash was thus nearly free to play the game just about whenever he wanted. He had even obtained and made a copy of the master key from a coach down the hall. Hayes wouldn't care. Farash figured that Richard was just as addicted to the game as he was—probably more. If he happened to find Farash in his room, he'd understand. Farash would make him understand.

One afternoon, Farash decided to "borrow" a computer from Hayes' classroom, rather than continue his clandestine visits under the cover of late hours. Farash had timed visits to Richard's classroom during different periods of the school day in an effort to determine which computers weren't being used. He no longer complained to Hayes about his frustrations with students. These were merely . . . friendly visits involving occasional questions regarding the vertical alignment strategies that the Social Studies department had set up for the year. In this way, Farash had determined that a few of the computers against the far wall remained unused throughout the day. They were extras. None of Hayes' classes contained more than twenty-five students and Farash could remove a computer from inside a desk console and the loss would remain unnoticed unless someone tried to turn the thing on. *That* would only happen if one of the other computers malfunctioned somehow. But these new computers were tanks. Aside from one catching fire some time back—which was apparently the fault of a storm, not the unit itself—they never seemed to need repairs, as far as Farhat Farash could tell.

It was no more than a matter of removing four screws from the metal plate in the back; detaching the relevant cables and wires; sliding out the gray brick of wires, fans, cable ports, and processors; then replacing the plate and screws. He also grabbed a pair of studded interactive gloves and an extra helmet from the back cabinet, bringing all back to his apartment in a cardboard box.

He set the gray brick in a shoebox upon a small desk, stacked with books in the corner of the second bedroom. It was referred to as the "junk room," though Mrs. Farash certainly didn't like the term, filled with boxes of clothes and knickknacks, most piled onto a twin bed. It was where the baby would sleep, were one ever to materialize. Farash made a small nook by piling up the boxes and books into two makeshift walls, hiding himself and his precious boon in the corner, away from the incurious eyes of his beloved wife. This was now his sacred "place of meditation." *Namaste.*

"Well?" Reichsminister Goebbels seemed more friendly than usual during their morning walk amongst the snow-laden trees around the former Leopold Palace courtyard. A statue of General Leopold stood in the center while SS men could be seen at nearly every building corner and on every rooftop in the vicinity. Only designated officials were allowed near the Ministry building.

Farash as Krafft began, "I have several quatrains that may interest you. This one foreshadows the Fuhrer's successful takeover of Britain:

The grand empire will quickly be reduced

To a tiny area, which shall soon after expand;

An unsavory place in a small country,

In the middle he will come to lay down his scepter."

The Reichsminister walked quietly, thinking, looking into the surrounding Linden trees that, undisturbed, might continue to grow for centuries. "I see," he remarked. "Britain is the 'grand empire,' which shall be 'quickly reduced' by the armies of the Third Reich. But what I don't understand is what makes the 'small country' unsavory? And, in what way will our Fuhrer 'lay down his scepter'? Seems to me an image of defeat."

Farash was silent. Both kept walking. The snow crunched beneath their shoes as they slowly strolled along the edge of the courtyard. Like Goebbels, Krafft wore a suit. "As you say, a man can paint a place as savory or unsavory, meager or powerful. 'A mind is its own place and can make a heaven of hell or a hell of heaven.'" Farash was quoting Satan from John Milton's *Paradise Lost*. The irony was apparently lost on Goebbels.

"And how would you do this?"

"England will be reduced by our bombing campaign. When we have destroyed it and made it 'unsavory,' we shall then 'expand' its potential by making it our jumping off point for an invasion of the Western Hemisphere. The scepter will be laid down by the Fuhrer—perhaps a giant statue of a man holding a burning scepter on the westernmost point of England, showing that we have taken all of Europe and will soon shine the light of National Socialism across the Atlantic."

"That could work," Goebbels remarked. "Or it could be interpreted as our creating a historical prognostication after the fact."

"Isn't that what we're doing? I . . ."

"No. Your job is to look into the quatrains for events occurring now and which could not possibly have happened as a consequence of active interference, not merely *creating* events to coincide with Nostradamus' four-hundred-year-old predictions."

The two were silent. His remaining ideas involving the quatrains surrounded just that—events to be soon created which *seemed* as if they coincided with Nostradamus' esoteric words, not events currently in play—or even any that would be.

The clouds over this section of Berlin were growing especially dark. In the "junk room" of his apartment, Farash could almost feel in his blanketed corner the chilling stillness of the morning air—though a warm and humid night infiltrated his apartment.

From conversations with his guard detail, the SS men who interminably stood outside his office door, Faresh gleaned that, occasionally, Krafft would sometimes awaken from a nap confused, having no idea where he was or for whom he was working. Thus, Farash made it clear to orderlies and the SS guards that the cause of this behavior was as unknown as the sources of his paranormal abilities, that during such bouts of amnesia he was to be physically restrained, gagged, and kept detained in his office, and that under no circumstances, while he was in such a mental state, were he to be told anything regarding why he was there or what his duties might be. He was not even to be allowed to speak until he gave a specific hand signal, indicating his rational self was back in control. They had accepted all of this without comment.

When Farash was not Krafft, Krafft slept on a cot unfolded from the wardrobe opposite his desk. Farash kept the physical body of Krafft exhausted through his continuous playing, so managing that Krafft actually slept during these three or four hour stretches of time. Whenever Farash as Krafft went anywhere, which was rare, he was accompanied by armed SS guards. Farash had actually insisted on it. Of course, Goebbels also knew of Krafft's strange amnesic episodes, but thought it merely part of the game a self-styled mystic might play, one who clearly wanted desperately into the Leader's inner circle. Farash knew this to be the Reichsminister's thinking, so he downplayed his "powers." Primarily, he must be what Goebbels wanted of him while perhaps still attempting to grind away slowly at the man's incredulity.

For Farash, the real problem with making any prediction and seeing it actually come to pass involved time. It took time for a significant event to play out once he "predicted" it. Some events might be fated to happen only days after a prediction, but these seemed always to be something anyone might derive from a general knowledge of preceding events, obvious causes. Other correct but highly sensitive predictions might be too risky, making the incredulous listener soon begin to question the man's background and cast about for some hidden political connections. And how did one reveal things that the Reichsminister himself could have (or should have) known without stinging the man's ego? The egos of evil men are fragile, for they operate against the whispered conscience of their upbringing, which experience and self-deception can never wholly extinguish.

Goebbels was becoming impatient. "You are wasting valuable time. This war will last as long as resources last—men, machinery, raw materials. The nature of consumption involves using up what cannot immediately be replaced. We need a message that will make Germans work harder for the Fatherland, dig deeper for iron, and accept greater sacrifices as the scarcity of basic necessities increases."

This gave Farash an idea.

"Norway and Denmark are deep sources for iron, coal, and wood. These countries can be taken almost without a shot fired."

Goebbels stopped and turned to look at him. No one outside of the cabinet knew of the Fuhrer's immediate plan to invade Norway and Denmark simultaneously, certainly not this wild astrologer who couldn't do so simple a task as invent convenient predictions regarding Germany's affirmative place in history from the nebulous words of a fellow counterfeit astrologer. "And?" Goebbels looked Krafft up and down, as if visually dissecting the man to extract more relevant information.

Faresh continued. "The Fuhrer should have no worries regarding Britain and France if he chooses to invade Norway and Denmark. None of them have anything with which to stop us and they know it well. They'll think of nothing but bolstering their own defenses. Why didn't these 'Allies,' for instance, declare war on Russia for invading Poland? They declared war on Germany for doing the same thing only a few weeks before. Of course, nothing came of it."

"The British and the French aren't idiots. They fear such a move would bring Germany and Russia closer together. Germany doesn't have an actual alliance with Russia, and they want to keep it that way. The Allies have no idea of the hatred Hitler has for Russia, nor the extreme differences between National Socialism and the idiotic notions of Stalin's communism. It's all socialism to them, so there are some who think we're linked ideologically. They don't want that link to grow into something more material. Hitler will never ally with . . ." Goebbels stopped mid-sentence. He seemed to have said too much and turned to continue the walk. The Reichsminister was agitated now. Perhaps he was beginning to see Krafft as someone with a truly special talent, maybe even someone who could be trusted. The Minister of Propaganda had let Krafft into his confidence, but just for a few seconds. Now, Farash just wanted to grab a pistol and blow off the man's head. Unfortunately, the Fuhrer wouldn't approve.

Farash knew he was safe, for now, but he would still need to offer reassurances to bolster the man's ego by reinforcing his sense of superiority.

"Can I be forward?"

"You are always forward, Mister Krafft," replied the Reichsminister, clearly annoyed.

"I need you to hear me. What I'm saying right now. Keep this information between us, if you like. You need not act on anything I say."

"Obviously. Go on."

"Germany will invade Norway and Denmark on the 9th of April. Our Fuhrer will be very successful, and the Brits and baguette-munching French won't lift a finger, just as they did nothing when we took back the Rhineland, just as they did nothing but talk when we took Poland and shared it with the Russians, just as they won't on April 9th, just as they won't . . ." Farash was about to predict the invasion of France. No, it was a card to be saved for later. "If I am wrong, execute me."

Goebbels thought. "April 9th?" He smiled faintly. "Complete success? Would you be willing to put it in writing, Mister Krafft?"

"Yes, in writing."

"Then you have a deal. I will keep the information to myself. If all happens as you predict, I will be your biggest supporter when in the company of the Fuhrer." Goebbels knew that the invasion had been put off until June, if it were to happen at all. The Fuhrer had formed a custom of making last-minute changes, negating months of hard planning. Farash saw in his face that Goebbels was sure it wouldn't happen on the given date and was fairly certain that the English and French would indeed get involved somehow.

For Goebbels, this would be a perfect opportunity to show up the sham astrologer. He would show the Fuhrer the document, perhaps on April 10th, signed by Krafft, detailing when, where, and how the invasion would take place. That way it would mean Krafft's incarceration when the date and outcome were incorrect. It wouldn't be much of a loss, really, since the man had no real gift for propaganda. It was dangerous to trust these Rasputin types.

Fall, 2033

Mr. Hayes sat cross-legged on his colleague's desk at a front corner of the classroom and listened as Mr. Perry delivered his short lecture.

"Can *love* be a theme?" he asked the class.

Many low yeses could be heard.

"No. It can't. Love is a concept. A literary theme must be expressed as a complete sentence, a statement about life. So . . . can this be a theme: 'Love between children and their parents'?"

Some yeses could again be heard.

"No. That's still a concept. A theme in literature should always be expressed in the form of a *statement*, a complete thought, like "Love between children and their parents can sometimes be strained when children show disobedience." The students were silent. A few were looking in Mr. Perry's direction.

Karen Perez sat in a middle row. She hadn't taken Hayes' class since the 2032-33 school year, but she *was* enrolled in Mr. Perry's class this year. She nervously watched Mr. Hayes, who seemed to be staring through the side wall and into his own classroom. He detected her gaze and looked back, raising his eyebrows in an obvious attempt to find out what the scrutiny involved. Did she need to leave the room? The student looked down again at her desk and pretended to take notes from Perry's lecture.

Hayes looked around the room. Like Karen, others still sported the green "*Schlaf!*" buttons, some on their shirts but most attached to their backpacks. Likewise, "*Erwachen*!" could still be found on backpacks, armbands, and binders. It was silly. He and Principal Mason had expected the Game-induced fad to peter out once he resumed the game. It did, for the most part, with this year's seniors. The juniors had taken it up.

After class, in the hallway, Karen dropped a folded note into Mr. Hayes' hands. *Never a good thing*, Richard thought. All the students had filed out, and Perry had gone back to his classroom and closed the door behind him, locking it and turning out the lights for his daily conference period nap. After the girl had turned a corner, Hayes stood in the hallway and unfolded the note. It read, "I know who you are in the game. Maybe we can help each other."

The next day, during his morning bus duty, Karen approached Mr. Hayes. Hayes stood by the curb, appreciating the cool morning breeze coming off the Gulf of Mexico. "I've been wanting to talk to you. It's about the Game," she said.

Thoughtlessly, Hayes replied, "If it's about your character, you should know that we don't discuss it. We just play it. Everything stays in the game. No unfair advantages. Wait . . . you haven't played it since the year before last, when you were in my class. Or have you . . . ? And weren't you supposed to graduate last year?" Hayes knew the advanced student, like others, had been playing with a bootlegged copy of his browser—or perhaps she'd discovered the actual URL. Karen was a bright one.

"I decided not to go with the three-year plan, so I'm graduating this year." She ignored the rest of his queries. "I think we both know it's more than just a game."

Hayes was silent for several seconds.

"You're Heinrich Wicker, the camp guard, aren't you?"

Hayes was taken aback. Such a thing had happened, he knew, avatars meeting in the same camp, though not his camp. "How did you know . . . Yes, I was Wicker. He's dead now. *Er ist tot.*"

"*Nein, er ist nicht tot.*"

"No, Karen, I watched him die. Actually, I killed him myself with a phenol injection."

The buses were starting to clear, and most students were already making their way into the hallways just before the first release bell.

"OK. Your rules. So I'm not going to reveal my character, but I saw Heinrich lying in the hospital ward. He's in a coma," she said.

Hayes considered. "Assuming he *is* alive, which he isn't, you've just revealed to me that we work or at least did work in the same camp. So, you might as well tell me, are you a prisoner or a guard?"

"When you come back to the game, we can help each other. Nothing weird or anything." Karen smiled and walked into the building, ignoring his question.

Mr. Hayes thought about following her but decided against it. *When* he came back into the game? . . . She knew Mr. Hayes better than he knew himself. If Heinrich was alive, assuming she was right, it wouldn't matter for long. If the upper brass in the SS feel he has any remaining use, they'll send him to the front, which will put him far away from Savina. If not, he'll likely wake up senseless, sent to an asylum, and eventually be "euthanized" by one of the doctors—with a legitimate dose this time. Either way, none of the camp officers could have any lingering respect for him now, and at some point they'd realize that he was just taking up space.

Hayes had learned so much about the Nazi way of doing things that it was hard for him not to sympathize with Wicker—a little. There had been hundreds of thousands of German citizens deemed "*Lebensunwertes Leben*," especially children and the elderly. Whole wings of hospitals in some of the larger cities had been filled with persons mentally and physically unable to contribute to society in any meaningful way. They were considered *Parasiten auf die Volk*. Doctors and scientists made use of their bodies—especially their brains—for scientific research, usually after they were poisoned, gassed, or starved in their beds. Heinrich Wicker would likely go this route. He was either dead or as good as, so that story was over. . . . Was it over? He could not completely convince himself of the imminence of this scenario.

Instead of returning to the Game, Hayes needed to find other interests with which to occupy his time. It was essential to his own mental and emotional well-being to find something else. But there wasn't anything else, no other focus that might drive away the obsession to see Wicker dead and Savina safe.

Back at home that night, Hayes detected consciousness in the screen of his helmet, a vague faintness registering black and white, pixelated with haze in the blackness of the surrounding enclosure. Karen's words, and those of the camp Doctor, had made his return inevitable.

It had been weeks since his attempt to kill Wicker. The murkiness of the interaction made it clear that Wicker's body was not completely healthy, but he was definitely alive and somewhat conscious. There was static in the audio, accompanied by a ringing that he couldn't shake off. After some hours of vague lucidity, Richard Hayes found himself standing over a hospital bed, several beds away from his own. He watched her breathe, following the thin, white sheets as they moved slowly and rhythmically up and down over her chest, her head turned toward him, eyes closed. He suddenly felt like an outsider and quickly realized how terror-stricken she would be to wake up and see Wicker staring at her from above.

He stood barefoot in a hospital gown and looked at his hands. They were big hands. The hairs on the backs of his wrists and arms were blond and thin. His palms were pale. He looked across Savina's form, small and dark. She lay in a short row of beds usually reserved for officers and guards. Savina wouldn't have received this level of treatment had she not been extremely useful.

He touched her cheek. She was unresponsive. He wanted to lie next to her, like in his dream, with the ceiling lifted away to expose the stars of the chilly night; he wanted her to respond as she had in his dream, willing to believe him, open to his crazy story, in the midst of a vast and empty camp. A beautiful thought—the two of them, free, far away from the camp, lying under stars, sharing ideas beyond the chaotic situation in which they had found themselves. But what explained these intense feelings? He knew little about her. She was a Pole, brought here by train when Warsaw had been invaded, had had medical training. That was pretty much it. If he were to get her out of this situation, it would have to be soon, before she was fully healed, before she again joined the general population of the camp.

"The vodka is here, Herr Wicker," whispered a uniformed soldier who had walked past but then stopped to grab Heinrich's arm, smiling a lipless smile. "I'm assuming you're back to what you were before your two weeks off? . . . crazy bastard. By the Kettle. Tonight. We'll all be there. Your . . . farewell party." The shorter enlisted man seemed quite familiar and patted Heinrich on the arm before walking back in the direction he had come. He showed no condescension or irony toward the officer, only familiarity, too much familiarity from an enlisted man nowhere near the regulation height of an SS officer and nowhere near Wicker's rank, even now. Wicker's standing had indeed fallen—to be spoken to so casually by a mere corporal of the regular army.

For a moment, Hayes had no idea what to do with himself. He decided to lie back down on his bed and watch for Savina to awaken. After some hours of watching her sleep with almost no detectable movement, he decided to explore areas of the camp with which he was least familiar. He needed to find blind spots, ways of getting someone out of the camp without being seen and without being followed. He had some ideas about how this might be accomplished, but no definite plan as of yet.

By nightfall, Hayes had explored many of the camp's more hidden nooks and eventually found his way to the rear of the general kitchen, not far from the hospital. It was in the back of a broad canteen, filled with stainless steel counters and wooden chairs. Giant ladles hung from hooks on a circular wheel depending from a beam overhead. In the larger of the several kitchen areas, an immense black kettle stood in a huge alcove of the back wall. A fire was lit beneath it and several *Wehrmacht* soldiers and a few SS men stood drinking just outside of its warm circumference. He was somewhat late for his "farewell party."

"Herr Wicker!" shouted the short corporal who had told him of the gathering. "You made it! And without bumping your head or stabbing yourself with poisoned needles. They really don't know what a fine officer they're sending away." The five men making up the assembly laughed. One handed him a clear bottle, apparently vodka, from which they had already begun taking drinks. This wasn't the first of such meetings he'd attended as Wicker. He had in fact gained a great deal of information about this world of Germans, Nazis, and death camps from these encounters. At such events, characters would often drink heavily, and the more they drank, the looser their tongues became. However, the company was usually not so mixed.

He pretended to join in and attempted to play his role to perfection, abashedly downplaying his antics and the rumors about him as mere "propaganda" created by his enemies to persecute him. All laughed. Once several bottles had been passed around, with Hayes pretending to drink on each occasion, he got into a conversation with an officer who rode a military-issued motorcycle with a sidecar, one the man rarely used but was known to brag of on occasion.

The conversation eventually became an argument about whether the man's standard issue BMW R75 was a better machine than the Zündapp KS-750, which, Hayes said, had been issued to a friend of his (Wicker's) just last month. Richard's regular reading of the *Munich Illustrated Press* online magazine during times of low activity in the Game had aided him in creating points specific to the machine in question. Better horsepower, smoother gear-shifting, better steering control—these were only some of the reasons, according to Wicker, that the R75 would eventually be replaced by the KS-750 in only a few years as the Reich's motorcycle of choice. The motorcyclist gave in on some points, specifically those involving modifications regarding the final drive differential, expecting Wicker, in the spirit of camaraderie, to ease up on some of his points and point out at least one way the R75 might be a better bike, perhaps with regard to style or color options? Hayes refused to concede any point of inferiority with regard to the KS-750, gradually irritating the young officer.

At one point, the man pulled out the keys to the machine and swore that the keys were Wicker's and his friend's if either of them could beat him in a race around the camp on their bikes. His bike was in the back barn and ready for the race whenever he or his friend could produce their beloved KS-750. Of course, the motorcycle wasn't the officer's to give away, so those listening knew the statement to be a mere gesture, the words of a bruised ego, but this gave away the location of the keys and where the machine had been kept during the winter. It was only a matter of waiting until after the officer had drunk a few more toasts, and all became engaged in a singalong of all three stanzas of "*Deutschlandlied,*" when, arm-in-arm beside the man, Hayes lifted the keys out of the distracted man's coat pocket.

It had taken some work, but Richard had gotten to the motorcycle in the barn in the late hours of the frosty night without being missed. It was, unfortunately, located at the back of the general camp, past the corner where the two small crematorium buildings sat, now cold and empty of human trace. It was now a matter of getting Savina to the building by early morning.

Savina had been groggy. Richard had intended to wrap her in as many blankets as he could and bring her, carrying her if necessary, to the lonely barn behind a thin copse of trees just inside the camp's perimeter. At this hour, all that stirred were a strong, frigid wind from the north and four of the camp's searchlights. The brick towers would be manned with one, maybe two persons, with one or two soldiers resting below, playing cards or simply napping on bunks.

The biggest problem of getting her there involved the sheer length of the camp, the entirety of which he would have to cover with Savina possibly draped over his shoulder the whole way. As thin as she was, it was nevertheless quite a distance to walk.

In the ward, no German doctors were in sight, only a few prison orderlies who needed only a brief look to silence any questions forming in their minds. When he entered, he stared two of them down until they dropped what they were doing and left the room, closing the main door behind them.

When Hayes reached Savina, she was awake but groggy. He grabbed a considerable stack of blankets and threw them into a backpack he found in a footlocker. He put this around his shoulders and across his back. He then walked up to Savina and put his hand out for her to take it. She lay still, staring into his face.

"I'm taking you out of the camp. You have nothing to lose if you trust me. Either way, you'll rot here." She smiled, ironically, apparently drugged. She put her hand out, only semi-consciously, and dropped it. He picked her up off the bed and put her on her feet; she immediately fell back onto the bed. There was no way she would be able to walk. He had had the idea of walking her to the back of the camp at gunpoint for "latrine duty" with a few other prisoners he could pick up along the way—to make it look legitimate. But if she couldn't walk, the plan would be null.

Hayes sat by her and looked around. He put the blanket around her, covering every part of her but her head. He then took another blanket off of one of the other beds and wrapped her in it as one would shroud a corpse, covering her head. He grabbed some white surgical tape from a nearby kit and wrapped it around the blankets, covering her ankles. He then wrapped it around her covered upper arms and chest. He made sure there was only one layer covering her face, checked her breathing, and put her over his shoulder with as much care as he could manage.

A recent snowstorm had finally let up, but the wind hadn't, stirring up the fresh snow around them as he carried his bundle. Visibility was further limited by a fog that had settled in, but he knew where he was going. With the double-rows of endless barracks on his right and the long ditch on his left, he trudged through the snow with his package. As he neared the first of the towers from which spotlights attempted to pierce the cold early-morning fog, Hayes walked closer to the tower, expecting to be halted and questioned. A spotlight had been directed squarely on them for a distance of about 20 meters. He approached the tower with his bundle and stopped, looking up. A window cracked open from above and a voice yelled out in German, "A bit late for hiking, isn't it?"

"Dead body," he replied. "We found it stinking up a closet in the Kettle room. Oh, and here's a little present from Herr Commandant." With his gloved left hand Hayes produced a small bottle of vodka from his left waistcoat pocket, showing it to the guard.

The window opened wide, and a man's head and arms appeared. "Throw it to me!" He tossed the bottle to the man and began to walk on.

The same man called out again after receiving the bottle. "Hey wait! Why not just throw the body outside into the snow? It's not going anywhere."

"Doctor says she died of Typhus. The body is covered in fleas. Needs to go to the stoves for burning." The tower window shut quickly. Hayes walked on with his load. Were it Hayes himself carrying Savina, he would have collapsed from exhaustion before reaching the first tower. Wicker's six-foot body suited the purpose much better. By the time he reached the second tower, the spotlight was dancing in front of him, moving side to side from his feet to the direction of the crematorium, as if to say, "Go quickly!" He waved at the closed windows with his left hand and kept walking. From there, it had been relatively easy getting Savina past the crematorium and into the old barn behind the trees, but what he didn't notice was the person following him.

The keys to the barn had been on the same ring as the key to the motorcycle itself. The heavy padlock had yielded, and the half-rusted, frozen hinges creaked as he swung one of the doors outward. Placing her on a bed of cold straw, he exposed her pale face. He then closed the barn door and began checking the tires and oil of the motorcycle.

Other machines lay scattered throughout the barn, now a place of refuge for the working and derelict equipment sheltered there. A typewriter lay on a rotting desk in a corner. The hammers containing the letters were rusted together, frozen in a clump just above the roller. A cabinet contained painters' equipment—rollers, old five-liter cans of light-blue paint. Richard caught the vague smell of turpentine. He rifled through the shelves, looking for gasoline. He found a two-liter can labeled "Benzin" and poured its entire contents into the gray teardrop tank of the vehicle.

"What are you doing?" Savina spoke, vaguely, for the first time since her abduction from the warm hospital bed. Before this moment, she had simply complied, not conscious enough to know what was happening. Now she was watching him from the bed of straw, wrapped in blankets against the stinging cold.

"Getting you . . . us . . . out of here."

She raised her head and then let it fall back down. "Why?" she murmured.

"Because you'll die here if I don't, and I'm not going to the front." He lied about the second part. It was all about her. He didn't care where his avatar went as long as she was safe.

"You talk differently, I've noticed," she said faintly.

"What?"

"Your German is more basic when you're being decent."

"And when I am not being decent?" he prodded.

"You don't do much talking," She replied sleepily.

"So you have not had much to go on."

"Not much, but I do know a German accent from a non-German one." It was true that Richard usually spoke German through the headset directly. He had, off and on, for quite some time. When he did so, nothing had to be translated; it was truly his voice. His German accent was at least plausible. He'd received no such comments from other officers.

She paused for a few moments. "Who are you? I mean, who are you . . . today?"

Hayes stopped his work and looked back at her. "You won't believe me, but I had intended to tell you."

"So."

"So it's a crazy story, but here it is. I'm a middle-aged man from your future named Richard Hayes. From my perspective, this whole thing, this reality, you, this camp, are part of a game played out on a computer through the Internet, and you are the part of it I'm trying to save." He knew that to her this would probably make no sense—unless her programming code decided otherwise.

She let her head fall. "Well, I am very relieved. You're not a psychopath . . ."

He grinned. "I said you wouldn't believe me."

"How can I believe anything that doesn't sound like anything that means anything? Internet? Computer?" Richard stopped and looked at her. He shook his head and continued working to free the machine's kick start.

The motorcycle finally roared to life. He let it run, re-covering it with a tarp to hide what noise he could. He squatted near Savina who watched him from the cold mound of hay. He looked at her for a few moments. Her eyes narrowed, then smiled wryly. She coughed and spoke. "You highborn Germans are so full of *Schiss*, but there's something wrong with you in particular, or at least different. That's not a compliment by the way."

Hayes replied, "How about we get the hell out of here and then we can talk about it later. Or would you prefer to stay and outlive your usefulness in the camp?" Savina became silent.

As Hayes began transferring blankets from the backpack to the sidecar, the barn door opened slightly. A female figure appeared, closing the door behind her. She wore a gray nurse's dress covered with a white smock. An oversized armband on her left arm bearing a red cross read "Deutsches Rotes Kreuz." Hayes' avatar looked up and froze.

The nurse spoke in German: "Officer Wicker, how quickly will they send you to the front when they learn that you have stolen *Wehrmacht* property?" Hayes looked at Savina and back at the nurse. He pulled out his Luger. "Not so quickly if you don't tell them. Hands where I can see them."

The nurse smiled and laughed. "Mister Hayes, you play the role well. It's me, Karen!"

Hayes thought for a second, grinned, and relaxed, placing the gun back in its holster. "Karen Murphy. You know you scared the crap out of me, right? Don't forget who'll be grading your history final."

Karen shook her head, still smiling. "Well, I'm here to save your ass. Yours and Savina's. You might wanna keep *that* in mind when you finally recall that I'm not in your class anymore."

Savina, still swaddled in blankets on a bed of hay, looked puzzled. "Who the hell are you Wicker?" "It's what I've been trying to tell you. Karen here is going to back me up, right Karen?"

"You got it, *mein Lehrer.* Now how about we vámonos!"

Hayes nodded. He took a few quick mental measurements and decided both could fit into the sidecar though it would be a tight squeeze. "Who are you anyway? In game, I mean," he asked. Karen replied as she began climbing into the sidecar, "Nurse Gretchen Haas, yours to command, *Sturmführer* Wicker." He told her that he thought she was overplaying the role a bit as he went to help Savina.

Hayes lifted Savina's tiny body into the sidecar, and she snuggled in beside Gretchen deep into the hollow space, turning on her side, leaving almost no outward sign of even being there. The remaining blankets, the darkest ones, were used to cover their heads. These Hayes pressed into the remaining spaces and underneath their shoulders. The sidecar looked as if it merely carried a large bundle of blankets.

Getting out of the camp was easy. Wicker was dealing with an infected body; the message had already made it around to the perimeter guards. A few SS men had already been made seriously ill by Typhus in weeks past, so no one was taking any chances. When he approached the main gate, he was briefly questioned though his bundle wasn't searched. No one went near it. He merely repeated his story, pretending anger that no one had been on duty at the crematorium. He'd have to take the body outside the camp, to minimize the contagion, and burn the damn thing himself. The can of gasoline attached to the back of the bike confirmed his story. He was waved through.

About two hours later, well before dawn, the three found themselves hiding behind a pile of brush and snow at the foothills of the Bavarian Alps. The snow was gently falling on the dirt road directly ahead. From behind the mound, they could see a cabin of some sort, possibly a small farmhouse, half-hidden by a patch of evergreens. No smoke poured from its stone chimney—a particularly good sign. After riding for some ninety kilometers southeast from Dachau through the wind at frigid temperatures on icy roads, Wicker's gloved hands were becoming unresponsive. Richard's nerves were frayed, but they were far enough south to hazard a rest, and this cabin would be perfect. It wouldn't be long before the endless roll call of prisoners would soon begin for the day at the Dachau camp, where they would stand for hours, if they could make it—which was an effortless way of culling out the unhealthy. Wicker and Savina would soon be looked for—probably Gretchen as well—hunted down like a virus by a swarm of antibodies. An SS officer and a camp prisoner wouldn't be allowed simply to disappear.

They trudged their way over the road and towards the dark cabin, the motorcycle hidden in an indentation behind a hill of snow and brush. Richard carried his Luger under the high mound of blankets, in case he was wrong about it being uninhabited. They walked up the sloping hill of trees. Savina whispered, "Are you still the good Heinrich?" He thought for a moment and replied, "If I weren't, would I be here trying to get you safe?" She squinted through the snowy flakes in the direction of the cabin. "Stay the good Heinrich, OK?"

"I'll be making sure of it," Karen said.

"Count on it," Hayes followed. He was, however, getting sleepy.

Richard kept his word until three days of fatigue and a splitting headache took the choice from him.

Chapter 7

The German scientist heard raucous cheering from the control room. He listened and watched from behind stacks of empty crates, one of which, upturned and facing the wall, he had made into a home of sorts. It was an area near a massive roll-up sheet door some fifty meters away from the Bell enclosure. Numerous unopened crates were also lined up against the walls and stacked up around the area almost like a maze.

Leaving the glass enclosure several days ago wasn't difficult. He had waited until the rows of windows near the ceiling of the giant warehouse had gone black for some hours and few fluorescent lights illuminated the dusty air. He had spent much of the ensuing days taking note of those inhabiting the facility. There were four rotating guards in total, two usually staying outside and one seated in front of screens; a fourth usually slept in rotation. There were also three scientists, always in lab coats, and a fourth man invariably dressed in casual attire—American jeans and a t-shirt. That made only eight people running the entire facility, as far as Debus could tell. It made no sense for a project of this apparent magnitude.

Debus had quietly thanked the gods when he found a pallet of bottled water in a corner by the roll-up door, carefully removing a pack of the refreshing though lukewarm substance from the back of the pile to bring back to his crate. The trash cans kept near the door gave him access to another convenient yet essential staple—food; thankfully, these Americans seemed to waste more food than they ate. For other needs, there was a small restroom on the ground floor behind a staircase and beneath the control room that he was careful to use only at night.

He was wearing a t-shirt and boxers, socks, garters, and patent leather shoes. That was all he had worn under the rad suit, which he had left in a garbage sack behind a barrel in a far corner of the warehouse. He wasn't really uncomfortable though. In fact, while it could get quite warm during the day, there was little humidity.

Debus was eager to find out how the Bell was being used. No one ever entered it, yet its humming was constant, its rim plates ever aglow and spinning. Frequent checks were made at the glass enclosure, cables and hoses tested, console staffed and manipulated, clipboards marked, so why hadn't anyone ever gone in? Perhaps they would now as the joyous noise from the control room might presage.

The German scientist longed to be back home, back in his chaotic and delightful 1943. He *would* go home, but he knew that he had little chance of making the necessary adjustments to the Bell under the present circumstances. Just what *had* the Americans done to it? After whatever modifications they'd made, *could* it be directed back to 1943? Or even better—to 1939, so that his mission might be completed. He had to find out what progress—or regression—had been made and then do what needed to be done.

The control room of the facility stood around ten meters high above the floor level. It had two metal staircases with landings on either side. Debus could see some of its occupants through the tall windows that looked out upon the Bell and the vast area surrounding it. He could even hear the laughter and loud discussions, though he couldn't make out the words, of those leaning against the windows and the tables as a bottle was passed around.

SOUTH TEXAS, NOVEMBER 2035

The young man and the elderly woman were engaged in a conversation about the Old Days.

"Poor Hans vas very shy. He couldn't get a word out. He just stood there. My father got angry. He thought he was selling brooms or something. 'If you can't speak properly,' he said, 'you have no business being in my house.' He opened the front door with one hand and grabbed Hans by the suspenders and swung him avound with the other. He tossed poor Hans onto the sidevalk and slammed the door. I vas crying, 'Papa, Papa, no! That's my fiancé!' Hans vas so embarrassed that he never spoke to me again."

They both laughed. Selma's life had been a pleasant one despite the fact that her father had had a bit of a short fuse.

A moment later, the door opened and the nurse appeared, followed by a young lady wearing a white blouse and a tan skirt. "Three visitors in one day! You're popular, Mr. Hayes." The nurse smiled and closed the door behind her.

The young woman looked around. "Where's Mr. Hayes?"

The old woman and the young man looked at each other. "In there," the woman said, pointing to the box.

The young woman gave her a puzzled look and approached the box. She walked around to the side and found the little door cut in the middle of the box, a kind of window flap, which was how Hayes received his food bowls and water cups. She gently pulled it open and looked in. She gave a quick gasp and stepped back. "Mr. Hayes?"

The young woman turned and looked at the young man with a frown. She went back to the box and cupped her hands around her mouth. She began whispering something into the box. All the others could hear was "It worked . . ."

Abruptly, she stopped and turned to the young man still sitting on the bed next to the old woman. "What are you doing here?"

"Um, what?" the young man replied.

"Why are you here?" she demanded.

"Same as you, to visit Mr. Hayes."

"Do you really think he wants to see you?" She then continued speaking into the box.

Selma looked at the young man and then at the girl. "Vell that is a thoughtless thing to say. You should be ashamed."

"It's OK," the young man said. "I expect as much. Goodbye, Selma. It's been a pleasure." He then left the room.

FALL, 2033

On the back glass of the burgundy Ford Ranger pickup, a statement in white hand-placed block letters stood out: "NO FAT CHICKS." Kevin Daniel got out, slammed the driver's side door and walked around the truck bed, lifting out a duffel bag and slinging it to his shoulder. He had just gotten home from football practice, such as it was, where he had been unsuccessfully fighting for the position of first-string tight end for the varsity team. Scowling, he thought, *I'm just meat.* During practice and especially at the games, he was rarely put in to play. And when he was put on the field, he never got the ball. It always went to someone else, usually the fullback, while Kevin's job was to block for the guy. It wasn't fair at all. Kevin was a fairly big guy for his age, stronger and almost as fast as David Marquez, the first-string tight end.

The boy unlocked the front door of the double-wide trailer home and jogged upstairs. Once in his room, he closed and locked the door, tossing his duffel bag into a corner and dove into his bed. He turned over, staring into the white, smooth ceiling, placing his hands behind his head. His walls were covered with posters displaying metal bands, female models in bikinis, Dallas Cowboys notables, and a few old-school blacklight posters. It was already 6:30 PM, and he was well behind on his homework for the week. He didn't care. Throughout the summer and into this semester, Kevin kept thinking that he'd get his chance to prove what he had on the field, *but the coaches are fools, just a bunch of fatasses who couldn't do anything but coach high school kids—and they suck at that.*

A large mirror stood along the wall behind his computer desk. He got up and sat at his computer, staring at himself in the mirror. Kevin's hair was shoulder length. His follicles were thin, so his hair was wispy. He pushed it back over his ears and booted up his gamer rig. As he reached for his interactive gloves, he knocked over a tube of lipstick. He slid this into a drawer and donned the headgear. He logged in to the game that he had learned to play in Mr. Hayes' class last year.

Kevin recognized where he was. It was "The Bunker," a set of rooms near the front gate of the Buchenwald camp, located just east of central Germany. The Bunker was used for torture, pure and simple. He was standing over a prisoner in blue and gray striped pajamas who had been shackled to a wooden platform made from two-by-four planks. The man's head hung over a stand-alone clawfoot tub. A single shower head dripped water from above, splashing against the man's forehead. Kevin could almost feel his own hands embracing the screw clamp fitted to the man's skull. The man was already screaming when Kevin entered the avatar, and after only a slight pause, he kept tightening the clamp until he felt the head pop. He kept screwing as bone cracked and brain matter fell off in chunks.

This was new, he thought. Kevin had always relished the occasions when he would enter into character during a hanging or, best of all, a whipping session where Martin Sommer, his avatar, would force the victim to keep count of the lashes. When he or she would forget—or become too frail—to count aloud, the count would start over, frequently resulting in their death. Martin Sommer was one creative sonofabitch. He took brutality to the level of high art, such as in the case of his "singing forest," where men hanged on trees by their wrists tied behind them would cry and wail as they suffered—a harmony of the damned. But the screw clamp was just pure genius.

After about an hour of Game time, Kevin took off the helmet and placed it on his desk. He was the "Hangman of Buchenwald"; no one else's avatar compared. He was good at it. First-string. A bonafide SS Nazi guard with probably the worst reputation in the camp, which meant being the best. Kevin felt grimy from practice and needed a shower. He looked at himself in the mirror and grinned. A mask placed over his bedpost grinned back at him in the mirror, just over his right shoulder. It had the jagged teeth and menacing eye holes of a sadistic clown.

It was a wind whose sand would rip the skin from one's body. It was the Mongolian waterless rain. A storm of hot, stinging glass. The tent whipped violently and ripped in places, filling quickly in its recesses with heavy mounds of lacerating sand. It was in everything and began weighing down on the tent from above. Savina was smiling at Richard's determined scowl. He was determined that they would survive the night. There was simply not enough cover in this strangely wooded desert to risk leaving the tent for more than a few seconds before being ripped to shreds. Staying meant being buried alive.

The dream quickly faded.

When Richard finally awoke in his futon that morning, he sat up and stared into the circular window just below the triangular roof. Nails stuck out from the plywood overhead—one day he would install a proper ceiling. He watched the particles of dust in the air shift in the hazy light. He thought back on the dream, trying to recall its allure—and menace. After a vain attempt, he refocused on the dim and open spaces, boxes piled against the edges of the A-frame loft, floating dust. "There must be more than this," he thought. "There must be more."

There was more. There was the Game, the corner of his cabin where he had played, and lived. He began to climb down the narrow stairs and stopped midway. When he saw the computer, it came back to him in flashes. Where had he last seen Savina? There was snow, cold and hunger. It had become so real for him over the last several days that while his avatar ate, from some of the stores he could find in the winter cabin, he, Hayes, had forgotten to do so. He hadn't eaten for . . . then he remembered . . . "Savina!"

Normally, Hayes left himself logged into the Game overnight. This way, his avatar wouldn't regain consciousness. He must have forgotten to leave his computer running. Richard surged forward, tripping down the stairs, and fell hard on both palms. His arms ached to the elbows. He dragged himself across the room, to the corner, and into the squeaky black chair. He squashed the helmet over his head and hit buttons impatiently.

When he reached her through the wires, diodes, and chips, she was asleep. He could now feel the cold intensely. *This is new*, he thought vaguely. Or was his aircon turned up too high? Only a second's pause occurred, less than a second, and he was there, stroking her hair, now as Richard. His head throbbed with pain and dizziness, which began as soon as he entered the avatar. His avatar's right ear was damp. He touched it—blood. It explained the headache and the dizziness, but it didn't explain why Hayes himself was feeling it. A voice yelled, "Touch her again, and you'll be getting some of this!" Karen, as Gretchen, sat facing them in a rocking chair by the fire; she was waving Wicker's Luger in one hand, and an iron poker lay across her lap, its tip slightly bloodied. Savina was clothed and bundled in the blankets on the floor in front of the fireplace, apparently fast asleep, breathing slowly. She didn't look hurt.

"Karen?" Hayes panicked.

"Thank God. I thought I would have to shoot you, and I've never driven a motorcycle before. Probably wouldn't get her very far. Hey, don't you stay logged in?"

"I must have forgotten."

It was midmorning. A small cord of logs sat next to the stone fireplace. On top sat a box of matches. The window behind Karen's avatar looked like a painting—idyllic mountains towered in the distance behind a few trees draped with snowfall. They talked as Savina continued to sleep. How Karen had found out about Mr. Hayes' avatar went way back to an event that occurred near the "commissary," as it was called, where mostly articles of clothing, glasses, and shoes were stored for distribution after being taken from the newest inmates of the camp. As a nurse, she had been in the process of recovering cloth to be disinfected and used for bandaging. She heard Mr. Hayes say his own name in an attempt to bring this female character into his confidences.

The sun shone down on the courtyard and on the statue of Leopold II. Linden and Maple trees were increasing in foliage, shading the paths amongst the statues lining the sides of the Ministry courtyard. Farash entered the avatar of Karl Ernst Krafft who thus awoke on his cot from a troubled sleep and glanced at the thick curtains shielding his eyes from the approaching dawn. Barely a ray of light could be seen through the two tall windows of his pitifully small office.

Folding his cot and gray woolen blanket, he packed these with a loose pillow into the wardrobe across from his desk and asked the SS guard standing outside his office for his morning coffee and perhaps a warm bun with butter. Since his stay here began, he had had no access to a newspaper, a radio, or a single visitor. "He is the astrologer," Goebbels had remarked to one member of the inner cabinet, "His *stars* can give him news of the world." Actually, Farash preferred this isolation, which would make his predictions and their outcomes all the more incredible in the eyes of his superiors since it seemingly left him nothing more than his own inner oracle to guide him.

Throwing back the heavy curtains and cracking open a window slightly to allow in a bit of the early morning chill, Farash regarded the Berlin dawn. It was clear and crisp without a single cloud lingering in the sky.

After a few hours of work with the Nostradamus text, pouring over a quatrain he had marked as intriguing for perhaps the dozenth time, Farash leaned back and stared at the high ceiling with its intricate white squares set deep into their framed edges. He closed his eyes as Farash fell asleep in his chair, his VR helmet still on.

When he awoke, he was being half-dragged up a flight of stairs to a large office in the rear of the building. Two tall SS men had hold of his upper arms, and a gag had been placed over his mouth. Farash quickly moved his left hand in several turning gestures and was thus given the freedom to walk up the stairs the rest of the way. The guards, silently, and now gently, led him into the wide office of the Reichsminister. Goebbels was looking out a window, his hands behind his back. Krafft, his hair in disarray, had just enough time to remove the gag when the Reichsminister turned around to greet him.

"Another attack of epilepsy?"

"Yes. Well, I think so." He was still breathing hard.

"You say interesting things when you aren't . . . yourself."

"Doctors call it split-personality, schizophrenia."

"Indeed. Let's get to business, if you're up to it."

"I'm feeling better, thanks."

Goebbels frowned. "Your prognostications, so far, have been exact." He waited for a response from Krafft. Krafft, Farash, remained silent.

"Norway and Denmark were a significant addition to Greater Germany. The raw materials will continue to resupply the war effort.
"

"And Britain? France?"

"The usual rhetorical saber-rattling. Nothing significant. No troop movements. Some attempts at bolstering Western Norway. It won't last."

"I was accurate on the exact date and on the events of the campaign." Krafft narrowed his eyes. It was a statement, not a question. Farash was learning to show complete confidence in his own predictions though he knew now that history was at least somewhat malleable. It wasn't a stagnant sequence of unalterable events; otherwise, even the conversations that Krafft and Goebbels were having could have never taken place, could not be taking place.

Still, the greater events depending on variables well outside the effects of his own tiny manipulations of history might be well beyond the reach of these the smaller causes—what type of shirt he put on, how his occasional "amnesia" affected the SS guards, the birds scattering as he walked with Goebbels in the courtyard. The greater events were far more difficult to change, if they could be changed at all, which made them predictable. This was a good thing. Farash would occasionally consult more detailed histories on the era via the Internet at work and in a few books he had at home, but otherwise, he knew the basics regarding troop movements, invasions, broken treaties, and now knew he could rely on them.

"The charts don't lie, but they can fluctuate," Farash offered.

"Odd. I never see you with charts of any kind. Perhaps if I saw these charts of yours, it would make the entire process more credible.

You could even teach *me* your methods. I'm a quick study." Goebbels knew that the man used no charts.

"The charts are in my head. They fluctuate," Krafft added hastily, "so if I taught the matrix to someone without the proper gift of spotting and nullifying subtle variabilities, a prediction would be worthless days later, sometimes even minutes later. Some things cannot be taught and must therefore die with the knower, Herr Reichsminister." In a way this was true. There was no method to learn, only a knowledge of the events in a causal stream as they unfolded in the mid-20th century. Also, the fact that there was no method that he could possibly "teach" the Reichsminister had the added benefit of requiring that Goebbels' seer remain alive for further prognostications to be "revealed."

Goebbels was silent and seemed somewhat disappointed. But after some moments he smiled and walked over to his desk. On his desk was a small bust of the Fuhrer's head being used as a paperweight. He picked it up and sat on the edge of his desk, as he frequently did, staring into it as if it were a crystal skull, a tool of his own necromancy.

"I want you to stop work on the Nostradamus quatrains."

Farash felt instant relief.

"Instead, tell me everything you know about the future of the Reich."

Krafft, standing several feet away, listened to the Reichsminister but appeared to be distracted, gazing into the corners where the high walls met the white ceilings, where dusty webs were forming. Finally, he nodded. "I can do that. It comes in pieces, but perhaps I can put together the complete puzzle in a sitting or two. I'll need time."

He knew, however, how tricky it would be. Everything happening in Europe and the world was historically correct up to this point, as far as he could tell. The Norway/Denmark conquest, accurately predicted for the exact day, was additional proof that events must be flowing according to historical fact. However, were anything amiss in this virtual world, significantly different from what was known in the early 21st century, his lack of newspapers and radio would keep the knowledge from him.

This was 1940, the year Hitler's biggest tactical mistakes would, in essence, begin. Hitler would consider an invasion of Britain, Operation Sea Lion, and then postpone it dozens of times. He would finally take it off the table, preferring to position three million troops, the bulk of the *Wehrmacht*, his regular army, in the East for a June 1941 attack on Russia, creating a second front that would eventually see disaster, particularly once the US got involved, starting in December of that year. Hitler would be surrounded by enemies that in several years would close both fronts and ultimately meet one another in Germany, in Berlin. They would then break the country into four sectors of control.

Up to this point, Hitler's successes might have rendered anyone invincible in his own thinking. There was the Fuhrer's taking of the Rhineland, Austria, Czechoslovakia, Poland, Norway and Denmark, all without meeting any serious resistance. Britain and France, regardless of their harsh language and war declarations, showed no real ability to significantly aid any of these countries directly, so far, and could only do so at the expense of weakening their own defenses. Stalin showed little interest in attacking Germany and wouldn't, so long as Russia wasn't attacked first. The Russians had plenty to snack on with Poland, Finland, and a host of other Eastern European delicacies for potential conquest. The United States currently showed no interest in aiding Britain as they themselves had not yet been attacked by Japan and weren't as yet on a war footing, not yet having been dragged into the war and having little confidence in Britain's ability to do its share in a potential joint campaign. No, Hitler was as successful up to this point as he could ever possibly be. Soon, his successes would give him the temerity to backstab the Russians, despite the Nazi-Soviet non-aggression pact of 1939.

It might be impossible to convince the Fuhrer from this point on that any tactical error on his part was even thinkable, even if it involved attacking the Russians, but, in his mind, this was Farash's only means of becoming the next Fuhrer of a country which would one day rule over all humanity. He must convince Hitler not to attack the Russians; otherwise, as Hitler's eventual second, he might end up ruling an empire in its last dying gasps—once the Fuhrer decided to opt out with a cyanide capsule and a bullet.

Krafft sat heavily into the chair before the Reichsminister's desk. "Attack France," he said with the utmost confidence.

Goebbels was silent.

Krafft continued in the calm, confident tone he had used during his last successful prognostication. "Germany will attack France, Luxembourg, the Netherlands and Belgium beginning on the 10th of May. The Fuhrer will walk beneath the *Arc de Triomphe* as the decisive victor."

The Reichsminister sat back at his desk, never taking his deep-set eyes off of Krafft whose own eyes stared continually toward the edge of the ceiling, as if attempting to conjure more details.

Goebbels covered his mouth with his fingers, as if keeping words from spilling out. Krafft had indeed identified the day that Hitler planned an attack on France, but the Fuhrer was as yet unsure whether or not to carry it out. The Maginot line of defense was strong, protecting France from any direct, even massive, incursion. It was all they really had—and still possessed—as these troops were never involved in the defense of Poland, a promise on which France had reneged.

"How?" Goebbels asked. "How will it be done in a way that ensures complete success?"

Farash had him.

"It will take a little over a month." Farash continued, "Would you like it in a quatrain, Herr Reichsminister?"

"Are you toying with me, Mr. Krafft?"

Farash continued:

Yellow lightning will fall on the Ardennes.
Then red fire will pierce the virgin's left rib.
She will withdraw from Siegfried though his spear is weak.
Vichy will carry the hammer of Thor.

After Krafft's recitation of the lines he had composed for just this meeting, Goebbels was dead silent for several minutes. Krafft allowed him time to let it all sink in.

The Reichsminister finally broke down. He saw plenty in the quatrain to know that Krafft was indeed the seer he claimed to be. No man could know so much with so little information at his disposal. This wasn't simply bogus astrology—Krafft wasn't just inventing phrases around a scatter of goat's entrails. The last two lines of the quatrain were a mystery to him, likely regarding outcomes of the campaign, but Goebbels knew well the meaning of the first two lines. They referred to Plan Yellow, which was to be executed first and involved attacking through the Ardennes. The second plan to be executed was Plan Red, which would involve flanking the Maginot line to its north side, the weaker side . . . the left side . . . where the "war virgin" France was personified as facing Germany.

In the quiet exaltation experienced during the head-first fall of faith's triumphant leap, Goebbels took Krafft into his confidence: "It is a plan over eight months in the making and remaking. The Fuhrer expects one million German soldiers to die."

"Execute it as is, without changing anything, and he will lose only fifty thousand soldiers. Heed my words and Germany will lose less than ten thousand."

Farash could see through Goebbels' controlled demeanor that the man was elated as he pressed for more details. Farash told him everything he knew, historically, regarding the coming months, while the Reichsminister wrote feverishly in a thin leather-bound journal. He knew about as much as Goebbels did regarding its planning, which didn't involve a great deal of detail regarding strategy, but he knew far more regarding its outcomes, both successes and foibles, particularly involving where Germany would lose the most troops and machinery. He pointed these out so that different arrangements could be made during the invasion. Krafft's warnings would prove to be true during so many phases of the campaign that denying his supernatural power of insight would simply amount to sheer lunacy.

FARASH AS KRAFFT WAITED out the next few months in his office at the old Leopold Palace. He had now, however, been given a radio and access to daily newspapers. France had been attacked, as planned. All was going far better for the Reich than even he or Goebbels had expected. As the months progressed, he noticed waning interest in his activities during the rare occasions that he left the Ministry.

Krafft was directed to take up residence in a small house in a wooded area just east of Berlin. Here there was one armed guard, but one acting more as an attendant than a gatekeeper. Here he stayed through the summer months and into October, traveling back to the Propaganda Ministry perhaps several times per week, sometimes less often. This wasn't what Farash was after, though it did give him time to repair the damage of long absences from his wife, who was still learning to tolerate her husband's odd habits of seclusion.

Away from the Ministry, he swallowed pills keeping the real Krafft unconscious or heavily sedated for eight, ten, even twelve hours at a spell. When this began to wear on his health, he simply had the SS guard put him in a cellar, gagged, for a given period of time, on account of his "episodes." He even kept in touch with a doctor whom he paid to provide ready-made explanations for any ensuing fits, should any be needed. At these times of Krafft's sedation, Farash slept (usually around four hours a night), taught, and spent time with Amala, though just enough to keep her from bringing up his "computer addiction" as she often referred to it.

While at work one morning in Berlin, Krafft was led away by four SS guards who suddenly appeared at his tiny office. They escorted the astrologer across the courtyard of the Ministry of Propaganda and continued to walk a half block west until they reached the imposing *Neue Reichskanzlei,* the New Chancellery built by Albert Speer for his Fuhrer, the only Berlin structure that Speer would ever see erected, unless of course history was altered. The bone-white Chancellery had been recently built according to Speer's exact specifications, with four high, square pillars at its entrance above a short flight of stairs. Three rows of high windows on either side of the pillars stretched interminably into the distance. The Imperial Eagle, the *Reichsadler,* stood chiseled above the entrance, guarding it with its angular and menacing spread of wings, carrying the symbol of the country's only political party on a circular wreath in its cold stone talons.

Through the portico, Krafft was led across a long entryway, through a single, tall door and then down another short flight of stairs into an open courtyard. At this end of the stone courtyard, on each side of the entrance, stood a bronze statue of a naked young man in perfect physical health. The statue on Krafft's right held a sword, the one on the left, a torch. The long courtyard was flanked by two rows of windows on both sides and a double-door at the center of each. Taken through the left set of double-doors and turning right, Krafft was brought by the four SS men into a long hallway. A double door on the opposite side was open with SS men in black uniforms standing at either side. He was motioned to sit on an elaborate studded leather bench just outside. Farash could hear men inside the room holding a quiet conversation.

Krafft didn't sit long before Joseph Goebbels came through the doors to sit beside him. His demeanor was profoundly serious. He whispered, "You are to meet the Fuhrer. Don't speak to him as you speak to me. In fact, don't speak to him at all unless he asks you a question directly." Farash nodded. Goebbels motioned for Krafft to follow, and they both walked into the room. The booted footsteps of the men were echoed throughout the wide room and in the thumping chest of Farhat Farash.

The two men turned to the left, their tread now muffled by a thin but ornate red and orange carpet. They had come through double doors at the side, but Farash noticed four more sets of double doors, two at each end of the room. Above each set hung a different armorial crest. Above the door through which he had entered, Farash saw the familiar angles of the *Reichsadler*, this time made of bronze. Lamps resembling candlesticks, but with small shades hovering over them, stood ensconced beside each set of doors. At the far end on the right side of the room sat a sofa and some chairs in front of a grand fireplace. A huge globe, bigger than the one Farash had seen many times in Goebbels' office, stood in its heavy enclosure at one side of the sofa.

On the left side of the long room, not far from Farash, men sat in thick leather chairs and talked casually. A wide wooden desk stood on a black granite floor, just outside the range of the carpet. Three men were seated in three studded leather chairs in front of it. The chairs were exactly the color of pale, white human skin never exposed to sunlight. As Krafft and the Reichsminister approached these men, Krafft noticed that the chair behind the desk was empty. The men became silent as the two approached.

Goebbels introduced Karl Ernst Krafft to the men in the three chairs before the desk. The man seated in front of the desk and on the left had low, thick brows, a tall man were he standing, good looking, wearing the black uniform of the SS though highly decorated. "Herr Krafft, Deputy Fuhrer Rudolf Hess." Farash pondered the man's good-natured countenance as he struggled to remember the details of the man's bizarre fate. Here was the man who would embarrass the Fuhrer by flying alone, unarmed in a stolen plane, to Great Britain in effort to negotiate an unauthorized peace. A hypochondriac and amateur mystic, if anyone were sympathetic to Krafft's claims to astrological powers, it would be this man. He nodded slowly toward Krafft, a nod which Krafft returned.

In the center sat the second most powerful man in Germany, a large figure in a double-breasted gray uniform, worn under a fleshy smile supported by a double-chin. The thin hair he had left was brushed way back, through which could be seen a few dark spots of age. "Herr Krafft, this is Reichsmarschall Hermann Göring."

A morphine addict, Göring's incompetence in directing the Luftwaffe could work in Farash's favor, but it would be another two years before his weaknesses as a military strategist would become most apparent. Göring, smiling, nodded curtly to Krafft.

Finally, the man on Göring's right looked up from a small book he had been reading. "Herr Krafft, meet Albert Speer, Chief Architect of the Third Reich." Well-dressed as a civilian, Speer stood and silently held out his hand. Krafft took it. Though Speer had no official power, he had Hitler's ear in a way the others didn't, making him possibly the most influential man in the room. Speer was the architect of this magnificent building and the future skyline of Hitler's Germania though it would never materialize, at least not in *this* future. Farash had seen a model of his plans for a new Berlin in a documentary he had once watched. It was stunning. Speer would one day become *his* architect, *his* archetypal builder of the Romanesque thousand-year Reich.

Goebbels looked around. "Where is the Fuhrer?" Two of the men seated chuckled.

"Behind you," came the steady voice of the Fuhrer. He had been admiring a painting near the corner of the wall and was thus invisible to both Goebbels and Krafft, while the introductions had been taking place. He walked slowly up to Goebbels as the Reichsminister and Krafft turned around to greet him. They shook hands. The Fuhrer then turned to Krafft and held out an unsteady hand. Krafft took it.

"This is your astrologer?" he looked unsmiling into Krafft's eyes. "The man who saved my life once. The man who made interesting contributions to Germany's war effort. The man who . . . I will just say it . . . can see the future. Is that not right, Herr Goebbels?" "It would appear so, mein Fuhrer," the Reichsminister replied.

Krafft, as instructed, remained silent. He returned eye contact with the Fuhrer, bowed his head, and then looked again into the Leader's eyes. The Fuhrer's sky-blue eyes were magnetic and piercing. It was as though he could see into the man wearing the helmet on the other side of the planet and nearly a century away. Farash wanted to look away again in a show of deference, but there was something there, attractive and empowering, like all wishes granted, like a license to do absolutely anything with impunity.

The Fuhrer did not yet release his firm grasp of Krafft's right hand. "Herr Krafft, your predictions were inhuman in their accuracy. I salute you. The people of Germany salute you." He gave Krafft's hand a final shake and let it drop. Farash's own right hand tingled. The Fuhrer then walked behind his desk and took a seat, spreading his hands upon his desk after he did so, nodding slightly in approval of something formulating in his mind.

At this brief meeting, Farash, or rather Krafft, was given an official place in the Reichsministry. He was to be Goebbels' secretary, an "Adviser on the Ontological Sciences." It was of course a euphemism, giving him a seemingly philosophical role in government when he was really more of a soothsayer, at a time when such were being whisked away to places like Bergen-Belsen and Dachau at gunpoint.

"The Fuhrer wants to attack the Soviet Union."

Goebbels and Krafft had been discussing various topics when Farash became impatient. The propaganda minister was quiet for a few moments, taken back by the outburst and the quick change of subject. Farash immediately regretted it and decided to try to play it off with downcast eyes as merely the eccentric behavior of a soothsayer in the throes of a vision . . . if he could.

Goebbels responded after a few moments. "We've all read *Mein Kampf.* He sees the East as a vital piece of the *Lebensraum* during the Thousand Year Reich. That will of course happen long after you and I have passed on."

"He will begin his attempts to make it happen only six months from now."

"Absurd."

"The Fuhrer will invade Russia in six months, to be exact on June 22 of this year."

Goebbels' hollow, deep set eyes stared at Krafft in their usual way. He knew of the Fuhrer's plans to attack the Russians. He and most of the cabinet were opposed to the idea though were wary of ever saying so too directly. "You have somehow been following troop movements. Not the most difficult thing to do so near the Chancellery."

"I follow the stars," Farash replied.

"Yes, and your 'charts' as you call them. And the stars have told you . . . what specifically?"

"That the Fuhrer will launch Operation Barbarossa against the Russians, that the vast majority of the Germans who die in this war will die fighting in the Eastern Front. The Russians will ally with the West, who will create a Western Front. D-Day . . ." Farash was getting way ahead of himself and decided to stop short rather than risk sounding like a total lunatic in front of the Reichsminister.

"Go on."

Farash hesitated.

"Please continue."

"Hitler's plan to invade the Soviet Union. Barbarossa. It won't work. It will lead to Germany's downfall within four years." He had raised his voice without realizing it. He could hear murmuring between SS guards standing just outside the open door. Goebbels looked in their direction and back at Krafft. He then stood up and walked to his office door, closing it gently. Goebbels walked back over to the standing Karl Ernst Krafft and stared into his eyes. The slap was a quick, backhanded one. Krafft stumbled backwards, holding his right cheek. The avatar had reacted to the blow before Farash was able to do so. This was new.

"You will learn to shut the hell up when and where it is appropriate to do so, Mr. Krafft, or I'll shoot you myself." Goebbels continued to stare at the man and then sat back at his desk. Krafft had barged in—the first time he had attempted to do so. He hadn't even thought to close the door.

Farash had taken too many risks. He frowned inside his helmet, sitting at a small desk surrounded by boxes and books, his "place of meditation." The spongy pads inside the helmet were getting drippy and somewhat rancid with the sweat produced during such moments of confrontation with his immediate superior.

He waited for a word from the Reichsminister. It never came. The Reichsminister motioned for Krafft to sit silently in his usual chair in front of the desk. He did so, looking down at his shoes. After a minute, he said, "My apologies, Herr Reichsminister. I thought it important enough to tell you as soon as I knew for certain."

Goebbels, still quietly fuming, showed guarded interest. "Everyone has read *Mein Kampf.* You're not saying anything . . . even Stalin himself has read it. Even *he* knows of the Fuhrer's hatred of the Communists and his ultimate intentions regarding the East."

"Herr Reichsminister, would it be safe to say that Russia has always been the Fuhrer's *primary* objective?"

"Wouldn't we have attacked them from the beginning if that were the case?"

"No. The plan was and has been to create a cushion of German satellite states between Germany and Britain. Now that such a cushion exists, Hitler can go after his main target—Russia." Krafft's manner remained intense.

Goebbels replied, "How could the West do anything more than they are already doing if there were to be a war between Germany and Russia? Don't you think that they would see it as in their best interest to sit back and watch us tear each other to pieces? They distrust the Russians maybe even more than they distrust us, despite the fact of our having annexed most of their neighbors. If anything, our attacking Russia would give them reason to pause the war and watch us bloody each other—and then come and try to finish off the winner."

"Which is exactly why now would be the opportune time, in our Leader's eyes, to attack the Russians."

"Or," Goebbels responded, "it might encourage the US to finally come to the aid of Britain and together invade Germany through France and create a true Western Front while all of our resources are aimed against Russia. You see, the Fuhrer would never take such a risk." Goebbels lied. Of course, he knew Krafft was perfectly correct. Hitler had already put the suicidal plan in motion. He also knew that it would be impossible for him to change the Leader's mind.

Farash had had enough of Goebbels' duplicity. He knew from history that Goebbels was lying through his little rat teeth. "It will happen, and it will be called War Directive 21."

The Reichsminister stood up. "How did you hear this? Who have you been talking to?"

"No one. How can you still doubt my powers of insight?" Farash paused, pretending to be utterly offended, and then proceeded. "You've got to convince the Fuhrer that *if* he must go on with this suicidal plan, he can't split up the army to do so. It will . . . it *would* result in complete failure. I know he intends to drive the northern army group into Leningrad, the central group into Moscow, and the southern group towards the Black Sea to take the oil fields.

"Instead, the three million men that he sends must all drive immediately into Moscow to take out Stalin and the Central Government. Otherwise, dividing the army into three army groups will slow the attack on Moscow and the Russian winter will do the rest. Still, the *successful* plan would involve the creation of a permanent alliance with the USSR and the launch of operation Sea Lion against Britain as originally envisioned. Once *all* of Europe is ours, and the United States is unable to establish a beachhead in Britain, keeping them out of the war, *then* the Fuhrer can focus exclusively—and successfully—on Russia."

The thin-suited Reichsminister again appeared stunned at the man's array of intimate knowledge. Only a handful of men at the top knew about such plans, and even fewer knew specifics to *this* degree. There was potentially more detail implicit in Krafft's schemes than even he himself was privy to. He could check into the validity of these additional bits of information, but he knew already that they would be verified.

Goebbels sat back into his chair. He tapped his desk and tried to smile. Farash knew what was probably going on in his mind. Were military officers intentionally feeding this Swiss seer a list of command strategies in order to trip up his supervisor, the Minister of Propaganda? Convincing him to produce ideas disdainful to the Fuhrer and then discrediting them in the Fuhrer's hearing as cowardly, showing a lacking faith in the Fatherland? He could be hanged for insolence.

This was the moment. If Krafft were to convince one of Hitler's most trusted voices that an Eastern Front would lead to inevitable chaos for Germany, it would be now. He *had* to seal the deal.

"Magda Goebbels will poison your children."

"What did you just say to me?"

Farash paused. "If we attack Russia as currently planned, then in the last days of the war, in the Fuhrer's bunker, your wife will give your six children a drink causing them to fall sleep. While they are dozing off, she will crack cyanide tablets into each of their mouths. Afterward, she'll play cards. You will know about it and won't do anything to stop her. By then you'll know it's over. *That's* the chaos I'm talking about!"

Goebbels was visibly shaken. "Why would she . . ."

"The Russians will surround Berlin in the spring of 1945. Eisenhower will allow the Russians to enter Berlin first, letting them do their will on the women and children of Berlin. Many will commit suicide, including yourself and your family. In your eyes and in the eyes of your wife, your children would be better off dead."

"If that were the case, we'd be nowhere near Berlin. We have a far more secure . . ."

". . . bunker near Berchtesgaden," Farash finished his sentence. But Magda will want to be near her Fuhrer until the very end. She will insist on it. And he will want to make his last stand in Berlin. She's his most ardent supporter. Certainly you know this since all your children's names start with 'H.'"

"You take too many liberties, Mr. Krafft," he said in almost a whisper. Krafft frowned and returned his gaze. "I can speak to the Fuhrer directly, leaving you out of every part of it, if you like."

Goebbels began to smile in earnest. This relieved Farash and he returned the smile and nodded just as Goebbels reached over to his phone and said a few low words into the receiver. An SS man came in within a few seconds and stood behind Krafft. Farash was relieved. He would be escorted to the New Chancellery and given a *real* audience with the Fuhrer! He knew far more than Goebbels about the chain of events about to take place. Goebbels possessed channels of information between members of the Reich Cabinet, most of whom didn't like him very much. But Krafft had an excellent knowledge of history. Finally, Farash would have his chance to rise to a position of power even above that of Goebbels, perhaps becoming Deputy Fuhrer.

An SS officer entered the room and stood behind Krafft. Goebbels, still smiling, shook his head, reached into a side desk drawer and produced a black pistol and aimed it at Krafft's chest.

Farash was plunged into a black oblivion.

Chapter 8

Debus studied the area. There was no one in sight outside the control room. In socks, he ran to the nearest staircase and carefully made his way up to the gray door. He peered through the wired glass window as the laughter and loud conversations continued.

The three in lab coats were gleefully boisterous. Talk revolved around the project: Space-time fluctuations and manageable perturbations, singularities and tidal gravity, geodesics and time dilation. Several bottles of champagne stood on the tables, most empty. The younger man in casual attire sat in front of a screen, nodding and laughing along with the rest.

Closest to Debus, as he peered through the narrow door window, was one of the guards, dressed in military fatigues, his back to the door. He sat in front of three screens, each divided into four quadrants rotating through what appeared to be CCTV transmissions. Debus was vaguely familiar with the concept, invented only a year before the Project Reise event by an electrical engineer named Walter Bruch. Debus himself had recently seen film footage of it being utilized in the monitoring of V-2 rocket launches. The internal and external views of the facility were displayed in marvelous detail. None of the camera angles directly concerned the area of empty crates comprising his habitation, which was a relief.

Looking over the man's shoulder, Debus focused on the external views. He had not dared to venture outside as, for one thing, at least two guards were always patrolling the area. For another, the doors were locked, requiring a passkey to exit, which he had found out after trying a few of the main doors. He watched as some of the cameras panned across the sandy landscape. Aside from some distant hills and far off mountains, the land was flat, scrubby, nearly treeless. He even saw a few cacti in the foreground.

He felt an even greater sense of isolation, not only because there seemed to be nothing resembling civilization even far into the distance, but he was struck with the sad realization that this wasn't Bavaria. He had not only traveled in time but also in space. This must be a covert American base somewhere in the North American Southwest, and the thought filled him with a fearsome dread. While ruminating on how things couldn't get much worse, the scientist squinted at the bottom of one of the CCTV screens. He could barely make out the yellow digits in the right-hand corner: 5.10.2031. He hadn't traveled backward in time but rather *forward*—some 88 years! It explained much about what he saw, but also gave him some relief. Perhaps the Americans *didn't* win the war after all but instead had somehow procured a copy of the Projekt Reise schematics. It was all so confusing.

Debus knew that eventually he would be caught. Getting caught meant never completing his mission or even making it back home. Going home would be the most likely outcome since the two Bells were clearly linked somehow. He would need to make better use of his time in preparing *this* Bell for his departure, and the sooner this happened, the more likely he could get away.

Fall, 2033

Early one morning, Hauptscharführer (Master Sergeant) Martin Sommer awoke in his bed with a folded note sitting on his chest. He was still tired from all the demanding work he had done the day before—much of the evidence of which currently lay under his bed. He tossed the note onto his desk and raised himself up. He walked into his private bathroom and glared at the handsome devil in the mirror, picking a piece of meat from between his teeth. He brushed his teeth and walked back to his bed. He felt beneath the bed for a ragged pair of shoes and then grabbed at the ankles, dragging the striped corpse out feet first. Then he grabbed the other one and did the same. He stuck his head out into the hallway and called for a kapo. He then went to his desk and took an ice pick, a leather strap, and several syringes in hand. He kneeled down, lifted a plank with his other hand using his fingernails, and placed the items under the plank beneath his desk. Two men wearing stripes soon appeared and were directed to drag out the bodies.

Martin Sommer began to pull up his uniform breeches when he saw the note which he had briefly forgotten about, probably a new duty arrangement, maybe a light reprimand. He was used to these. Karl-Otto Koch, Camp Commandant, was constantly on his ass for being "too severe." What a laugh—Koch, the man who shot a hospital orderly and attendant after they treated him for syphilis, to keep word from getting out. And then there was Ilse, his wife. *Even the guards refer to her as the "Bitch of Buchenwald." Man does she hate me. Ilse and her tattoo lampshades made from prisoners' skin. They are impressive though. I give her that.*

He picked up the note, which was written on his own stationery, and read. It was written in poor German, but he understood its essential meaning.

Dear Mister Sommer,

You may be wondering why you don't remember things sometimes. You have blackouts, right? That's me. My name is Kevin. I am an American. I live in the 21st century. I play a computer game that allows me to take over your body for as long as I am logged in. I just wanted you to know you are not going crazy.

Kevin

The Hangman of Buchenwald sat on his bed, holding the note. It was almost a regular occurrence, these blackouts. He'd be patrolling the fence one afternoon, and the next thing he knew, he was beating a prisoner with a pipe or eating dinner in the mess hall. He'd gone to see Doctor Hoven about these spells, but the tinctures he'd been given had no effect. In fact, they seemed to increase in frequency. There was only one real possibility—Doctor Waldemar Hoven and his "medical experiments." It was bad enough that he had apparently taken to experimenting on SS men now, but this *Scheiss* about someone from the 21st century taking over his body involved messing with his state of mind, which was taking it *way* too far. He'd find out for sure, one way or another. Sommer stuck the note in his pocket and went to find the good doctor.

Kevin Daniel logged in, finding his avatar in bed, apparently in the middle of the night. It had been a few days since he had found himself using a screw clamp on a prisoner and had decided to write a note to his avatar. *What was he really like?* Of course, it was impossible to talk to the man, so he had decided simply to write him a note, let him know he wasn't crazy. That sort of thing. What he found today was unexpected, to say the least.

Looking around Sommer's barracks room, Kevin immediately noticed a folded note, like the one he had written earlier, sitting on his chest. He opened it. It was in German, an ornate cursive script; he had to Google many of the words:

Dear Kevin,

Thank you for informing me of the situation. I thought I was losing my mind; however, you will forgive me if I do not completely believe what you wrote to me. There are many more plausible reasons for my blackouts than the fact that a person in the 21st century is taking over my body against my will. And it IS against my will. However, assuming this is not a hoax created by Doctor Hoven, who assures me it is not, I ask you to refrain from continuing to do so. I have no means by which to stop you, as you know. I only appeal to your sense of decency and respect.

Martin Sommer, SS Hauptscharführer, Buchenwald

Kevin read the note several times. It was *insane* how realistic this game was. This was an absolutely mind-boggling level of artificial intelligence. When he had written the note, he hadn't expected a reply of any kind—much less one so detailed. He'd play along, but he had conditions. He went to Sommer's desk, took out a bottle of ink and a pen, and wrote on the back of the note:

Dear Martin,

I understand. I will stop entering your body, for now, except to write notes. That doesn't take long so I doubt you would even notice. I feel like we have a lot in common and I want to correspond with you if it is OK. You and me could work together. Also, do you speak English? I am slow with the German translations.

Kevin

The next evening, after logging in, Kevin found another note on his avatar's chest:

Kevin,

I am writing this in English, obviously. I speak OK English. Not great. I am flattered that you want to know more about me, but there is not much to tell, really. What about YOUR world? What is it like living in your century? Are there flying cars?

Martin

Kevin kept his word. He only entered the avatar to write notes, and so long as Martin kept up his end of the deal, it was all he would do in the Game at this point. The letters were friendly and casual. It would be a growing friendship.

Farash lay in bed, staring at the ceiling. Despite his wife's words of concern, he rarely ate anything, slept most of the time and rarely removed the helmet, lying in a sort of half-conscious state.

He was an adviser to the Reichsminister of Propaganda, who had shot him, probably killing Krafft, his avatar. He wore the helmet even when he slept, lying on the little bed in the spare room, subconsciously tuned into any faint sound, any small glimpse of change appearing on the wide band of screen wrapped ear to ear across his closed eyelids.

Amala came into the room every day to bring him his home-cooked meals, aromatic and very spicy, often retrieving the untouched plate hours later. She loved her husband and sympathized with—though could not understand—his addiction. She, found barely a teen by a decade-older Farhat Farash while still an orphan on the streets of New Delhi, was once addicted to the nicotine-like pull of betel quid, which had permanently stained some of her teeth. But this was much more. Farash had usually met her with a smile and a hug at the end of a long day—recently, not so much.

Amala saw it simply as an addiction to his work, his "research," his quest to create an ideal mix of technology and teaching, as he had put it. He worked hard to be the best teacher at his campus. Whatever had driven her husband from her for days on end, it was something he needed. And if he needed it, she would support him in his pursuit of it. She still wore the traditional dress of the Indian wife and would forever be his loyal Amala. He would come out of this. He would be the man he always had been, better, for all long journeys bring but a greater understanding of oneself.

Farash dreamed always, whether awake or asleep, of becoming the ruler of Germany, and ultimately the world. Isn't that what the game was about? And then it would be over. His character was perhaps not dead but merely in a coma. He would awaken.

One night, asleep in the little guest bed, helmet on, Farash felt a glow against his eyelids. He awoke. Foggy and unfocused, the image before him was accompanied by the sound of shuffling feet or perhaps the movement of some padded object being dragged along a smooth floor.

"Herr Krafft." The sound was garbled. "Herr Krafft." It was a male, talking to him from his left side. He continued to see nothing but a gray, moving blur.

Farash moved his avatar's head to the left and down. A variety of pale colors came into view, surrounded or perhaps embedded in a rectangle of metal. He leaned his head back and a brighter picture emerged. A circle this time, piercingly bright. Farash squinted in his helmet.

"Herr Krafft. Are you awake now?"

"I am," he responded.

"Good. That is good. You have been out for many days. Now you must eat to stay conscious." The words were good-natured and came broken and short from an elderly man who himself did not sound completely well. Farash moved his helmet in all directions until stopping on a face. Though blurry, it was white with age.

"Is this the Ministry?" Krafft asked.

The old man seemed amused. "Ministry? Hmm. What ministry would this be? A ministry of pain, perhaps. You are in a cell under Gestapo headquarters."

"Under?"

"It's a dungeon, my friend. But you have been well-treated. Your head. They hit you on the head. Do you remember anything?"

Krafft felt his chest. No wrappings were there, just a thin button-up shirt. No wounds. He hadn't been shot, at least not in the chest. He tried to sit up. The screen and audio went dead.

"Damn it!" He slapped at the helmet. Farash had finally gotten back in the game and was out just as quickly. Next time he would be more careful.

It was an hour before the screen lit up again and the audio returned within the black helmet. Farash was ready. The images weren't quite as blurry this time and he was alone. There was a metal tray of food next to the old mattress on which he lay. Light streamed through the bars of a small window at the top of the cell. He lay there, resting his avatar very carefully this time, trying to think what specific error of his resulted in this, his new condition. He ate the hard bread and overcooked carrots from the tray.

There was another mattress against the wall opposite him. Between the two mattresses was a doorway. The door, a foot deeper into the wall, was braced with metal strips and rattled slightly with the movement of a subterranean wind. A day of semi-consciousness followed.

Eventually, a man in a black coat and gray hat unlocked the door and appeared in the doorway. The other mattress had disappeared.

"Herr Krafft. It is good to see you awake. Can you walk?" With some effort, Farash was able to lift up his avatar to a somewhat standing position and shuffle his feet towards the man. "Good. You will be so kind as to come with me."

Krafft followed.

He was led to a table in a tiny room and bade to sit down. He seated himself in a plain metal chair behind a small fold-out table. Farash could himself feel the pounding of Krafft's skull and resisted the urge to take an analgesic. The man simply dropped a fountain pen on the desk and walked out, locking the door behind him. Farash waited. Surely the man would return, and he'd be given something to sign. He waited. After half an hour, the man still hadn't returned. Impatient, Farash inspected the pen. Eventually, he took it apart. A tiny, rolled up slip of paper was found in the empty chamber of the pen. Farash unrolled the note and read. It was in Goebbels' jumpy handwriting:

He believes you. – JG

That was all there was to the note.

This was particularly good news for Farash. He would be released. He would be placed in an office of real power, perhaps just above the Reichsminister of Propaganda himself. He would be more careful with how he addressed his superiors and perhaps one day become Deputy Fuhrer. If the note read true, Hitler had called off Operation Barbarossa. An eastern front would not be created with Russia, at least not yet. Germany just might win the war. Farash's avatar pocketed the note.

Soon, Krafft was taken back to the cell. Now all there was to do was to wait for his release. His release never came.

Spring, 2034

It was mid-January, a Tuesday. Richard Hayes wove in lectures and other activities to balance against the time he had students playing the Game. He liked to begin with historical background to help them make correct in-game decisions, usually reserving Game days for Wednesdays and Thursdays—sometimes Fridays, if there wasn't an exam scheduled.

It wasn't until his third period—the Advanced class—that things got a little strange. Normally, Mr. Hayes kept the "regular" students in approximately the same place chronologically as his Advanced class, modifying study questions and other assignments according to their general abilities. It was just easier this way. The lecture on D-Day had gone off without a hitch for his first two classes. Students took notes on notebook paper and noted key events and dates on a map handout. Third period started off the same way.

"Operation Overlord didn't just happen," Hayes began. It took tons of preparation and military exercises to make it a viable plan. The Allies were dealing with fronts all over the place—Japan, Africa, and of course Europe. The Allies came up with a "Europe First" strategy before tackling the Japanese, for geopolitical reasons. They dealt with the threats in a kind of order of importance. Once the British general Montgomery kicked Rommel out of North Africa, exercises began near the county of Devon, England as a kind of rehearsal for D-Day."

"What's D-Day?" one student asked.

"Well, that's what we refer to when we talk about Operation Overlord. You see, before the Americans entered the war, there wasn't much to discuss. The Germans had already created a strong beachhead across the Channel in France. There was no way Britain was going to break through it without our help."

Cynthia in the front row raised her hand. "Is that why the Americans couldn't help the British and the French? The Germans were too strong?"

"Well, but they did help. D-Day was led by US General Eisenhower who was appointed Supreme Allied Commander . . ."

Brian interrupted, "So how did they help? Did they send relief to the people of Britain suffering under Nazi rule?"

"Well, yes, but it was the American military support which made all the difference, though the serious amphibious exercises in preparation for D-Day didn't happen until January 1944. And Britain was being bombed by Germany, but it would be a mistake to say that they were under 'Nazi rule,' Brian." Some of the students looked confused.

Cole raised his hand, "But America never entered the war, so how did they help?" Hayes let out a faint sigh. There were times when he really regretted not going to graduate school. Teaching high schoolers could be really frustrating. "Cole, the United States entered the War in December 1941, when Japan attacked Pearl Harbor in Hawaii. Not long after, they began sending significant military supplies to . . ."

"Yea, but," Cole countered, "We declared war on Japan, but not Germany."

"Well actually, Germany declared war on us *first*, right after the bombing of Pearl Harbor.

Cynthia spoke, "Was that before or after Germany conquered Britain?" Hayes paused, then rubbed his eyes with his right hand and shook his head. "Cynthia," he began with all the composure he could muster, "Germany never conquered Britain. When the United States . . ."

Cynthia held up a map she had colored in with map pencils. "Yesterday, you said Germany conquered Britain in 1942. See, you had us color it in!" Hayes walked over and gently took the map. All of Europe, including Sweden, was colored in blue. Hayes said sympathetically, "I think you might have heard wrong. I'll get you another map to color in, it's no big deal."

Cole showed his map, "Actually, mine says the same thing." Other students were taking their maps out of their three-ring binders and holding them up. All of the European countries were colored in blue on all the maps. The blue areas were overlaid with swastikas. Mr. Hayes was genuinely puzzled. He remembered yesterday's lecture quite well, including the mapping exercise. The students had seemed to be completing it correctly. *I must be losing it*, he thought. "Alright, you guys, who's the ringleader?" They were puzzled. "C'mon, who decided it was time to put one over on ol' Mr. Hayes, eh? And the rest of you, what, just thought it would be great fun to go along with it? I gotta tell you, you had me!" He laughed, briefly. "Yeah, hilarious. But it's gonna cost you a few points when I have to print out new maps for everyone. C'mon, let's have 'em. Pass 'em up." The students, still confused, were handing in their maps when the bell rang for the passing period.

Hayes decided that for the rest of the day his students would finish what was left on the Europe mapping assignment using their notes and then watch a 30-minute film covering Pearl Harbor with accompanying study questions, an activity he had planned to use several weeks from now. That was safe. Meanwhile, he could walk around and monitor their work, read the notes they'd taken from *his* lecture only yesterday.

It was the same. According to their lecture notes, Germany had successfully invaded Britain in May of 1942. America kept its hands full with Japan. Other than a few advisors and token military and humanitarian aid, the United States had sent *nothing* to Britain or any other part of Europe before or during the invasion. Over and over, he pondered the situation, but said nothing about it to his students. To himself, a repeated refrain: *I must be quite literally losing my mind.*

As students were shuffling out with their backpacks at the end of the final period, Hayes, exhausted, watched them and suddenly froze. He felt chills crawling up his spine and along his arms and legs at the thought, suddenly nauseated and weak. *It couldn't be.* The idea was so preposterous that it had never occurred to him to Google it during class time. Now, not so much. So he did. And there it was.

He walked over next door and caught Farash as the man was preparing to leave. "Mr. Farash, quick question." Farash smiled, "Mr. Hayes, what can I do for you?" He laid his leather satchel on his desk and waited, arms crossed.

"When did the US enter the Second World War?"

"Excuse me?"

"Just please answer the question." Hayes was shaking.

"December 8th, the day after Pearl Harbor was attacked. Roosevelt asked Congress to declare war on Japan. Only one congressman voted against it."

"And when did D-Day happen?"

Farash paused and then gave a big smile. "Ah, you're quizzing me! Well, let's see. I believe it happened in 1927 when everyone on the planet had an inexplicable stuttering fit. It was a s-s-s-ad d-d-d-ay for every w-w-w-one." Farash giggled at his own jest.

"I'm not screwing around, Farash, when was D-Day?" Hayes roared. Farash went quiet then sputtered, "June sixth, 1944." He looked hurt.

"You're sure?"

"Quite sure." Farash replied.

"Google it," Hayes demanded. Farash sighed and turned on his computer. "You know, I think the Game is frying your brain, Mr. Hayes. It's a lot of fun, I hear, but computer games can be addictive." Hayes was silent as Farash pulled up the screen. He could find nothing on D-Day or on America entering World War II on behalf of Europe. "No, this is wrong."

"Damn right it's wrong. D-Day never happened." Hayes responded.

"This is a joke of some kind."

"I wish it were."

Farash's eyes went wide, "Excuse me for a moment," and he rushed out of the room. Hayes sat on Farhat's desk and waited. Farash returned about a minute later, eyes still wide, closing the door behind him. "I asked coach Samuels." Samuels was a history teacher several doors down.

"Asked? Asked her what?"

"About D-Day and America entering the War."

"And?"

"Her reply was, 'What's D-Day'?" Farash crossed over to his rolling chair and melted into it, visibly shaking.

Hayes and Farash spoke more, discussing the possibilities of a hoax, of the "joke" Hayes' students had supposedly played on him regarding the maps, of concepts involving the Multiverse, alternate timelines, the stuff of science fiction. Eventually, they came around to the Game.

"You know," Hayes began, "Since I discovered the game and started playing it, a few things have changed which I can't explain."

"Such as?"

"Fraulein, my dog. One of her eyes suddenly turned blue."

"You saw it happen?" Farash seemed slightly alarmed.

"Well, no. I just happened to notice one day. Does that happen sometimes with dogs? Or people? I've never heard of it."

"No clue," Farash replied. "But surely *something* has happened, yet if, let's say, our timeline shifted somehow and D-Day never actually happened, how would *we* know any difference?"

"You mean, why is it you and I remember that there was a D-Day and that America fought with the British against Hitler but no one else does?"

"Exactly!" Farash thought he knew the answer but didn't dare share it. The Game was *real*. He had never even considered the possibility, but now, barring some really bizarre hoax, and considering the role he'd recently played in convincing Hitler to abandon Barbarossa at least temporarily in favor of attacking Britain instead, to call it a mere coincidence would be naive. The answer as to why he and Hayes remembered D-Day might have something to do with how close the two were to the Game itself. He especially.

Farash spoke slowly. "Richard, what do we really know about the human mind and its connection to hard reality? Can or does memory exist *outside* of reality, in some circumstances perhaps uploaded to the ontological Cloud of Being itself, outside of space-time?"

"Ontological Cloud of Being?" Hayes laughed. "Farhat, I think you're way ahead of me on this one. I need a drink."

The next day, Hayes apologized to his third period class. He played along with the new "reality" as best he could but kept any mention of it brief. Okay, there was no D-Day—he'd just been testing them with a brain exercise, he told them. They all passed with hundreds. Nicely done. He'd focus on America's history with Japan, which seemed pretty much the same, at least until he could get his mind around what was happening and could do some considerable research to get to the bottom of it. There were no parent phone calls. He could keep his job.

That morning, Karen Murphy, the senior class president, called a class meeting via the morning intercom announcements, also inviting the junior class. It took place in the classroom of the senior class sponsor, Mr. Perry, right after school. The room was packed full, with students sitting on desks and lining the walls. Karen shut the door and began the meeting.

"I called this special meeting to discuss a matter which many of you might find trivial. It concerns Mr. Hayes." There were some murmurings amongst the juniors. "Mr. Hayes is one of my favorite teachers, and I know that goes for many of you. . ."

"Except he's nuts," broke in one of the Advanced juniors. Some giggling ensued.

"Well, after yesterday, from what I heard, I'd say that he . . . has some interesting teaching techniques. I mean what other teacher lets you guys play a game two or three times a week and get graded on it? He's . . . eccentric, but he's not crazy." More murmuring.

"Anyway," she continued, "we all know he plays it himself. I happen to know which avatar he plays." Silence. That got their attention. "In fact, my character is helping him get a Lithuanian Jew out of a concentration camp. Actually, we succeeded, but it's going to be impossible to get her out of Germany without help. We can't do it alone."

"Who is he?" one girl asked, excitedly. A boy in the back row replied, "I bet he runs Auschwitz." Mr. Perry sat at his desk drinking a Diet Coke and reading a magazine. He grinned.

"Not quite," Karen continued. "I'll give you the details *if* you agree to help him. Now with juniors, it's not a problem—you can work on the details during his class. Seniors, those of you who had his class last year . . . shall we say . . . still have access from home?" There were general nods. Most of the seniors still played it, using copies of the clandestine browser.

"Alright, and I have to say, this is *really* important to Mr. Hayes. Don't ask me why. If you think he's losing his shit . . . sorry, Mr. Perry . . . *mind* . . . now, well let's just say she's important to him."

"Hayes got a girlfriend!" One senior exclaimed. A few others picked it up as a chant.

"Good for him!" another spoke out. "I mean, a grown man's gotta get it somewhere, right?" The room roared with laughter. Karen, stone-faced, waited. After a time, the room was quiet again.

"Look at it this way, here's a chance to kick some serious Nazi *ass* and do something good that matters to someone. And we do it as a team." Perry looked up but let the profanity slide. In the present climate—as had actually been the case for *many* decades of cold war—hatred of Nazis was ubiquitous, well beyond the Game. It was the Russians and the Chinese that had kept them in check since the 1940s—along with tens of billions of dollars in annual American military support. The Atlantic was a veritable minefield.

"So," Karen finalized, "If you're with me, stay. If not, the meeting's over." Several students got up to leave. The rest stayed, many of these wearing armbands and buttons. Karen closed the door and continued the meeting, answering questions, revealing the details of Hayes' avatar and their current in-game situation involving a cabin skirted by the Black Forest. She only had a vague idea of how it would all work and would talk to Mr. Hayes more about it, knowing that he would be sympathetic to the idea. Probably.

Once the meeting was over and another scheduled for the next day, Karen passed into Mr. Hayes' room across the hall. Hayes was still at his desk, apparently struggling with lesson plans. "Mr. Hayes," she said," I just wanted to let you in on something." She brought up the meeting.

Hayes listened thoughtfully, rocking in his chair, fingers touching. "This plan includes seniors?" he asked. He knew about the browser theft. "Yes, but I won't know how many until tomorrow. That's when we get into the nitty gritty." Hayes smiled. "Well, if anyone can manage this, it's you Karen. Care to hash out some details?"

They worked on a plan long into the afternoon. It would involve getting as many avatars as possible to meet near a small sub-camp, in a town called Balingen, not far from the Swiss border. As far as logistics, they'd have to square away which students played viable roles in the Game before talking strategy. Prisoners, for instance, wouldn't be of much use, but perhaps some could be smuggled out of their camps. It would take a few days to get started. It was dark outside once they had a general plan sketched out. On her way out the door, Karen stopped and turned to Hayes as he was putting on his jacket. "Oh . . . and . . . Mr. Hayes, I remember something from your class about D-Day . . . sorta." She smiled and left.

Chapter 9

Debus made notes on the back of an invoice using the pencil that had, essentially, saved his life. He carefully charted the movements of each member of the team, including the guards—especially the guards. One always manned the CCTV screens while two went outside and one slept, he assumed, in a room off to the side of the control center. It was on the same level as the control room and back behind it near the far wall, reached by a second set of metal stairs and a mesh landing. Below it, on the ground floor, was a storage room the lab coats sometimes accessed using a card they wore around their necks. This storage room likely housed what Debus thought he needed to get home.

He had seen the scientists regularly enter and exit another room just behind the control room and off of the same landing, presumably their sleeping quarters. All three worked together either in the control room or in the vicinity of the Bell for most of the day and apparently ate together in the canteen and kitchen directly behind the control room. The two subordinate scientists tended to go to bed at about the same time each day while the senior scientist kept working through much of the night. He was also the first to rise, followed soon by one of the subordinates. The other assistant tended to sleep for an extra hour or so.

Debus had done his late-night reconnaissance around the Bell, studying the instrumentation board on the massive control panel, inspecting the numerous hoses and cables connecting both the control panel and the numerous sets of free-standing modules located on a metal rack just to the side. He knew what most of the readings on the gauges meant. Understanding every toggle switch, dial, and button took much longer, requiring occasional late-night risks involving brief tests which modified sinusoidal wavelengths that might get noticed. They couldn't be avoided. The radiation and flow-speed readings were wrong and, among other maladjustments, always well below the necessary quantities needed to stimulate a quantum transportation event. The Americans' celebrations were premature. Each minute step in the process must, for them, seem a remarkable achievement. Debus would show the Americans how it was done. He'd show them the German way. *Alles oder nichts.* All or nothing.

One evening, Debus watched from a nearby stack of empty crates as the shorter of the two lab assistants approached the secured storage room on the ground floor. There were two red diodes lit up on the panel to the man's right. The man pulled out a card attached to a lanyard around his neck and inserted it into a slot by the wide door. One of the lights went green. He then moved a flap on the panel and stared into a faint blue light. The other diode lit up green and the door clicked open. The man flicked on a light switch as he went in. The German could hear the man rummaging around in boxes. "Where's the damn . . . ugh." Quickly, he exited the room, leaving the door cracked open, and headed for the small restroom beneath the control center, grabbing at his crotch.

Swiftly, Debus ran to the door, avoiding the security cameras, and entered. He quickly inspected the boxes and cubbies on rows of metal shelves. They were filled with manuals, cables, computer parts, extension cords, wiring modules, writing instruments, camera gear, and various modules appearing as if they would fit some of the sockets in the control panel. He committed all of it to memory, as best as he could manage, and fled.

SOUTH TEXAS, NOVEMBER 2035

The young woman had left, and Selma was about to get up to leave when the nurse reappeared with a clipboard. She briefly began to explain the procedure.

"As his aunt, you have the final say in how the medicine is administered," the thoughtful nurse replied.

The old woman hesitated. "Young lady, I must confess, I'm not really his aunt. I'm only a friend."

The nurse looked puzzled and then frowned. "There are only two days remaining until Mr. Hayes must be removed from this facility. We have tried to contact his family members but with no success. I'm afraid I'll have to ask you to make the decision anyway, if you don't mind. You're as close as we have to a relative, so . . ." She offered the clipboard and a pen.

The old woman nodded. There was no point in arguing. It simply had to be done if the law were to be followed, which it assuredly would be by the staff of this facility. Six months of critical health care—that was the maximum. Besides, they had to make room for the next patient who would likely, six months later, be "medicated" as a matter of course, making room for the next. Selma had been a nurse most of her life back in Switzerland. She knew how it all worked.

The young nurse treated the old woman as one would a 100-year-old tortoise, like one of the last of a dying species, with great gentleness and patient maneuvering. The nurse carefully explained the two options, regarding "the medicines," from which the old woman could choose.

The first method involved injecting a soup of chemicals directly into Richard's heart. The effect would be instantaneous, supposedly painless—considering his mental condition—and the most humane, but costly. What was left on his plan didn't cover it.

Upon arriving at the McAllen airport that morning, Selma had exchanged all her reichsmarks for geos and gotten a bad deal. reichsmarks were still being accepted throughout most of Europe, and the exchange rate would have been better there. Still, at roughly RM 3.00 to G1.00 it was a far better exchange rate than the poor American holdouts exchanging their dollars for geos in the line next to her, their practically worthless green and white currency now exchanging at almost a tenth of its value from just a few years back.

Nevertheless, she couldn't afford the first option proposed by the young nurse and still feed herself until the next quarterly check arrived from the World Bank. Since the man had been in the State-run asylum for almost six months and had thus maxed out his health care benefits package, she would have to pay for most of it—if he were to die with dignity. With the second method, well it would be the cheapest way to go, free in fact.

Finally, very hesitantly, the old woman checked a box on the page and signed it. She nodded towards the pillow. The nurse understood and smiled.

THE CABIN HAD NO ELECTRICITY, but candles and firewood were found in abundance. Water was pulled from the ground through an outside hand pump, and an attached root cellar had supplied most of their meals—potatoes, onions, cabbages, and carrots carefully stored under a wide mound of sand. There was a bed in the single bedroom, which the females shared while, in the living area, Hayes had slept on an old couch, its cushions stuffed with straw.

Savina was relishing the relative freedom she'd enjoyed since the trio had discovered the cabin several days ago. (Richard) had driven the motorcycle through the chilly night air while she and Gretchen (Karen) rode snuggled deep in the sidecar over dirt roads, trying to discover a bit of unoccupied shelter—a barn, a shed, even a drainage pipe—somewhere to hide. It was an unbelievable find that they had almost missed, and would have, had Hayes not spotted the red tile roof in the headlight when he had to make a sharp right to avoid a large rock. The cabin was almost as unbelievable as their story—two time travelers, a teacher and a student from the 2030s, playing a game in Savina's world. Thankfully, to them it *wasn't* just a game.

While Savina washed and dried the breakfast dishes, Karen and Richard were checking small animal traps and foraging for lichens and whatever else they could find in the woods along the base of the mountain range. Recently, Richard had caught a few rabbits using snares made from a roll of copper wire he'd found in the cellar. Once the pots and dishes were put up, Savina went outside to check on the drying blankets taken from the camp. They were hung behind the cabin on a clothesline just outside the shadow cast by the morning sun rising against the sloped roof.

As she walked around to the front of the cabin, Savina saw and heard a car driving up on the dirt road. Quickly, she ran around to the back, pulled the several blankets from the line, and went inside. She locked both doors and hid in the bedroom. Soon there was a knock on the front door, and after several attempts, a voice: "Fraulein, we know you're in there. We saw you as we pulled up. We just want to talk." After a few moments, there was a discussion taking place outside the door. A few minutes later, Savina heard Richard's voice.

Richard and Karen were walking up to the back of the cabin when they heard the knocking from some distance. Richard was carrying two dead hares by the ears. They stopped and hid behind a copse of trees. "What do you think?" Karen whispered. "I don't know," Hayes responded, listening to the voices coming from the other side of the building. "Sounds like they saw Savina outside." Both crept up to the back door of the cabin just as two men walked around the side and saw them. All four stopped cold. Hayes cursed the fact that he was still wearing Wicker's uniform—he hadn't thought to bring a change of civilian clothes. Both of the other men were wearing the uniforms of local police, and both had sidearms.

"Excuse me sir," one of the middle-aged men began. "This is Sergeant Kopf and I'm Lieutenant Schultz. We're from Oberaudorf. We got a visit from the owner of this property a few hours ago. He says he saw smoke coming from the chimney early this morning and said it looked like there might be squatters. Do you know the owner?"

Hayes had no idea who owned the property, so there was no bluffing there. Perhaps he could use the uniform, his SS rank, but whatever story he told, it would certainly be checked out. They'd likely already seen his name sewn onto his jacket. And his vehicle? A motorcycle suspiciously hidden in some brush rather than parked at the house . . . It was over.

Spring, 2034

It was Friday night, and in his room from three blocks away Kevin could hear the cheering of the crowds. Everyone in the small town showed up for the games on Football Friday Night—this was Texas. Kevin was playing the Game, trying to ignore the faint roars penetrating the thin paneling of the double-wide and the cushions of his headset. The coaches would do without him. *I doubt they've even noticed I'm not there.*

Kevin could smell the tacos his mother was making for just the two of them in the kitchen not far away. She was an excellent cook, having worked both as cook and waitress one time or another for the last six years in a cafe on the main drag. Kevin had no siblings. He'd never met his father.

His mother opened his bedroom door and poked her head in. "What kinda beans you want, honey? Charro or refried?" He pulled off the headset and looked up. "What?" She repeated the question.

"Charro, of course!" he responded, angrily. She silently closed the door.

Kevin marveled at the large pan of wedding rings. *There must be tens of thousands*, he thought. He was looking over the shoulders of several prisoners sorting through jewelry, watches, gold teeth, and lockets with little portraits inside. He didn't quite know what he was supposed to be looking for, but it was a new part of his duty shift to inspect the merchandise taken from prisoners. The three men in the striped pajamas didn't have pockets, so there wasn't much point in doing these inspections . . . but they did have orifices. Kevin barked at the men to open their mouths. He used a flashlight to look down their throats and around their gums. No loot. Well, that was the only orifice he had any interest in looking into. Job done.

Kevin took off his headset and looked at himself in the mirror. He stood up and walked forward for a closer look. He turned his head from side to side, stroking his chin. He smiled and went to his closet. A few jackets and several pairs of jeans were hanging there. An old shotgun leaned against a corner; several pairs of ragged sneakers were piled on the floor. He took out a pair and put them on over bare feet. He then went to his chest of drawers and opened each drawer. He chose a Black Sabbath t-shirt, slipped it on, and walked out his bedroom door.

As Kevin strolled the few blocks to the stadium, the crowd noise would fade and then crescendo in waves. He jumped over a ditch and looked through the chain-link fence at one end of the field. The Home side of the stadium was packed—it was the last game of the year, and though the team had barely won a game this year, the fans were loyal. The Visitors had also shown up in droves, filling the much smaller set of stands on Kevin's right. He looked up at the scoreboard. Home 3. Visitors 21. There were eleven minutes left in the second quarter. He continued watching the game.

The band of the visiting team took the field during the first part of halftime. All were dressed in black and gold uniforms, sporting green and purple feathers on their tall hats. The drum major mounted the stand before them while an obese band director stood beside her and watched through black horn-rimmed glasses, arms crossed. Once all was set up, the drum major flicked the wand a few times and the snare drums began. Soon the horns joined in with a fast-paced rhythm. "The Boogie Woogie Bugle Boy" began playing as a dozen cheerleaders danced a sort of Charleston on the track in front of the home section.

Crowds cheered as the cheerleaders joined with arms around each other's shoulders, doing rolling high kicks and then breaking off to dance in pairs. Kevin climbed the fence, and once on the other side, began stripping off his clothes. With nothing on but his tight, white underwear, he did a dancing run in the direction of the cheerleaders. The crowd roared in an apparent mix of appreciation and disgust as Kevin grabbed her hands and led her in a four-count swing. She looked petrified and started to walk away when he took her hands again, doing a push-pull, bringing her to him and then back, expertly twisting her around the back of him with a pretzel maneuver. She started to cry in sheer embarrassment as he put his arm around her and they turned through a cradle wheel. Gradually the band stopped playing as security guards walked up and escorted Kevin off the track.

Kevin had no idea what had happened—well, he had one idea. One minute he was playing the Game. The next, he was *in* it. Completely. He literally *was* Martin Sommer. It terrified him to suddenly be standing by a narrow bed looking at walls of peeling plaster and up at the beams of a wooden ceiling. In the Game, he had merely come back to his barrack room early after inspecting the prisoners sorting the stolen merchandise. He had ordered a Kapo to bring one of the male prisoners awaiting punishment to his room for "personal interrogation."

The syringes, jars of liquid, and other implements of his craft still lay hidden under the loose floorboard plank beneath Sommer's desk when the prisoner was brought in. Once the Kapo left, quietly closing the door, Kevin turned to look at the prisoner. He was a small young man, barefoot, shaved head, wearing the filthy striped pajamas. Kevin stared, expecting to see raw fear in his eyes, but this one seemed . . . resigned. Kevin approached the young man who was about twenty centimeters shorter than he was. He couldn't have been much older than Kevin and he smelled horrible. Kevin had him stand in the middle of the room and walked around him. It wasn't that the prisoner garb was oversized, rather there was barely anything inside to fill it. It just hung on him like a tent. The boy was a skeleton. His neck wasn't much bigger than Martin Sommer's wrist. Kevin sat on the bed and looked at the floor, shaking his head. This was all wrong.

He called the Kapo back in and had the prisoner removed. He then locked the door, sat back on the bed, and sobbed violently.

About twenty minutes later, Kevin was standing barefoot by a police car outside the football stadium. He was in his underwear, and Principal Mason was handing him his clothes. Once his mother arrived, they were informed that Kevin would likely be suspended until Tuesday, pending assignment to an "alternative educational environment."

Martin Sommer found a note on his chest the next morning.

What the hell did you do?

Kevin now had plenty of time to play the Game—at least until Wednesday, when he would be allowed back in school pending the outcome of a disciplinary hearing. However, he was angry and confused, and didn't feel much like playing. He only logged in occasionally to check for messages.

On Sunday morning, he entered the game as Sommer with a note on his chest. It explained it all.

Hello Kevin. How does it feel to lose control? How did you like being me for real? I admit I was also quite surprised when it happened. Please don't be angry. You're a legend now.

The messages went back and forth all day—the two agreed to leave them in Sommer's left jacket pocket. Sommers stayed in his room for most of his day off, temporarily giving Kevin permission to subject him to the regular blackouts. Over the course of that Sunday, Kevin began to cool off. Martin claimed to know nothing about how the transference of consciousness worked and was quite apologetic for his actions—actions that Kevin would have to take the blame for. Well, there was no way around it now. They spent the remainder of the day corresponding about the upcoming attempt by the juniors and seniors to get Savina to safety. Hayes wasn't going to like the outcome. After all, Mr. Hayes always said that he wanted students playing the game to stay in character. Kevin's avatar wasn't one to go against the principles of National Socialism.

It was Wednesday afternoon. Kevin sat in the back row of the meeting at a corner desk. As he watched Mr. Perry's room fill with juniors and seniors, two boys, one thin and the other a bit on the heavy side, looked around the room as they walked in. Both locked eyes with Kevin and quickly looked away, turning to sit in the front row by the door. *Cowards*, Kevin thought. *Couldn't go through with it. No balls.* The two boys, Jay and Thad, had been with him on the night they "took care of" Steven Berg last spring. The two had worn their own masks—Freddy Krueger and a zombie. But when it came down to it, they bailed out. Sure, they had kept Steven blindfolded and tied up in the back of the van, borrowed for the occasion from Kevin's unsuspecting neighbor, but once they got to the field, the two scattered into the brush, leaving Kevin to do all the work. He knew they would never talk—they were there and would have been considered just as guilty. Still, he'd never forgive them *for being such pussies.*

Karen Perez walked into the room, followed by Mr. Hayes carrying two large rolled up maps, which he hung from brackets in front of Perry's whiteboard. Perry sat at his desk as usual. Karen began the meeting, "OK, everyone. Let's get started. We have bad news and good news." It had been a week since the first meeting of the juniors and seniors interested in helping Mr. Hayes get Savina safely across the Swiss border. In the interim, students worked on getting their avatars in position to head to Southern Germany to meet up and launch a plan involving a caravan led by official-looking vehicles and a few cargo trucks. Karen and a few of her friends had tried to keep up with who would be available to play the Game at the designated time, as well as the feasibility of *which* avatars could actually make it to the chosen site—a massive but dilapidated barn discovered by one of the students about 60 kilometers west of the cabin. Unfortunately, of the hundred-plus students who turned out for the first meeting, there were only 34 in attendance today. Karen knew that most (though many were eager to participate) simply wouldn't have the in-game freedom to make the trek.

The usual *"Erwachen"* and *"Schlaf"* armbands and buttons were gone. In their place, Hayes noticed, were simple white stickers reading *"Einheit"* (Unity). Everyone was wearing one. He broke in, "Hi everyone. Thanks for staying after school and agreeing to this project. For you juniors, it's extra credit if you want it. Seniors, you simply have my thanks."

"How is Savina?" one girl asked.

"Well . . . fine for now, but that's what we need to talk about. The plan we had tentatively devised is scrapped. There have been new developments." Hayes turned and pulled down a map of Southern Germany. "Karen, Savina, and I got caught staying at the cabin without the owner's permission. We were taken to a police station in Oberaudorf, a town about three kilometers southeast of the cabin."

"That's the bad news, right?"

"Bad and good. We were held in a cell all day until a group of officers from Dachau showed up and took us to a sub-camp called Bayrischzell, which is where we are now."

"Were you hurt?"

"Not badly, not yet anyway. Now for the good news: it isn't the Dachau main camp. There are dozens of Dachau sub-camps all around Munich. Some aren't as bad by comparison—porcelain factories, farms, building projects. Some are just as bad or worse, like munitions factories, mines, and general camps. This one is neither. It's a research facility, only about ten kilometers from the cabin. I had no idea it was there." Hayes continued to outline the situation while pointing to the map. The three had been placed in the sub-camp until the higher ups could decide what to do with them. The camp, located in the mountains near the Austrian border, was run from Dachau by SS *Hauptsturmführer* Dr. Sigmund Rascher, who appeared there regularly. His "research" involved several prongs dealing with the harsh conditions faced by Luftwaffe and Wehrmacht soldiers stationed in the Northern Territories, particularly over the North Sea. One area involved dealing with the low pressures involved in flying at high altitudes. Another, surviving subzero weather and the effects of hypothermia. Not surprisingly, prisoners were kept on site for experimentation. Not far from Rascher's laboratory also stood a hospital where wounded German soldiers were sent for convalescence. When he had finished, Hayes sat on Perry's desk.

Karen spoke. "Alright, now we need to know who can do what at the Bayrischzell breakout!" There was an excited murmur amongst the students. Finally, Matthew Conn raised his hand and began in his deep Texas twang, "I got me a tank . . ."

"We got *us* a tank, you mean," immediately replied the brunette girl sitting next to the blond young man. Hayes smiled. This was Julia Dryden. The two were inseparable, had been since they were little. Both were highly skilled ropers; Matthew rode bulls, and Julia did barrel racing. Their relationship was purely platonic, as far as Hayes knew.

"Seriously, a tank?" Hayes asked.

"Yeah," Matthew continued. "I drive the tank, but Julia likes to come along for the ride. She actually drives a jeep, so we have that too." Hayes looked puzzled. "How did you two end up in the same regiment?" They looked embarrassed. "About three hundred different logins finally got me in one with Julia." Hayes frowned but said nothing. That sort of thing was strictly against the class rules, but today he didn't care.

Apparently encouraged by Hayes' silence at the infraction, another boy in the front row raised his hand. "Thad and me got death wagons."

Karen asked, "What's a death wagon?"

"It's a gas van, a mobile extermination machine. Actually, these are more like buses. Instead of taking people to the gas chambers, Nazis bring the gas chamber to them. They just put 'em in and drive around with the exhaust feeding into the bus—separated from the driver, of course. Takes about twenty minutes." Jay replied.

"That's what you two do in the Game?" Karen was horrified.

"Nah, we just do maintenance—mainly on officers' cars." Thad continued. "But we got access to the bus keys. We thought we could use 'em to round everybody up when we head to that Bay-rich-hell place."

Karen seemed relieved. "Well, make sure the exhaust is pointing outside when you scoop everybody up. Where are you two located?"

"In a small camp in Poland near the Baltics, so we're gonna need a schedule of who to pick up and where," Jay replied. "We'll be driving south picking up everybody, so we're gonna need a list. Gotta get started early too since it'll be a lot of driving."

Hayes interrupted. "Do you think you can get past all the borders and checkpoints? It's a long way."

"Well, Jay's got some forged documents which should get us down to Bavaria. We were also thinkin' about painting some skulls and crossbones on the busses so everyone would know what we were. People stay away from them *Sonderwagens*, as the Germans call 'em."

"I doubt regular Germans would know anything about them," Hayes said. "Forget the skulls. The SS don't advertise that sort of thing. Better stick to using the documents. Make sure they look legitimate."

"Oh, they look legit." Both boys nodded.

It was Friday, and the breakout, which the students had named *Aktion Einheit* (Operation Unity), was scheduled for a week from Tomorrow. Mr. Hayes would keep his classroom open the entire Saturday for those who didn't have the high-speed bandwidth to deal with the action-oriented movements required during the mission. He'd order pizza for everyone. As far as Administration was concerned, it was a last-minute makeup day to allow students to complete additional work to pass the class for the six weeks, which would be ending that week.

Karen spoke with the students individually and those who had partnered up, writing down all the relevant information needed. She had all their email addresses and would send them all the final plans within the next few days.

As students filed out, Hayes addressed Kevin, who hadn't said a word during the meeting, as he was walking out the door. "Kevin, nice to see you with your pants on." He laughed. "I saw the videos—that was some impressive swing dancing. Where'd you learn all that?" Kevin just stared at the whiteboard. "I wasn't . . . myself."

"Well, I'm glad they let you back in school so soon, for now anyway." He paused. "So, I understand that you work in a camp."

Kevin looked up and grinned. "I'm a Guard. Hauptscharführer at Buchenwald."

"Really? A master sergeant. And at Buchenwald. You must see some horrific stuff going on there. Try not to let it get into your head. It helps if you just concentrate on doing the right thing, which is what got me through Dachau."

"Yeah, it can get pretty gruesome. And don't worry about Savina. We'll take care of her."

Hayes returned to his room after the meeting to find Farash, sitting in his desk chair. Farash stood up and asked Hayes to close the door.

"There's something you need to see," he said. Farhat motioned Hayes to his desk and had him sit down. He asked him to log onto his computer, which Hayes did. Farhat then reached over and typed in a Google search: "political world map." He clicked the first result.

At first, Hayes didn't know what he was looking at. The map of the world was almost entirely in red. He checked the legends and went cold.

"Does this mean what I think it does?" Hayes asked.

"Ever since the day we discovered that D-Day never happened, I've been checking history sites several times a day. As of today, it's changed again. The timeline, or whatever you want to call it, is worse."

Indeed it was, unless you were a National Socialist. All of Europe and the vast majority of Asia had been conquered by the Nazis by 1943. Heinrich Luitpold Himmler, Reichsführer of the SS, had taken over as Hitler convalesced from what American historians had been sure was Parkinson's Disease. The Germans had garnered all the resources they could from Europe—all the tanks, guns, munitions, and men from both sides of an ended war—and drove them into Moscow. Though certainly a bloodbath, it was a relatively quick operation. Afterwards, Russia's invasion of China was a sure thing. America was—and had been for ninety years—almost completely isolated.

Japan had never been nuked in this timeline and had signed a ceasefire with the United States—while still part of the Axis Alliance. Africa was one giant resource of raw material and slave labor for the Axis powers. The major cities in Australia had been reduced to rubble by a Nazi-controlled China, and what was left could barely be called a third-world nation. South America currently fell under a kind of American hegemony though nearly all its nations, democratic in name only, were staunchly "neutral." The US, Canada, and Mexico were all that was left to defend the principles of a de facto democracy. After several skirmishes marked the attempts of National Socialist forces to invade America along the Atlantic and Pacific coasts, a peace agreement was finally formed in the late 1950s. Trade thus continued between enemy nations though heavily unbalanced in favor of the Axis allies.

"When did this happen?" Hayes asked.

"When? Nearly a century ago."

"No, I mean . . . why now? Actually, I'm not sure what I mean."

"I think what you're asking," Farash broke in, "Is why is it happening in increments? Since all this happened so long ago, why didn't *this* new timeline appear when the first shift occurred? If Germany invaded Russia and China so long ago, why wasn't it part of history on the day we found out that Britain had been taken."

"Yeah, I think that's it."

"I have no clue, but it looks like it's all happening in chunks, like history is slowly resetting itself—but in bursts rather than all at once."

Hayes asked, "Do you really think this has something to do with the Game? I mean we've talked about it, but it's just a stinking *game*."

"We agreed it might be much more. Either it has everything to do with the timeline shifts, or it has nothing to do with it. Either way, it makes me ill. I threw up three times in the last hour. I don't think I can take this."

"Nor can I. Without history, what is there to grab onto?" Hayes replied. "I hadn't really thought much about it before, but history cements us in reality. If it's fluctuating, then everything is chaos." He placed his forehead against the top of his desk and murmured, "If it's the Game, then someone's making choices that are changing the timeline . . . I can't believe I'm saying this . . . If that's the case, then we have to figure out how to change it back."

"I don't think it's possible. The Game follows the historical timeline. You've noticed that in the Game Britain is no longer independent?" Farash asked.

"I have."

"That's evidence of what I've been saying—the timeline in the Game is somehow speeding up. If we go into the game right now, I'd imagine we'd find Russia and China already conquered by the Nazis. Which means, to make things right, choices would have to be made to reverse everything—which can't happen since the Game is chronologically linear."

"So to fix things, an army would have to be formed that could conquer, what, some 60 or 70 percent of the World," Hayes mused aloud.

"Precisely. We passed the point of no return—probably when Britain was taken, and America didn't enter the war."

"Then we're screwed, and we're stuck with all of this?" Hayes thought for a moment. "OK, so what changed? As far as I can tell, it all leads back to Hitler not attacking the Russians until he had all of Europe under his control. He never created a second front." He paused and then spoke slowly. "Somebody manipulated the timeline, probably gave the Germans some sort of advantage, some information that would change Hitler's mind. *Who would do that*?"

Farash was silent. "Perhaps they thought it was just a game."

Chapter 10

Kurt Debus didn't have a watch though it had to be around six in the morning. Both the senior scientist and one of his assistants had made their way to the control center of the warehouse, which left the third lab coat still in bed. The German stealthily made his way up the stairs to the door and peeped into the narrow window. Both had apparently just sat down to their computer screens, side by side, sipping coffee from paper cups and snacking on bagels. Debus tiptoed to the apartment just to the left and tried the door. It was unlocked. He entered and gently closed the door behind him.

On the floor beside the bunk bed on the left sat a large bowl containing a metal spoon and the remnants of what looked like stew. Beside this was a digital clock reading 6:12. The smaller of the two assistants lay slumbering under a thin sheet on the bottom bunk, facing the wall. A second set of bunk beds, unmade, stood against the other wall. The sleeping man's lab coat lay folded over the back of a chair in front of a small desk at the foot of the bed. Debus checked the pockets. No access card. Opening the desk drawer, he found a notepad and some stationery along with scattered office supplies, but nothing else.

Frustrated, Debus looked back at the man and noticed an orange string at his neck. *Sheisse*, he even wore the thing to bed. This wouldn't be easy. Not that any of it was. The German quietly went through the room, checking clothes pockets, desks, even under the bunks. Nothing. He sat briefly at the chair by the desk and thought. He might be able to get some use out of the lab coat.

No, it would do no good. He couldn't think of any scenario in which simply disguising himself would get him what he wanted. He rose to leave but then stopped in front of the door. It couldn't end here. He needed access to the secure storage room, and nothing short of possessing that card would get him in. He had to do what was necessary.

Debus gently placed the pillow on the man's face. He stirred. Debus then sat on the pillow, pushing up into the bottom of the top bunk with his long arms, trying to get all his weight to matter as the man flailed. He bounced on the man's head, sandwiched between the two pillows, thinking it might break the little man's neck. He'd never killed a man, and it took everything he had, both physically and emotionally, several macabre minutes which seemed like hours. Finally, Debus felt—rather than heard—a crack, signaling through his buttocks that the man's neck had broken.

Feeling a chill, he went ahead and donned the lab coat which only covered to his waist and most of his arms. He took the card and made his way down the stairs. At the panel by the wide door, the card worked just as it had for the other man. One diode changed from red to green. He slid aside the flap, releasing the blue light into his eyes. He stared at it as the man did. Nothing happened. The second diode remained red. He blinked. Nothing. This wasn't something he had dealt with before, but it only took him a few seconds to figure out what needed to be done. It was somehow coded to the man's eyes. He needed those eyes.

Back at the bunk by the still form, Debus contemplated. He could drag the man's body down the stairs and prop up his head in front of the blue light. He'd have to perhaps hold the body by the neck with one arm while lodging open the eyes with the other hand, a trick entailing undue risk and consuming far too much time. He planned to leave this place within the hour if at all possible. It would be much easier to use the spoon . . .

In a box on the top left shelf, he found one crucial item. He picked up a device about the size of a hand-held transistor radio—one of two sitting in the box, held it up to the light, and stuffed it into one of his lab coat pockets. He found the other item, a cylindrical plug with a red cap, in a box containing identical plugs but with assorted colors and specifications stamped on their caps. The one he held, indicating the lowest possible resistance, was the one he needed. He slid this into his other pocket and left the storage room.

THE BAYRISCHZELL CAMP was surrounded by a fence primarily composed of cattle fence panels attached to thick wooden posts spaced three meters apart. The galvanized panels were grids of six-centimeter squares and were placed three high, reaching four meters to the four rows of razor wire beginning at the base of each curve. The fence spanned 100 meters on its widest side, built in the shape of a slanted parallelogram or a tilted rectangle. Four wooden guard towers stood just outside the center of each side.

Within the perimeter of the camp stood a single long, windowless prisoner barrack positioned north to south and stood about ten meters from the west fence. It had a wide door at the southern end, locked from the outside. The barrack, built more like a stable, housed 108 prisoners at capacity. The twelve bunks had been built three levels high and were arranged along the east wall of the narrow barrack. Prisoners slept three to a bunk on bare plywood in their striped rags. There were no blankets, and in the bitter chill of the Alpine night at an altitude of 1100 meters above sea level, only the sleeper in the middle could get a semblance of a peaceful rest, so they took turns.

In the early morning hours, some of the prisoners heard the sound of a small object striking the west wall of the barrack. It repeated several times in intervals.

"What is that racket?" one of the men in a lower bunk whispered.

"Sounds like a rock. Somebody is throwing rocks at us." replied one of his bunkmates.

"Who the hell would do that?"

"Why don't you go take a look?"

"If it's me, I get half your morning ration."

The man in the middle thought for a moment. "A third."

"Deal." The second man slowly got up and shambled over to the west wall. With one eye he peered through a knothole. He stood there a while and then returned to his bunk.

"What is it?"

"There's an SS man out there throwing rocks from the other side of the fence."

"What does he want? He must be drunk."

"Maybe. He was waving his arms and saying, 'Mister Haze' over and over."

"Definitely drunk."

"Mmm. Yeah, probably.

It was early Saturday morning. Richard Hayes had been on his computer and in the Game nearly all night. He knew it wouldn't be long before two SS guards would come storming into the barrack to drive the herd into roll call at the center of the camp. Lying on a top bunk between him and a Dutch man whom everyone simply referred to as 'Preacher,' his bunkmate beside him, a German Jehovah's Witness—most were in this camp—named Fritz, was already awake. "How do you do it?"

"Do what," whispered Hayes.

"You sleep like the dead."

"Oh, that. It's my . . . superpower," Hayes replied.

"Your super . . . what?"

As the men filed out of the barrack into the frigid snow-covered field, each thanked the Maker for the privilege of wearing shoes during this coldest of seasons. Most had purple triangles sewn onto the left side of their jackets, pointing down, with a number sewn just above it. This marked them as "Bible Researchers" as officially designated in the Camp logs. Witnesses were especially valued as prisoners—they rarely fought back, a tenet central to their creed. Thus, they were often found in sub-camps, like this one, where security wasn't quite as tight though their treatment was just as harsh as at any camp. Richard's triangle was orange—political prisoner. Unlike most of the others, he'd kill as many guards as he could get his hands on—if everything went to plan.

As the prisoners shuffled out the barrack door, Hayes noticed an SS guard to his right behind the fence and beside the guard tower, alternately waving his arms and folding his arms, shivering. It had to be one from his team, but he didn't know which one. He held up a hand in a "wait" gesture, but the young man shook his head and pointed to the latrine shack just north of the barrack. Hayes nodded and continued walking with the group.

After roll call, Hayes went to the latrine, but instead of going in with some of the others, he slipped around to the north side, out of sight of the closest guard tower. He saw the young man standing by the fence, looking up at the tower and back down at Hayes' avatar. Hayes decided to risk it and approached the fence.

"Mr. Hayes, I need to speak with you. It's important."

"We won't start the raid until noon our time, seven theirs. What are you doing here?"

"I'm . . . I'm . . ." the young soldier began to sob and shake his head. Hayes waited, surprised by the outburst. They were standing a meter apart.

The young man began, "Mr. Hayes, it's Kevin."

"Oh, hey Kevin. What's the emergency?"

"No, you don't understand. It's really me. I'm . . . literally in this body right now."

Hayes was completely baffled. "Um, yeah, you're playing Martin Sommer if I remember right from Karen's list."

"Mr. Hayes," Kevin was trying hard to get through. "Remember the thing I did at the football game?"

"I wasn't there, but yes. It was stupid."

"It *was* stupid. And it wasn't me. Sommer took over my body and did all those things. I was stuck in his body . . . for a while. He's done it again. But this time it's been days! I took a train and got here just last night. I . . . I don't know what to do. You gotta help me!"

Hayes' eyes narrowed. He frowned. "That's impossible."

"Oh God! You don't believe me!"

"Take it easy, Kevin. Man, you're really shook up."

"You would be too, if you were stuck in 1943 and couldn't get back home. I'm afraid of what he's doing in our time. To my mother."

Hayes shook his head and thought. He assumed it *was* Kevin speaking to him since there wasn't a trace of a German accent, and his mannerisms were all Kevin. But this was beyond unbelievable. Students love to play foolish tricks on their teachers—and are generally bad at it. However, Kevin was completely sincere. Those were real tears.

"OK, Kevin. Where do you think you . . . um, Sommer is now?"

"We agreed that I would be in your classroom today using your computers, so he might show up there."

"'We agreed'? Who agreed?"

"Me and Sommers."

Hayes' mouth fell open. "You . . . *communicated* with him?"

Kevin nodded. "I . . . wrote him messages. He started writing back."

Hayes tried to control his temper, but it was showing. "Kevin, do you know who that man is? I've researched the few well-known characters some of the students play. I checked yours a few days ago online. Do you know *what* that man is?"

Kevin replied, "I know who he is. He's the 'Hangman of Buchenwald.'"

"He's a fucking monster!"

"I . . . I know."

Hayes was silent. He was trying to organize it all in his mind. Kids could be so stupid sometimes.

"There's one more thing, Mr. Hayes."

Hayes sighed. "What is it, Kevin?"

"We agreed . . . that is, Martin and I agreed to sabotage the operation."

"Sabotage?"

"He might have sent word to Dr. Rascher, telling him about your plan to get Savina out."

Hayes was furious. He could barely trust himself to say another word, but he risked two between gritted teeth: "But . . . why?"

"You failed me the first semester in World History, remember? I had to make it up in summer school."

"I . . . failed . . . you . . ."

"I'm so sorry, Mr. Hayes. I'd spend the rest of my life making it up to you if I could. I just don't want to spend that life in *this* body. I know I don't deserve it, but I *really* need your help."

Despite everything, Hayes felt compassion for Kevin. He was an A-1 screw up, no doubt. He was possibly one of the worst students he'd ever taught. He was a bully, a braggart, and a know-it-all. Still, Hayes couldn't watch him suffer and do nothing—not that there was much he could do—assuming his story was in any way legitimate.

After a few moments, Hayes spoke. "I've got to get to school and open up the classroom. Let's hope that you . . . Sommer shows up. What I *should* do is call the police, but who would believe me?"

"I think he will. He wanted me to keep an eye on you and the others during the game. He was real serious about it. We planned that sometimes I would let him take over during the raid. I think he *wants* to be there when it happens, and that's the only way he *could* be, by logging in—unless he let me have my body back. Man, it sounds so strange saying it out loud."

"Again, let's hope. I'll confront him. Let's see what he says. I have to think about this. Stay hidden and group up with the others when they all get to the rendezvous point. After what you've said, I expect you to do your part in helping out, but if what you say is true, getting you back is the most important thing right now. Agreed?"

"Definitely. Yeah, agreed."

Kevin, in Sommer's uniformed body, slid into the woods. Hayes went around and used the latrine. He then went to join some of the others for voluntary exercises. As he performed the toe touches and knee bends, he remembered a quote by Frederick William Robertson: *"The truest definition of evil is that which represents it as something contrary to nature; evil is evil because it is unnatural; a vine which should bear olive-berries, an eye to which blue seems yellow, would be diseased; an unnatural mother, an unnatural son, an unnatural act, are the strongest terms of condemnation."*

How could this have happened? Hayes marveled at the possibilities and shivered. How could *any* of it be real? He knew from speaking with his students and hearing their reports that there tended to be an affinity between host and avatar, some sort of likeness in personality. But he definitely would have known if any of them had been "taken over" by their avatars . . . wouldn't he?

He saw evil in Kevin, if it could be called that. There was a subtle, inexplicable difference between him and the other students.

He'd seen it in a few others as well—students who had, predictably, ended up with prison sentences for violent behavior. Hayes believed in evil, that it existed in and of itself. It wasn't just a construction created through religions and social conventions to keep people in line. Perhaps evil is the absence of good, like cold is the absence of heat, but then it would still exist, just as cold exists. Or perhaps it exists in whatever is unnatural, as Robertson claimed. There was a definite affinity between Kevin Daniel and Martin Sommers, an affinity so strong . . . and unnatural . . . that it somehow gave Sommers the power to *do* the unnatural, to take over Kevin's body. To switch places. Evil for evil. But wasn't the Game itself unnatural and therefore evil? Manipulating the past, changing the present, destroying the future. These things were unequivocally unnatural.

Hayes got into his old truck and left for school at around 7:45. He had had to log out of the game at home in order to log back in at his school computer, and this made him nervous. Wicker would wake up in his own body after being absent from it for over a week. Hayes wondered if, for him, it would be an instantaneous transition from the cabin to the camp. Or would there be a period of fog in between, like sleeping? He suddenly realized that he had never really thought about Wicker's feelings on the matter. If it were happening to him—prolonged periods of blackouts, ending up in various places seemingly at random—it would probably drive him to the brink of insanity, if not over the edge. Was it fair what he was doing? What *any* of the players were doing? He wrestled with his conscience. The more he became convinced of the reality of Wicker, Gretchen, Sommer, and the rest, being actual people living in an actual past, the more diabolical all of his actions over the past few years seemed.

By a little after eight, Hayes was in his classroom logged into the Game. A few students had waited for him outside the school, and they were logging in now, preparing for the raid. Sommer wasn't one of them. Hayes decided to use his computer screen rather than don the headgear. That way he could keep an eye on things.

Richard looked around. He was in a shed, one of the "lab" buildings lining the eastern half of the camp from north to south. He was stark naked and immersed up to his neck in a large metal tank, suspended by straps which kept his feet from touching the bottom. A prisoner was shoveling snow into it from a bucket. To his right was a second water-filled tank of the same size, but steam was coming off of its surface. Wires were attached to his chest, head, and armpits. He reached around and felt something jammed up his rectum—also attached to a wire. The wires fed into a metal box sitting on a small table. Two men in SS uniforms were standing behind it, watching him. The room was dark, save for two low wattage bulbs screwed into crude light fixtures mounted to the wooden ceiling.

"Mr. Wicker, can you hear me? You seemed out of sorts for a second there. You must communicate throughout the entirety of the process," one of the men said.

Hayes knew this man from his stint at Dachau and as the "physician" in charge of the Bayrischzell camp—Dr. Sigmund Rascher, Dachau's version of the Angel of Death. A crackpot of the highest caliber, Rascher would inject victims with saltwater in an attempt to discover how to make soldiers adapt to drinking sea water. He would force prisoners to ingest a concoction including beet and apple pectin, a substance called "Polygal," which was supposed to aid in blood clotting, and then cut off their limbs or shoot them in the neck or chest—without anesthesia—to see how much of the substance was needed in the body to keep the victim from bleeding to death. And then there were the high-altitude experiments using hypobaric chambers. Apparently, he'd selected Wickers for one of his freezing experiments while Hayes was logged off.

"You were saying some crazy things, Mr. Wickers. So, how's the water?"

"Cold," Hayes replied. His avatar was starting to lose mobility.

"Yes, well, you're doing the Reich a service. You see, we need to find the best and quickest way to rewarm our Luftwaffe pilots who are shot down over Arctic territories. You're making history, Mr. Wickers. You're the first Arian we have used in our trials and therefore the best candidate to simulate a Luftwaffe pilot. You should be grateful for the recognition that you will receive when our findings are published."

"H-how long will I b-be in here?"

"Once you achieve the optimal hypothermic temperature for our study, three hours, no more."

"What temperature is that?"

"The water itself? Ten degrees centigrade. Your body temperature shouldn't go below 30 degrees. Any lower and you would probably die."

Within thirty minutes, the screen went black.

At 9:15, Mr. Hayes stood up and walked around the classroom checking on his students. There were twelve, all in headgear and wearing gloves, speaking occasionally, their hands motioning in the air or typing on keyboards. Two more came in as he made his way down the rows of desks—Matthew and Julia. Matthew spoke, "Howdy there Mr. Hayes, ready to kick some Nazi butts?" He smiled widely.

"Sure am. How close are you guys to the rendezvous site?"

Julia spoke as she found a desk and started donning her gear. "About ten clicks northwest. I'm driving the jeep and Matthew's in the Panzer."

Mathew continued as he logged in, "Yep, got me a Panzer Three. She's a bit worn, but she'll do the job. Thad and his death bus dropped off Ana, Jorge and Trace near the base to help me run it—couldn't use my usual crew o' course. Had to give 'em some quick lessons in gunnin', drivin', and loadin'. We could use one more, but I think we'll be OK."

As Matthew was speaking, Kevin walked through the door.

"Kevin! Glad you could make it," Hayes said. "Let's go into the hallway. We need to discuss your role in today's operation." Kevin allowed himself to be led into the hallway. Hayes closed the door.

"So, Kevin. How's your mom these days? What's her name, Pauline, was it?" Kevin nodded.

"She still working at the Firestone?"

Kevin merely looked down the hall.

"Cat got your tongue?" Hayes asked.

Kevin turned to Hayes and stared. "Are we playing the game today or just talking about my mother?" Hayes detected the accent he was expecting, but only slightly. He looked into Kevin's eyes.

"You're not Kevin."

The young man smiled. "You are crazy."

"Which is probably true, but you're not Kevin." Hayes put his hands on Kevin's shoulders, trying to see through the cold stare. He had to be sure. "Who are you, really?" he asked in German.

After a few moments, the boy pushed Hayes back with his left hand and then lunged forward and swung his right fist, connecting with Hayes' jaw. Hayes was knocked hard against the wall, hitting his head and then falling to his hands and knees. The boy was breathing heavily, staring at Hayes. "Jewish pig," he barked out in German and then fled down the hall. After a moment, Hayes got up with some effort and jogged to the window at the end of the hallway. He watched from the second floor as the boy ran across the street, climbing over a barbed wire fence, and vanishing into a field of thick sugar cane growing in rows across the street from the school.

After pacing a bit, trying to regain composure, Hayes re-entered the classroom and sat at his desk. The students were busy getting ready for the big event and apparently hadn't noticed that he'd even left the room. Some were already in place, waiting for the action to start, chatting either with the person next to them or to others in the Game. Hayes flipped through a textbook, keeping one eye on the screen.

After an additional hour of waiting, the screen showed a faint blur. He put on the headgear and gloves.

He was submerged to his neck in a steaming bath. The electrodes were still attached, and only Rascher watched him from behind the metal box. He could almost feel the weakness of his avatar, the nausea and stress.

"Welcome back, Herr Wicker. You did well. You lasted longer than most of my subjects thus far—a whole thirty minutes before losing consciousness—probably due to your general fitness and hearty German diet." He called in three prisoners to help get Hayes out of the tank and into his striped rags. Hayes' avatar could barely stand up and had to be dressed while sitting on a bench.

As Hayes was walked back towards the prison barracks, he noticed prisoners working to build igloos down the middle of the parade ground from blocks of snow and ice brought into the camp by flatbed. One guard at each of the five partially formed igloos was barking out instructions. *Another experiment*, Hayes thought. *They're gonna leave men in those to freeze overnight. Too bad it won't make it into Rascher's research.*

Hayes knew his avatar needed rest, but the camp was seven hours ahead, and the sun was already starting to set. He couldn't rest for very long. He'd give his avatar thirty minutes, no more. If that wasn't enough, he'd just have to rely on his team to get Savina out. She and Karen's Gretchen were working as orderlies at the nearby Mountain Lodge, a recuperation facility for German soldiers recovering from war wounds and battle fatigue, located just outside the camp on a lower ridge to the southeast, but separated by a thick growth of trees. The plan involved freeing them first. Afterwards, the camp.

As he rested his avatar, he heard his name, coming from the west side of his barrack wall. He had temporarily forgotten all about Kevin and the hell he must be going through. He got up and walked out of the barrack. He saw Kevin standing by the guard tower and made his way to the latrine. Behind the latrine, he motioned Kevin to the fence.

"So, did he show up?" Kevin asked.

"He did. I have a sore jaw to prove it."

"He hit you? That figures. What did he say?"

"Very little. Look, I think I know how to get you back." He nodded toward the SS dagger hanging from Sommer's belt. "You'll have to kill Sommer."

The young man in the crumpled SS uniform looked confused. He was scared and clearly very tired. "Mr. Hayes, I can't do that. I feel everything he feels."

"You'll have to. It's the only way to switch back. It has the added benefit of getting rid of Sommer."

Kevin pulled out the long knife and stared at it, reading its inscription. He looked back at Hayes. "How?"

Hayes tried to stay firm. "Wrists, neck, femoral artery just below the groin. Your call."

"But I'm gonna feel it!"

"Not for long. It's the only way."

"But what if I don't come back? What if I *actually die* and he stays in my body in our time?"

"That's not going to happen."

"How do you *know* that?"

"Look, I don't pretend to know how all this works, but your thoughts, your brain, what makes you you, are in the body I saw running through a field not too long ago. You're linked with him . . . somehow . . . but you're not him. His thoughts, his brain, what makes him the bastard he is, is in the body you're in now. If you kill it, he dies. End of story. You'll have to trust me on this. And you need to do it soon, before he does something to *your* body or someone else's. He's capable of anything."

Kevin looked again at the knife. Hayes nodded. "It's OK, son. You'll be back in Kansas in no time."

"Kansas?"

"Never mind."

"Can I be part of the raid first?"

"Now! Kevin."

Kevin looked again at the knife, sheathed it, and nodded. Head lowered, he walked back into the trees.

Robin Hatch, in the avatar of a communist Austrian partisan named Brenda, scanned the hill with a pair of binoculars. Through the trees she could see at least seven soldiers standing at the entrance of the Mountain Lodge. Along with the soldiers, a four-wheeled armored car, a Light Panzer, was parked out front along with several jeeps. Sure enough, they'd been tipped off, but it didn't look like they were expecting much. Robin, along with everyone else, had received a text from Karen who had received a text from Mr. Hayes that the Nazis might be ready for them. She rushed back down the hill to join Barry, the other half of her small recon group, and messaged the team.

The new plan involved the jeep, the two buses, and the tank moving in from the north in the shadow of a mountain peak called the Lacherspitze. It took more time, but this way they avoided the town and the more populated roads. Karen had already scouted with the jeep, mainly to see how much of the road was visible from the guard towers of the camp. It was an almost perfect angle of approach.

The sun had set in a cloudless sky. In the twilight, the caravan zigzagged down the east side of the Lacherspitze. The jeep and one of the buses parked off to the side of the road under some trees at the base of the steep hill leading to the north side of the camp.

The remaining bus continued southeast, followed by Matthew and his Panzer crew. Karen and three others left the jeep and stealthily marched up the hill, carrying two pairs of bolt cutters and their carbine rifles. Eighteen armed passengers left the parked bus at the base of the hill and climbed up, merging into the thick tree line along the east side of the camp. The remaining bus, followed by the tank, slowly proceeded south. It was up to Thad and Matthew to create the distraction.

Karen and Savina looked down onto the soldiers from the second story balcony on the east side of the lodge. Once Karen saw the bus round the corner of the tree line, slowly coming up the sloped road, she took Savina by the hand and smiled.

The bus rounded a growth of trees and stopped in front of the lodge, twenty meters from the front doors. Thad, dressed in an SS uniform, opened the door of the bus and stepped out. He smiled and waved at the soldiers who began walking in his direction. "I have orders to take twenty prisoners back to Dachau." He held up a blank sheet of paper.

The squad leader began walking up to him when eleven rifles fired from the open windows of the bus. Five of the men fell immediately while one ran for the armored car. Thad quickly retreated back into the bus as men in regular army uniforms began pouring out of the lodge, firing at the bus with pistols. Suddenly, the armored car exploded, throwing the man attempting to mount it against the front of the building. The tank, with Matthew in the command seat, rolled up from behind the bus and paused, shooting a second five-centimeter slug, this time into the top half of the guard tower up the hill and to the left.

In the camp, SS men were pouring out of the guard barracks, several falling to gunfire from the eastern tree line and from behind the east tower. The tank kept moving towards the gate standing just to the right of the smoking tower along the south side of the camp, its machine gunner pinning down Wehrmacht soldiers trying to take cover behind vehicles at the front of the lodge.

Karen took Savina down the stairs and past the laundering room to the back door. They fled into the tree line, meeting up with members of the team.

"Get that bus the hell outta here!" yelled Matthew from his classroom desk into his headset. "We need it to get those prisoners out!"

Someone sent Thad a text. Thad revved up the engine and began moving the bus, but the right front and rear tires had been shot, and he was having trouble with the steering and the clutch as bullets perforated the side of the bus. Nearly all the windows had been broken, and several avatars had been wounded. One was unresponsive. At least twenty German soldiers were shooting at the bus and the tank through the cattle panels and from behind the front gate as the tank made its way to the closed entrance. It stopped and fired at the west tower but missed. A few seconds later, another round was loaded, and a hole soon appeared in the upper half of the tower, shattering the windows. Prisoners watching from the doorways of various buildings in the camp, their cheering drowned out by gunfire.

The tank approached the gate and kept going. SS men scattered in its midst as the gate started to bend against the welded armor paneling.

Matthew, from his desk, coolly said, "Karen, text the guys at the north fence. That tower's comin' down." His headgear tilted in her direction. "You guys done yet?"

"Yup," Julia replied. "Nail it, Matt."

The gate was soon under the tank tracks when the tank stopped abruptly and shot a round at the tower one hundred meters to the north, nearly cutting it in half. Julia's group picked off two tower guards as they tried to escape the tilting mass, motioning prisoners toward the opening made from the detached fence panel in front of it. Striped forms converged on the north fence.

Jorge, the tank gunner, then took aim at the east tower, and after several shots, left it a pile of matchsticks and broken glass peppering nearby trees and fallen snow.

Emerging from the prisoner barrack, Hayes casually clomped through the snow, past a row of igloos, towards a windowless building resembling a shoebox at the northeast corner of the camp. Fritz was in there, and he'd be damned if he'd leave him behind. The metal door was locked, so he waved down the tank and pointed.

Hayes spoke from his desk, "Matthew, I need this door opened. Use a non-explosive round. I don't want anyone hurt behind it."

"Roger."

The turret slowly turned a bit to the left and then blew out the metal door.

Hayes walked into the building, sidestepping an SS soldier blown nearly in half. He looked around and opened a door on his left. When he entered, Dr. Rascher had a pistol leveled at his chest.

Hayes walked into the room and looked around. He pointed to his left. "Open it," Hayes calmly commanded, nodding to a sealed containment room. There were gauges on the wall by a door with a long metal lever. Rascher was standing next to a filing cabinet. In front of him was a desk piled with documents and folders. He stared at Wicker, his lips trembling. "Open it," Hayes repeated, "and you live."

Rascher, noticing that Wicker was unarmed, holstered his pistol and walked to the door and spun the wheel until it unlocked. The door opened with a hiss. A prisoner fell out onto the floor, unconscious.

"Now get out."

Rascher obeyed, leaving the room and carefully stepping over the dead guard and through the entrance. A few seconds later, Hayes heard a round fired from the tank.

"Got 'em!" Matthew called out in a whoop of joy.

Hayes went past the wreckage and looked out onto the parade grounds. Rascher lay in a mound of burgundy snow with a five-centimeter hole in his chest.

Hayes took off his headset and looked across the classroom at Matthew. "I told him he could live."

Matthew responded from inside his headset. "Oh. My bad. Gotta admit though, that was a helluva shot. Nice shootin', Jorge."

Back in the building, Hayes shuffled briefly through the desk drawer and grabbed a few items, including a rare (for the time) ballpoint pen. Hayes' avatar, still shaky from his ordeal with severe hypothermia, scooped up the emaciated man and put him over his shoulder. He barely made it to the north fence and handed him to two prisoners who put his arms around their shoulders, Fritz' bare feet dragging lines in the snow through the breach in the fence.

Julia spoke, "Mr. Hayes, Jay wants to know how Thad is doing at the bus."

"Matthew, do you have eyes on Thad?" Hayes asked.

"No, sir, but we will in just a sec," Matthew replied.

Ana, the tank's driver, began moving the tank forward, pulling hard on the right track brake, causing the Panzer to slowly rotate 180 degrees. The tank then headed back towards the south entrance. Once through, she made a hard turn to the left and drove parallel to the bus, stopping a few meters from its side door.

As Matthew, working the machine gun, pinned down the remaining Wehrmacht and SS men—about twelve still firing from behind vehicles and the entrance to the lodge—Trace, the loader, slid through a side hatch by the rounds-storage compartment on the right side, using the tank as a shield from bullet rounds, dragging his carbine behind him. He crouched his way into the bus.

"Damn." Matthew swore. "Trace reports that everyone in the bus is dead. Better tell Jay to pack 'em into the other one. It's gonna be a tight fit. Lucky they're all skinny."

At the base of the hill, Karen and the others were using flashlights to guide the last of the prisoners into the bus. Hayes was the last one down the hill. Savina saw him through the trees and ran up to him, giving him a warm embrace. Hayes looked her in the eyes; this was the last time he would ever see her. Karen and a few others would soon be taking her in the jeep to the Austrian border and *hopefully* get her into Switzerland.

"I have something silly to give you," he said, and pulled out a small booklet from the side of his waistband. On the front cover was a German soldier, its title: "Heroes of the Wehrmacht." It was a small token given to financial contributors to the war effort. On the inside front cover, he had printed his name and address:

Richard Hayes

1206 Farm Road 709

Rio Hondo, Texas

Savina looked at him questioningly. "I know, it doesn't make any sense," he said. "But if you have this, I'll feel like we'll still be somehow connected." He smiled and gave her a bear hug. He whispered, "Look me up next time you're in the States—in about 90 years."

Hayes watched as Jay drove the bus away in the dark. It was packed with prisoners, some sitting on each other's laps, some four to a seat, some sitting along the aisle. The bus would meet up with Mathew and his crew and take a westerly route directly toward the northern border of Switzerland. It would be a slow journey behind a tank, but there would be few who would stop them to ask for documents, particularly at night.

He made his way back up the hill towards the camp, his pathetic shoes getting tangled by weeds as he tried to use the starlight to find his way. This was best, he thought. He could have gone in the jeep with Savina, but the fewer the better. Besides, he had to get rid of Wicker.

On his way past the smoldering tower and through the broken fence, he looked for Rascher's body, and, finding it, pocketed the Luger. A dozen guards were lying near the smashed gate one hundred yards away to the south, a few lay scattered around the camp. He also noticed several prisoners lying in the snow, taken out by crossfire. *At least they died knowing that someone had come for them; someone had given a damn.*

Hayes shut the door to the hypobaric testing lab and sat behind the desk. He looked to the spot where the prisoner had fallen out when the chamber had been opened, hoping he had gotten him out in time.

Hayes placed the Luger under Wicker's chin. He thought about Kevin and the SS dagger. Kevin had really wanted to be a part of this, despite his original intentions. Not such a bad kid.

Still holding the gun with one hand, he took a small mirror that he had found in the desk and held it up with the other—strong jaw, chiseled features, piercing blue eyes, the ideal SS man for Hitler's Third Reich.

He thought about the Heinrich Wicker from history—at least the history before everything went to shit. He had looked him up early on—a member of the Hitler Youth from the age of 12; a member of the SS *Totenkopfverbände*—the Death's Head Units responsible for administering Nazi concentration and extermination camps— surprisingly from the age of 15. He had fought in the Battle of Demyansk, and, after being encircled by the Red Army for three months, he was wounded and shipped back to work as a guard in the camps. And when the Americans liberated the camp, he was there, had been quickly promoted to commandant after the commandant had fled. They executed him, along with fifty others, without a trial.

And yet, at one time or another, he must have done *some* good. He was someone's little boy at one time, wasn't he? Wasn't it Marcus Aurelius who said it? He wasn't sure: "I have seen the beauty of good, and the ugliness of evil, and have recognized that the wrongdoer has a nature related to my own." Considering all that had happened those years since he had brought the Game to his classroom, to his students, Hayes' "nature" wasn't so great either.

Hayes tossed the Luger and reached for a packet of stationery. When he finished the note, he folded it and put it in Wicker's lap. He then logged off.

Kevin found himself sitting by a resaca. It was early afternoon, and the mosquitos were swarming. He scratched at a few bites and stood up in the brush, suddenly realizing where he was, approximately. There was a trail leading from the bank, which he followed until he came to the side of a recognizable street. He followed it. He looked down at his clothes—his Metallica t-shirt had rips and his cargo shorts were dirty. *Damn Sommer.* He loved that shirt. Still, he smiled. He was back in his own time, back to his own crappy life, sure, but it was *his* crappy life.

Determination began to set in as he walked across the yellow bridge and looked down into the deep river. He had a thing to do, and there was nothing he wanted to do more. Every other urge was subsumed into this one thing, this one perfect, self-destroying, liberating act that would put him in more trouble than he had ever been in in his life, which was saying a lot.

At the police station, he walked up to the counter. "What can I do for you sweetheart?" asked the friendly female cop in a black uniform.

"I'm the guy who attacked Steven Berg, and I'm here to turn myself in."

Chapter 11

Minutes after retrieving the items from the storage room, Kurt Debus grabbed his radiation suit and slid into it. He carefully made a crouching run along the wall to the control panel beside the glass enclosure. The Projekt Reise Bell was humming faintly, its rotating cylinders barely emanating a pinkish glow. Behind the wide gray box, he bent his nearly two-meter form to avoid the cameras and the direct viewing of the men in the control room. He made a few adjustments and plugged one of the items into a slot in the panel, the rectangular cuboid taken from the storage room. Its digital readout lit up. He then held up the cylindrical plug and looked up at the control room windows. Some of the faces he saw—that of a guard scanning the CCTV monitors and the young man in jeans, arms akimbo, standing at the window and looking down into the wide ground floor area. He also saw the tops of the heads of the two scientists, one nearly bald, behind their computer screens.

Debus flipped a switch, causing the humming, counter-rotating cylinders to begin to slow, their aura fading. He quickly yanked a cylindrical module from the panel and replaced it with one identical in all but color, flipping the switch again. He returned to the cuboid and pressed the right arrow until its countdown read 2:00. He was about to press the black button below the arrows on the inserted device when he heard a booming voice which seemed to come from every direction: "Paul, is that you? What the hell do you think you're doing? The tests aren't needed until next week."

At the sound, Debus involuntarily left his crouch, and his eyes went to the control room windows. Both scientists were standing facing him, the eldest with arms folded. *Scheisse!* He quickly checked the panel. He had done what was needed. He gave a clear nod from within his rad suit and accentuated it with a thumbs up gesture using both hands. He clicked the back arrow on the cuboid device several times and pressed the black button. It began counting down from 00:01:30.

Pulling out the access card, Debus casually walked to the glass door, holding up one hand toward the windows, nodding. He murmured to himself, "*Warten. Warten. Nur eine Minute, Arschlöcher.*"

Once he had crawled into the Bell from under its standing platform, he closed the airtight hatch and spun the wheel until it locked. They couldn't get in, but they might shut it down. He was fairly certain that once the process was started, enough inertia existed to keep things going for at least a minute after shutdown. This should give him enough time. The humming suddenly increased in pitch as the rotating cylinders picked up speed. He visualized what was happening outside. The men would be running down the metal stairs, tripping over each other trying to shut it off, maybe even banging on the glass, as if he could hear anything above the gut-shaking whine sending razor blades into his eardrums.

＊＊＊

SOUTH TEXAS, NOVEMBER 2035

At the soda machine in the lobby, the young man pulled out a few coins and shoved them into the slot. He then made his selection. After a second or two, a line of fat, white cylinders began to spin behind a scratched piece of clear plastic. Five seconds later the tumbling cylinders stopped and

- G Ø 1 . Ø Ø

was displayed across the cylinders in black lettering. A red and white can of soda rolled out into a small tray. He grabbed it and returned to his seat.

He sat in the dim lobby, if it could be called that, with its four plastic chairs, a fake plant sitting on a small fold-out table, and reception window perpetually closed. Long neon bulbs, their fixtures exposed just under the sagging ceiling tiles, represented the only light brought into the room. Only one of the four bulbs was actually working.

His heart was racing. He was angry. The caffeine wouldn't be much help to him in that regard, but he didn't care. He sat and meditated, staring at but not really seeing the fake fern on the table in front of him. Karen could be such a bitch. *"Well, I deserve it,"* he mumbled to himself. *Six months in lockup was probably less than he deserved. The chaplain had told him he had already been forgiven and now needed to forgive himself, quit beating himself up. He doubted that would ever happen.*

Kevin's train of thought was broken when the remaining bulb went dead. After a few seconds, however, he could hear a generator kick in from somewhere below the floor. It vibrated his seat just slightly. The bulb came back on, though dimmer than before.

SPRING, 2034

Only four weeks were left in the spring semester. Farash, interminably depressed, had fitfully slept through much of the weekend, unfazed by the likelihood that Krafft, his virtual counterpart, would be screaming all sorts of outrageous claims during the interval. In the Game, for days, Krafft had only received food in his cell. No letters. No visits from the Reichsminister. In a sense, Farash was stuck there, sharing a cell with Krafft. He had sent many letters addressed to the Reichsminister and one even to the Fuhrer himself. He received no responses.

Even before his imprisonment, Farash had wondered at the peaceful state of Berlin. There were supposed to be hundreds of bomb attacks on Berlin between 1940 and 1945. Yet though some bombing had occurred over the preceding years, Berlin remained completely intact. Farash, languishing in his cell, had started to rely on Berlin's destruction as a possible means of getting free of the cellar. It wasn't happening as the chirping birds outside his window daily testified.

Mr. Farash entered his classroom. He hadn't prepared lesson plans for the week, so he'd try to wing it with material from last year. He walked to where his filing cabinet was supposed to be and stopped. His room had been completely cleaned out; the floors were polished, and the walls were covered with new paint. He walked back into the hallway, thinking his cabinets and other missing materials might be stacked up someplace. Nothing.

He descended the main stairs into the cafeteria. It was still early enough that only a few dozen of the student body had yet been dropped off by parents and buses. He watched as students retrieved their breakfast plates, chatting in groups at the heavy fold-out tables. Then, as he was about to head over to the teachers' lounge for a cup of coffee, he noticed the redundancies. Had the District instituted a campaign for the wearing of uniforms? Certainly, *he* had not been informed. And yet there they were. The cafeteria began filling with students wearing khaki pants or knee-length shorts, and brown long-sleeved shirts. Their shoes looked like hiking boots. Even the girls wore them, their uniforms identical to those of the males though cut shapelier.

It was first period. Once the bell rang, all became attentive and completely silent, looking up at their instructor. This startled Farash more than anything he had seen thus far. "I hope everyone had a nice and restful weekend." He paused and looked around the room. He recognized most of the students, but not all. Had some of their schedules been changed? He decided to ignore the fact for now.

He continued, "But what I would really like to know is how did you all find out about the new policy on uniforms? I didn't see any notices going out." The students remained silent. A few in the front row looked questioningly at the teacher and at each other. "Your uniforms. Certainly, you didn't all go out and join the Boy and Girl Scouts over the break?" He grinned but received no like response.

"The what?" a boy in the second row asked almost in a whisper. There was a brief murmur among the students. A blond, female student from the back row stood up. "Sir. Our uniforms haven't changed since last year . . ." Her words trailed off. The student sat back down out of what seemed like embarrassment.

Farash was perplexed. The students seemed more so.

"One moment, please." Farash went out into the hall. From the hall, looking into another classroom, he viewed through the narrow window a male teacher speaking to his class. He was tall, young, dressed in a dark suit, white shirt, black tie. He looked down at his comparatively woeful combination of button-up shirt, khaki pants and black sneakers.

When he returned to his classroom, his students fell completely silent again. Farash decided to wait until lunch to ask about changes in dress-code policies implemented, apparently, over the weekend. Most students took extensive notes as he began to lecture on supply and demand, bringing up terms from the previous week. By near the end of the period, he had gotten completely off track and was discussing the base-12 system of the Babylonians, emphasizing its influence even today, with our 12 months in a calendar year and 12-hour clock. That was until he glanced at the 24-hour clock above the whiteboard at the back of the room.

"Aren't there 24 hours in a day?" one boy in a front corner seat suggested as he slowly raised his hand." "The sub obviously refers to the clocks from the old days," came the voice of a small girl in the row behind. At that moment, the classroom door opened. A large, ruddy-faced woman came in with an apologetic look, closing the door behind her, dealing fitfully with the several handbags she was carrying. "*Es tut mir leid*. My tire was low, but I thought nothing of it until . . . oh, I almost ran off the road. A kind field laborer helped me with the tire. It was so frustrating trying to speak with the man." She tiptoed up to Farash and stopped, still fiddling with a huge bag which contained several paperback books and a newspaper. She looked up at his face with a startled hush.

Farash looked at her, annoyed. "Do I have a meeting that I need to attend?"

"Am I in the right room? Is this E2005?" she asked.

"Yes, it is," he responded. The students giggled.

"I thought you needed a substitute. You *are* Herr Schreiber?"

"No ma'am. I do not need a substitute and I am not Herr Schreiber. Are you lost?"

"Are *you* a substitute then?" she asked in a high-pitched tone.

"No."

"There must have been a room change. Herr Schreiber needed a substitute for today with his wife giving birth and all. That's why I'm here. Are you sure this is E2003?"

Farash turned and looked at the students and then at the woman. He began to panic. "This is Herr Schreiber's room, you say?" he asked.

"According to the Assistant Principal's secretary."

"Actually . . ." Farash was flustered. He looked around for his satchel. "Actually, I was asked to fill in until you got here. And now that you are here, I will be going."

The large, ruddy-faced woman smiled and nodded, seemingly less confused. Farash picked up his bag and left.

Farash thought to look into Hayes' classroom next door, not having seen the man all morning. Someone else was teaching his class. The computers had been removed. It was a normal classroom, desks in rows, uncluttered, floors well-waxed. Twelve or so students sat in the first three rows while a woman wearing a white blouse and a black skirt walked amongst them and spoke. Students perused the handout she had handed them.

"Can I help you, sir?" a tall, attractive middle-aged woman asked, smiling, walking towards Farash in the hallway, towering over him. The woman wore a black dress suit resembling a uniform. Farash asked her about Richard Hayes. The woman hesitantly replied that Mr. Hayes had taken the week off, due to an illness. The assistant principal had taken Farash for a substitute teacher and watched him doubtfully as he made his way down the stairs. Farash stumbled to the parking lot looking for his subcompact and then remembered his having walked to school that day.

Once home, he mounted the stairs to the apartment above a derelict shop, mulling over the story he would tell Amala, about the students, the smaller numbers, the new dress code, why he was home so early. When he got to the door, his key wouldn't work. He tried the handle and, thankfully, it was unlocked.

In the living room of their two-bedroom apartment, everything looked fairly normal. Still, there was a television—an old one Farash didn't recognize. A pair of bicycles he didn't recognize sat leaning against the wall behind the old sofa. Having woken up late that morning, on the bed in the spare bedroom, he had rushed out without noticing any of this. He glanced into their small kitchen. There was a hot-plate on a flimsy fold-out table where a four-burner stove should have sat crusted with char from countless customary Indian meals.

He walked into their bedroom. Amala was sleeping on a full-sized bed, not a queen-sized like he was sure they had owned. She was somewhat smaller, had certainly lost a few kilos. Timidly, he closed the door and walked back into the living room, dropping into the old, familiar couch, confused, shaking, wishing his character wasn't wasting away in a cell under Gestapo Headquarters. Farash got up and went to his corner in the spare bedroom, stopping short. It was completely empty save for a bed and a few cardboard boxes.

Farash had been to Hayes' house a few times to play cards with several other instructors. Farash was bad at cards and didn't attend further games after some heavy losses made him rethink Texas Hold-'em as a pastime. After a brief but unnerving rest on the sofa, Farash decided to drive to Richard's house. As he stood up, his wife of 12 years walked sleepily from the bedroom.

"Amala!" He cried. A surge of positive emotion swept through him. She looked at him curiously.

"What's wrong?"

"I am so sorry. So, so sorry."

"For what?"

"For . . . for not giving you the attention you deserve all these many months. Well, it's done. You deserve better and I'm going to give it to you now. My . . . research is done. No more computers. I am back for good, my sweet, sweet, beautiful Amala."

She looked at him quizzically for a second time and then walked into the small kitchen to pour some hot tea, shaking her head. "Would you like some tea, my husband?" she asked.

"What happened to the oven? And when did we get that TV?"

"Oven? I'm not sure what you mean, Farhat. The TV still works, doesn't it?"

"Yes, I'm sure it does. Never mind."

She handed him a small cup of dark, steaming tea. He took it and a saucer and sat at the small bar separating the kitchen from the tiny living room. He sipped the tea and flipped through a small stack of mail. Nothing important, just some insurance papers and a brochure ad for a department store he'd never heard of called "Wohl's."

He hated junk mail, especially when the address reflected such a lack of regard for the recipient that the sender hadn't even bothered to double-check the spelling of the recipient's name. They had spelled her name "Amaia Farash."

He ripped open the next piece of mail, one from the Renter's Association, whatever that was. There was a short, handwritten letter inside.

Dear Amaia,

We had intended on having the farewell party for Juan and Esmer on Friday. But it will have to be postponed until Saturday. The time hasn't changed. We'd love to see Farhat as well if he isn't too busy with his lawn service on that day.

Tschüss!

Lupita

"Amala . . ."

"Why do you call me that? It's like you have a lisp today my husband."

"What should I call you?"

"What you've always called me—Amaia."

"Did you change your name?"

"What has gotten into you today?"

Farhat stared at the letters and then at his wife. His eyes were bulging with confusion. "I have to go. I will be back by tonight. Then we will go out, ok?"

"That's fine but..."

"We have a lot to talk about." He no longer wanted to mention the incident at school. He had much to iron out before such a conversation could take place.

"But your tea..."

Farash was out the door and down the narrow staircase before she could finish her sentence. He pushed open the old door to the flats and ran into the bright sunlight, almost hitting an old man on a three-wheeled bicycle sporting an orange flag and a large, empty basket in front of the handlebars. Farash reached in his pocket for his keys. There were no keys and he saw no car.

He fled back up the stairs, taking them two at a time. He opened the front door and yelled, "Where's the car?"

Amala looked at him from the kitchen. "What car?"

"What car?" *Could it be possible that we don't even have a car?* "The car... I kept seeing... going up and down the street yesterday. I thought I told you about it. Ugh, sorry. You're right, I'm not myself today." He grabbed the bigger of the two bicycles from behind the sofa and made his way to the open front door. "I'm going to a colleague's house. I'll be back this afternoon. Let's go out! I'm thinking seafood. The Galley?"

"Sure..."

Farhat recalled the way to Richard's cabin as he rode down the main street of the little town. It was maybe eight miles away. He noticed little going on around him as he rode, gradually taking to the shoulder when there was one.

Crossing the yellow bridge and walking his bike to the other side of the two-lane street, Farash remembered a short cut over a gravel road which would probably cut the time to Richard's cabin by a third. The wheels of the bicycle were fat and knobby enough to take the punishment of the caliche, so he decided on the shortcut and did a quick U-turn. Passing some dilapidated buildings which had, only yesterday, been operational stores, he made a left turn and then gradually another left and a quick right. He followed the dirt road some distance until he came to a cattle gate.

It had only been a year since he had been to Richard's little piece of land. All had been cactus and weeds with a few crooked mesquite trees littering the fields and a halo of pepper trees surrounding the small dwelling. Now, beyond the gate to his far left, he saw two rows of makeshift dwellings, most of which looked like sheds practically sitting one on top of the other. Most had tin corrugated roofs held up by walls of gray cinder block. Tarps and thick blankets covered some of the openings. Tiny trails amongst the shacks were beaten down earth, broken toys and other useless refuse littering the edges. Dogs barked and half-naked children played along a narrow dirt road formed between the two rows of dwellings. To the right, almost covered with weeds and brush, a small, cubicle A-frame cabin sat dug in next to a long ditch of stagnant water shaded over with scrubby trees.

It was about midday when Farhat pushed past the half-open gate and walked the bicycle along the groove of some tracks. As he reached the part of the trail running parallel to the wide ditch, the fetid stench of human waste wafted up with a brush of warm air into his face from the makeshift hills of refuse along its other side. The repulsive odor caused Farash to veer away from its source and into the left track through the weeds without noticing that he had done so.

Approaching the cabin, he threw the bicycle into a patch of weeds and knocked quickly at the door. There was no response. He tried again, calling "Richard . . . Richard Hayes." Still, there was no response or sound of movement. A dog barked from within, echoing size and ferocity.

He tried the door quickly in effort to forgo the need to take another breath in the fetid breeze. It was locked, but there was a large pet door he could just squeeze through. He was a thin man, and, so long as his shoulders would fit, the rest of him would follow. He crawled through and brought his feet in last, letting the flap close behind him.

He looked up and into the eyes of a large black dog, a Rottweiler. The dog was growling a few feet from his face. "Fräulein!" came a welcome voice through a rough cough. The dog sat down on the linoleum floor, but the stare and the growling continued. "Fräulein! *Kommst du hier*!" The dog turned and walked toward the couch from whence the voice had come.

With breathless relief, Farash got to his feet. He brushed grit off his knees and peered into the cabin. He couldn't see much in the darkness and didn't know where the voice had come from. He looked closer as his eyes adjusted. "Thank God! I thought I was a dead man! How have you been, Richard?"

There was a pause. "I'm still here. Farash?"

Farash walked into the open square room. Despite the dust, the cabin was quite uncluttered, not from the tidiness of its inhabitant, but rather from having an inhabitant who didn't seem to need much. He could barely see the man sitting against the far corner of a couch. He was staring at the blank screen of a small, old television propped up on a wooden crate. His face had a week's worth of beard growth, at least.

"Have you decided to quit the profession?"

"The profession?"

"Teaching."

"Oh. I suppose so." Hayes paused, then said, "Yeah, I'm not going back."

Farash was silent. He indulged in the thought of never having to go back, though, as of today, he couldn't even if he wanted to. He looked at Hayes sympathetically. "What do you plan to do?"

"Well, right now I'm sitting here staring at a television set that doesn't belong to me. Someone took my TV and left me this one, I guess to make up for it. I've been here for I don't know how long trying to figure out why anyone would do that. I mean, if you're such a jerk to steal a guy's flatscreen, why would you care enough to replace it?"

Farash thought of the old TV now sitting in his own apartment. "Richard, what's my name?"

"Your name."

"Yes, what is my full name?"

"Well, as far as I know, it's Farhat Farash, unless you've changed it."

"What is my wife's name?"

"Um." He had to think for a second, feeling somewhat embarrassed. "Give me a second. I know this one. . . Amaia . . . no, Amala."

"Is it Amala with an 'L' or Amaia with an 'I'?"

"I'm pretty sure it's Amala, with an L." Hayes looked away from the old television set and to his former colleague now sitting at the end of the couch. "Did I pass?"

"Yes. Thank you. Thank you. *Thank you*, my friend!" Farash was beaming though he looked exhausted.

"For what? Reminding you of your wife's name?"

"For reminding me that I'm not an insane man."

"Well, let's not jump to conclusions . . ." Hayes smiled vaguely. "Want a beer?"

"No, thank you. Have you been playing the Game?"

Hayes was silent for a while. "By 'game,' I assume you mean Valkyrie?"

"Yes, if that's what you call it. I didn't know it even had a title. The kids just called it 'The Game.'"

"I was playing it until recently."

Farash paused. "Richard, I have a confession to make. I used one of your computers to play it. I did so for many months. I even took one home."

Hayes looked at him. "Well. That solves the mystery of the missing computer. I figured it was one of the tech guys who forgot to bring it back after making a repair. I know you play the game; I saw you once in my classroom. It's not a big deal. Nothing's a big deal, really, if you think about it." Hayes scratched his bald spot, frowning. He hadn't meant to get philosophical. "What is your character?"

"A Swiss Astrologer named Krafft," Farash replied.

"Hmm. Sounds innocuous enough."

"What is yours? If you don't mind my asking."

Richard stared off into the distance. He didn't appear to have heard the question. After a while, "I was an SS guard at Dachau. I met a girl." He looked down and slowly shook his head. "God, I miss her."

Farhat was silent. He had never considered a romantic encounter for himself in the game. He looked around the room again. The dog was lying by the wall next to the television, his head propped against the milk crate upon which the TV was sitting. No one spoke for a while.

Farash stood up and looked around the room and saw the computer in a corner area of the cabin. "May I use your computer? he asked.

"Go right ahead."

"Who do you think took your things?" Farash asked as he made his way to the table. The computer looked like an antique. He doubted it would be of much use and soon returned to the couch.

"I have no clue. They didn't even leave traces in the dust around the things they took. The stuff just disappeared. Gone." He thought for a moment. "They also left me this dog."

"That's not Fräulein?"

"No."

"You called this dog 'Fräulein.'"

"She seems to answer to it. Takes to me really well, for some reason. I just woke up this morning, and I had a new dog—scared the shit out of me at first. Some stuff missing, no flat-screen, and a god-awful stench when I opened the windows. Do you smell it?"

"So, you were last logged on to . . . Valkyrie . . . a few days ago?"

"Just a few days. I'm not really sure. I've been sleeping a lot. There were some weeks when I didn't sleep at all, so I guess now I'm paying for it." Hayes thought as he looked down at his filthy t-shirt. "It's over though."

"What?"

"The Game. For me anyway. But don't ask. I'd rather not talk about it."

"Richard, I want you to see something."

Richard Hayes looked at him questioningly as Farash stood up and held out his dark hand. "I think I can get up on my own. Hell, I'm not *that* far gone." Farash continued to hold out his hand, and Richard took the man's arm by the wrist and allowed himself to be pulled up heavily from the couch. "Thanks."

They walked around the old television set and into the corner area. To the right was a window covered by two layers of aluminum foil taped to the glass. A set of horizontal blinds hid most of the foil. Farash lifted the blinds and ripped off a section of the aluminum sheets, revealing the scrub in front of the cabin, the darkly foliated drainage ditch on the left, and the property gate in the distance. Not much light poured in, due to the overhanging bowers. There was another window on the other side of the corner. Farash lifted the blinds and removed some of the foil from this window as well, motioning for Hayes to look through the window. Hayes saw a line of shacks through the weeds. Gray smoke rose from some of the low shanties. A baby was crying.

"Holy shit! That's my land!" Hayes was starting to look much more awake. Farash caught the acrid smell of the man who apparently hadn't bathed in some time and backed away a few inches. "*That* wasn't there yesterday," Richard said.

"Richard, do you remember any discussion at school about a change in dress code? Anything about switching to uniforms?"

Hayes was still overwhelmed by the changes that had taken place, seemingly overnight, on his once untamed land. He stared at corrugated roofs and walls formed by wooden pallets covered with colorful Mexican blankets. "I. Um, no. We tried it several years back. The kids wouldn't have it. Parents complained."

"The kids at the school were in uniforms today, Richard. They don't seem to mind. They act like they've always had uniforms."

"What? Oh. Well, who the hell cares? Look at my land!" He continued peering through the window.

"Richard, my friend, It's my fault."

Hayes turned. "You invited those people here?"

"I think I've screwed up far more than that."

Hayes narrowed his eyes as Farash closed both sets of blinds. He then turned and sat on the floor, leaning back against the wall beneath one of the windows. Farash remained standing, silent, trying to put words together in his mind. Finally, Richard got up and walked to the refrigerator and found a liter of water. There was nothing else inside the warm and dark appliance. He returned to his seat beneath the window and gulped down some of the tepid liquid. Farash sat on the wooden chair by the desk, rubbing his hands nervously.

"What the hell is going on, Farash?"

Without hesitation Farash replied, "The Game. It's real. I'm absolutely sure of it now."

Hayes looked at him for a moment and then nodded. "I know. I've known it for some time now. But these people living on my land has nothing to do with the Game."

"It has *everything* to do with it. There's been another time shift. This one is *big*, but I haven't had a chance to check on the new history. I can't find a computer anywhere. I was hoping to use yours."

Richard continued to reflect. "Well, it's over for me. It ended and . . ." He looked over at the computer. "That's not my computer. What a piece of crap. Well *that* makes sense, somehow."

Farash turned and stared hard at Richard, his voice now quite shaken and loud. "Richard, *I* changed history! *I fucked up the world*!"

Both were silent. Both knew with absolute certainty that what Farash was saying about history being changed, yet again, was completely correct. It was another jump. Still, it wasn't likely that Farhat Farash alone was responsible.

"Whatever it is you did, or others maybe, since you don't necessarily know it was *you* who changed history . . . anyway, it's permanent, if things are as bad as you say." Richard got up from the floor. His legs were starting to cramp.

Farash gave Richard a look of panic, even mania. "It *was* me though. I was a part of Hitler's inner circle, sort of." Farash then gave Hayes a brief summary of the part he had played in changing Hitler's mind, of a Barbarossa much delayed, of the full-on assault of Moscow after Hitler's total conquest of Europe. Richard started to ask for more specifics, but Farash was sobbing and had difficulty speaking, so he held off.

Richard hung his head, scratching at his bony legs. He shook his head for a long time. "She was real. I *knew* she was real." He hesitated, then spoke. "I killed someone, Farash."

Farash nodded. They were all real. The idea of harming computer-generated players, changing a merely virtual world, had made it easy to do what they did. But there had never been computer-generated players. That was clear now.

"Let's see if this thing works," Hayes said, taking a seat at the old computer. He logged into the machine. *Same password, that's some relief.* He then typed in the Valkyrie URL. It took minutes to load up the login screen. "Well, Valkyrie still exists," he looked at Farash, "but I doubt this bandwidth can handle it."

"Try the search bar."

Hayes typed. Up came "Reichstaat Information Services." He sighed. "No Google. This is bad." He tried various search terms and found what they were looking for.

Essentially, in 1952, the Axis Powers, involving a host of National Socialist nations—with Heinrich Himmler acting as Supreme Commander—attacked the United States' Eastern Seaboard. Though the US had some nuclear weapons at their disposal, it was unanimously decided between the President and the Joint Chiefs that their use would have no significant effect on the outcome, so they were simply dismantled and hidden. The takeover was quick and decisive, and all US territory extending west to the Rocky Mountains fell under Axis hegemony. What was left of a Free America was considered not worth the effort to subdue. Canada and Mexico became "Neutral Powers." The NSSA, the National Socialist States of America, had been formed.

"It doesn't make sense," Hayes said.

"Which part," Farash threw in with some irony.

"They wouldn't have stopped at the Rocky Mountains. They have everything, including China, Japan, Southeast Asia. Why would they stop?" Hayes paused. "Even if they didn't want to expend the effort to forge ahead through the mountains, the Axis could have easily taken California from the Pacific."

"Then you're thinking what I'm thinking."

"I believe so."

"We're in for another shift."

After a while, the man from (what might still be) India stood up and left into the late afternoon without another word. Richard, still trying to put all the pieces together, turned again to look out the window in the direction of the murky water as the Rottweiler snored peacefully by the milk crate.

Chapter 12

North America, 2031

The German scientist puked into his face shield. The agonizing screech had brought him to his knees, his hands pushing hard at the sides of his hood in a failed attempt to turn off the tumultuous dissonance. It had been too much; he had allowed the massive beast too much power; he was lucky to be alive, impossibly conscious. After what seemed like an eternity, the humming began to subside. He waited, expecting a shift or perhaps a bump against his knees and feet, indicating an event, the reentry after a quantum perturbation.

He fought the urge to just open the hatch and rush out as the whining lowered in pitch and volume. However, he waited until there was absolute silence, aside from the pulsing of his heart throbbing with a directionless echo. He was vaguely aware of sharp pains all over his body, needle pricks stabbing at his skin and internal organs. As the tall scientist painfully slid from the hatch and wriggled into a prone position beneath the platform, he was blinded by three dancing lights coming from one general direction.

Debus held up one hand to ward off the lights, pulling himself along the concrete floor until he was stopped by . . . glass. Five figures moved off to Debus' right, three holding flashlights. One opened the door for him, the others lining up well behind the first. The glass door closed behind him once he had crawled through. One member of the group approached gingerly, waving a clicking device from a few meters away. "He's hot. Hey buddy, you need to get out of that rad suit pretty quick."

Debus complied while still lying on the floor, quickly ripping off the fetid hood before painfully removing the rest. One member ran off and came back with a shovel, using it to carefully drag the parts of the suit well away from Debus, and returning. The man with the Geiger counter approached more closely. "Still hot—just don't get too close to him. Man, he's in bad shape." Indeed, bleeding pustules had formed over most of his body; his boxer shorts and t-shirt were spotted with dark patches.

"Let's get a clean suit on him. That should protect the rest of us," an older man suggested. A suit was found and dropped next to him. "Put it on." Debus attempted to comply, barely able to pull on the heavy coveralls before blacking out.

Kurt Debus awoke wearing radiation gear but without a hood. He was seated in a wheeled office chair, his wrists cuffed behind him. Seven men and one woman stood in a half circle around him, whispering and pointing, all staring in disbelief. He recognized the control room. His head lolled on his shoulders as his eyes opened. His face was a bright red, and pinpricks of blood stood out from his facial pores. "He's back." "That didn't take long." "Who the fuck is he?" "Hey man, who the hell are you? How did you get in here?"

Debus coughed, trying to clear his throat. His body was a fiery hell. He managed a whisper, "Mein name ist Kurt Debus. I came through die Bell."

"He's German," said the female soldier. "Can't be," replied another soldier. "The Germans don't know anything about this." "Yeah, well listen to his voice. Are . . . you . . . German?" the woman asked slowly, as if speaking to a child.

"Yes."

The older man wearing a lab coat broke in. "You say you came *through* the Bell?"

"Yes."

"From where?"

"*Deutschland* . . . Germany. 1943."

They all stood in shocked silence. Finally, one of the four soldiers spoke, "Well, that would explain the outdated rad gear." After a few moments, he continued, "So you're a time traveler." He didn't seem convinced. "So *why* are you here?

Debus remained silent.

"Well," the younger scientist began, "It's not too far-fetched. We know that that was the original Nazi plan, wasn't it? Project Rise or something. I gotta go wake up Pauly. He's missing out." The man walked around Debus and left through the gray door. The German let his head tilt back. "Morphine," he whispered.

"The man wants morphine. I'll go get him some," said one of the soldiers. "Just don't give it to him until he's answered our questions," replied the older scientist. The soldier left.

"This is nuts," snorted the older man.

"Amazing is what it is," replied the man in jeans, arms folded. "The damn thing transports matter, people even! It actually works! And we were just using it to . . ."

"That's classified information, son, and this guy isn't cleared," roared the sergeant, his hand secured to his holstered pistol. The young man in jeans appeared to be thinking. "Well, he ain't got much time left. No reason not to tell him. He's probably curious. Besides, if he does make it, he won't be holding any press conferences."

Debus nodded vigorously. He *was* curious, despite feeling that his entrails were being cooked from the inside.

The older scientist spoke. "I'm the lead in this operation, and it's my decision." He looked Debus up and down for a moment.

"Hell, show him what we've got, Stamitz. Maybe he's got some ideas."

Stamitz, the young man in jeans, walked around to the back of Debus' chair and pushed him up to a computer screen. Stamitz sat in the chair next to him. He pulled up a login screen and typed.

"It's an interface. We call it Valkyrie. It uses modulated waves of space time harnessed from the Bell to allow us to interact with the past. You came here from the past, I'd assume to make some changes. Well, we're already doing that!"

At that moment, the gray door opened and the young man in the lab coat walked slowly to stand behind Debus' chair. All eyes were fixed on the screen—except his. Suddenly, he spun the chair around and stared fixedly at Debus' sanguineous face. "You sonofabitch!" he screamed as he planted his right fist into the German's brittle skull.

SOUTH TEXAS, NOVEMBER 2035

"Mr. Hayes, is everything okay?" The nurse put down the clipboard and retrieved a water bottle and a straw from a pocket of her white scrubs, dropping the straw into the bottle. She gently pulled open the cardboard flap and inserted the bottle. She seemed genuinely concerned. She looked at Selma, still smiling. "He may need to be alone right now. He's not used to having so many visitors."

The nurse retrieved the bottle, closed the flap, and left the room.

After a few moments, the old woman shuffled up to the flap, opened it, and looked into the empty eyes, attempting to make contact. They met, for a few seconds, and then his eyes fell again.

The old woman whispered into the box. "Mr. Hayes. Richard." She said it in German: "I have come to thank you, but I must go now. I am Savina's daughter."

"ICH BIN DER GUTE ARZT." He repeated it in his mind. "I am the good doctor." He brushed some lint from his military cap with a gloved hand, polished the metal insignia with his left sleeve, and positioned the black cap onto his head. He heard cheering meant for him alone. He had succeeded. *"Ich will.* I *will* wipe this plague from Germany. From Europe. From America! I will wipe it from humanity. I am the healer. *Ich bin Übermensch!"*

As Farash looked out from his balcony, the street was peopled mostly with brown-shirted students in khaki shorts making their way to school, mostly in pairs or threes. Flags stood dead of wind above the sidewalks of vacant shops. They were predominantly striped white and red. But in the upper left corner, a square blue field sported a design of white stars forming four bent arms, each pointing in a diagonal direction.

He was standing above a burgeoned populace come to greet him. It was Munich, 1945. *"Meine guten Deutschen!"* My good Germans! The crowd noise began to surge into a roar. They saluted in 45-degree angles, palms down, in his direction. Red flags whipped loudly above the crowds in the heavy breeze, bringing mist to his eyes. He had finally been named the Leader of the world's greatest power. He would make everything right.

Through the crowd noise, a gunshot could be heard. The slug penetrated the new Fuhrer's neck. Blood poured quickly into the neckline around his white shirt. He stumbled backwards from the balcony, half-supported by SS comrades hovering over him with immediate concern, but already his brain had begun entering the blind, oxygen-deprived purgatory of graying death.

He made his way to the bedroom he shared with his wife, Amaia. He leaned against the wall, leaving a smear of blood on his way to the closet. His comrades were there to assist but could do nothing.

"*Mein Führer!*" they exclaimed as their hands held him, one holding palms against the entry and exit wounds made by the bullet that had pierced through the pale, white neck of Karl Ernst Krafft.

The ice pick fell from his hand into a small pile of shoes. Hanging work clothes and button-up shirts fell in folds around him as his body dipped into the gentle, swathing darkness of the closet.

The day after Farash had visited the cabin, Richard Hayes took a walk through the early morning dew. He had no real hope regarding what his place might be in this new . . . reality.

He walked through the slum of poor, discarded shreds of humanity who returned his glances with kind smiles. They seemed to know him, and what they knew had been positive. That morning, he was dressed no less shabbily than they were. He wasn't wearing shoes either. He had forgotten to put any on. His wispy hair was unkempt; his graying beard hid half of his face. The food they made smelled good, though bereft of any scent of meat. Behind the two rows of makeshift homes lay vegetable gardens stretching back to the fence line, where scraggly trees had once stood.

Richard Hayes looked 70. His eyes were hanging bags of red crust. He sat on a bench, not far from the yellow bridge, as the wind blew through the park against the back of his hairy neck. He had not much remembered the walk getting here, but he certainly remembered the images boring into his mind during that walk. Most were of Savina, some of the woman he'd killed at the parade ground.

He had walked to the main street of the little town. He had watched the flags in wonder; they had barely moved in the cold, gray morning sky. Billows of smoke poured into the dark clouds from distant South Texas fields while black wisps of ash floated down into the streets. Sugarcane fields were burning to make room for the next planting.

On his walk, he saw bicyclists, some students, and a few cars. Hayes had come to the bridge, crossed it, and veered left through a passage in the broken links of a chained fence behind an important-looking white building, probably still a city hall. The fence had been overgrown with weeds. The park constructed parallel to the deep river was deserted. He sat at the end of a park bench, viewing the scrubby foliage along the river. No boats went by.

After a while, a light-skinned woman wearing a purple dress and a white hat waddled up and sat at the opposite end of the bench. Two young boys, also pale, ran up and down some slides while a young girl sat spinning in a swing, dragging her feet as the chains untwisted themselves above her, looking down at her shoes.

After some moments, the woman looked toward Hayes but not quite at him. "You know, that town (she pointed south) was named after the first resident to be born there." Hayes was unresponsive but listened. She continued despite his silence. "His first name was San Benito. That was the name of the boy and so it became the name of the town."

"Didn't know that," Hayes responded noncommittally. He suddenly realized that they were both speaking in German, she with a heavy Russian accent. She continued, "Most people don't. They think it was named after a famous priest." She paused thoughtfully. "Or someone who used to do miracles."

Hayes balanced his bare feet on the top guard rail, keeping himself steady with his right hand clutching a girder. He looked down into the water some distance below. He didn't like swimming, which was OK since he wouldn't be getting wet. Tied to a crossbar above his head was one end of a blue nylon rope, a castoff amongst the heaps of garbage found during the hours of walking along the shore of the river. The other end was around his neck. He had forgotten how to make a noose, but he'd figured that several square knots should do it.

It was high noon, and the sun was intense. He'd always hated the heat, the humidity of this place. And there wasn't much in the way of picturesque landscape to speak of. *Why had I chosen to live here? Of all the places I could have ended up—with towering mountains and broad trees . . .* He thought of Bavaria, the ideal place to retire. Of course, now . . . was there anywhere left without a *regime* in place? He could look at textbooks, ask people, but they'd all be full of lies, beaten down by propaganda. He'd seen the flags lining the main street. The good ol' Stars and Stripes. The stripes were the same. The stars formed a swastika. This wasn't America anymore.

His head hit concrete before the rope snapped on his way down.

A few years after the German-led European assault came across the Atlantic in 1952, the Cino-Japanese coalition attacked from the Pacific and conquered what was left of a free America. Whole cities were leveled, and millions died, particularly in California. The Americans had never discovered the plans for the Nazi Bell, and the Germans discontinued the program in the mid-1940s, once all of Europe had fallen under the Reichsstaat. Thus, the Valkyrie Project never existed.

There was an angry flash lasting for less than one millionth of a nanosecond as the past finally caught up with the present—the Universe allows no contradictions, only misinterpretations. The paradox in spacetime had triggered a reset back to the first perturbation.

Hayes heard the beep, despite the hard blowing of the huge window unit. He stared hard at the screen. Again, the scrolling froze on one suffix: ".allein," at the top of the endless column of possible letter combinations. Only slightly curious about what was probably a glitch, some for-next loop ending sooner than it was meant to, he started to open another window on the screen in order to type the suffix into another gray box which would allow all addresses actively using the suffix on the Web to appear in a separate column. This would take hours as every possible web address would have to be checked for an active response during the subroutine.

He thought about running it. It wasn't just that it was a waste of his time. Something was wrong, something very odd about what he was doing, but he couldn't pinpoint what was gnawing at the back of his mind. He closed the program and decided to take a walk.

On his return to the cabin, Hayes descended to a path next to the still water and halted, watching minnows swim near the hard, clay-dry edge of the water. Several grackles squawked from the trees above, then louder, as the German shepherd approached a black bird on the little trail. It was beautiful in its bluish blackness, Hayes reflected. It was also enormous, for a grackle, appearing more like a small raven or a large crow. The sad thing attempted to flap a wing that would never again touch sky or cloud. Fräulein sniffed at it and then backed away, watching attentively the bird's failed attempt at flight.

He had not heard the grackles until he noticed Fräulein looking toward him and then up into the trees at five or six black shapes, squawking as if for a fallen comrade. Fräulein, receiving no sign from her companion whether or not to approach the broken bird, apparently decided that the easy kill wasn't worth the noise and simply trotted on ahead past the thing. Hayes pitied the poor creature and knelt down. "Poor little guy."

He scooped up the creature, careful to keep the wings gently pinned under his grasp. He reached up and placed the bird on a horizontal limb of the mesquite and walked back to the cabin.

We were born to work together like feet, hands and eyes, like the two rows of teeth, upper and lower. To obstruct each other is unnatural. To feel anger at someone, to turn your back on him: these are unnatural. The best revenge is not to be like your enemy.

—Marcus Aurelius
Meditations